THE ELEVEN HOUR FALL TRILOGY

ROBERT APPLETON

This book is a work of fiction. Characters, names, places and incidents either are the product of the author's imagination or are used fictitiously, and any resemblance to any actual persons, living or dead, events, or locales is entirely coincidental.

THE ELEVEN HOUR FALL TRILOGY

ISBN-13: 978-1494901370

Printed in the United States of America

Copyright @ Robert Appleton 2014

All rights reserved.

No part of this book may be reproduced or transmitted in any form or by any means, electronic or mechanical, including photocopying, recording, or by any information storage and retrieval system, without permission in writing from the publisher.

Published by Mercury Seven Books
2014

Contents

Book One: The Eleven Hour Fall 1
Book Two: The Elemental Crossing 92
Book Three: Kate of Kratos 195

About the Author 315

BOOK ONE
THE ELEVEN HOUR FALL

Chapter One
Falling for Remington

Spindrift from a nearby cornice curled out over the edge of the mountain and streamed into the violet unknown. A bottomless unknown. For Kate, performing her umpteenth scheduled check on her wrist gauges—O2, suit pressure, biometrics, comms signal strength, all fine—it wasn't the most perilous scouting expedition she'd taken part in, but it was the most dangerous she'd ever volunteered for. The punchy, unpredictable winds up here forbade anyone from venturing near the edge.

As the most experienced scout in the team she'd demanded point position, but some clever dick back on board the *Fair Monique*, probably never planted a boot on alien soil in his life, had given that responsibility to a rookie pair not yet a month out of Basic, hoping it would give them much-needed experience. Um, yeah, they'd get experience all right—of the plummeting kind, if they weren't careful.

Hmm, just as she'd thought, the tracks ahead veered way too far from the bisecting course she'd plotted. If they kept this up, she'd have to—

Kate lost her footing in the snow and toppled straight onto Remington, knocking him flat. She helped him up and wiped his visor clean, but soon recoiled. After all, it wasn't exactly what she'd had in mind for sweeping him off his feet.

Katie girl, you've just done the dumbest thing since volunteering for this hike. Stay calm. Say something, quick.

"Wow, you okay?" Remington's grim, no-nonsense tone still managed to cut through the crackling reception.

"Ask me again when we're some place warm."

What she really wanted to do was warm things up then and there. To hell with the mission plan. Everyone knew Kate Borrowdale was the most qualified, the fittest, the most competitive terrain scout of the group, but only she knew the one thing that outmatched them all—her feelings for Jason Remington.

Way to drop a hint. Dusting herself off, Kate cursed her footing for blowing her chances.

Remington, though, stepped closer and, to her amazement, grinned through his helmet.

She beamed a smile back, bowed to say thank you for helping her up, and fought the urge to tear off both their suits. The insanely low temperature, off-the-charts altitude and lack of oxygen might have dissuaded her, yet it was still a close call.

At the very least, it would be one way to get warm in a hurry.

The wind speed picked up, buffeting her sideways as Kate fell back in line. All she could think about was the tall, stern man a few steps behind whom she'd watched from afar for over a year now, in her own bottled-up, intense way. But...but had that genie just been unleashed? He'd certainly never grinned at her this way before, at least not since their maybe-flirty pursuit race in the low-g velodrome, which she'd let him win on the last stretch. The whirling indigo sky grew deeper; her head felt lighter than the atmosphere at any peak.

"All right, the weather's turned. We're putting up the shelters," blurted a voice over the com-link. Sounded like one of the rookies. A smart call, one she'd commend in her report.

Remington immediately broke back to join his expedition partner while Kate ploughed ahead through the knee-deep snow. Her designated partner was Jill Qualen, another scout with limited experience in the grind. In fact, Kate trusted Jill about as much as she would a loose crampon on a wall of wedding cake icing. It was therefore imperative to take charge of the shelter before the weather hit, as she knew full well the dangers of a blizzard at high altitude.

Soon, clouds hurtling overhead blanketed the last hint of sunlight. Violet and violent. Kate gritted her teeth against a flurry of wind blasts. Resistance to her every movement increased exponentially. Their destination, the west ridge itself, faded in moments under a swathing swirl of ice.

She shot her tent clamps into the rock and, hustling Jill inside the shelter, fastened it shut behind them.

The two women checked their equipment in silence. Kate had done this a million times before, but knew it was the most crucial part of any expedition. Oxygen...fifteen hours' worth. Suit integrity...fine. Suit temperature...fine. Altitude...still no reading. *I wonder how high we really are?* The ship's probes had only managed to explore the highest peaks of the planet. Electromagnetic interference in the thick layers of cloud had scrambled any data retrieved from the few probes able to penetrate the lower strata.

For all she knew, they might be setting a record for the highest ever climb. *I'll bet we are. The largest planet ever explored...near the top of a high mountain...eat your hearts out Geary and Musampa! Olympus Mons was kitten play.*

Jill gave the thumbs up, and Kate responded in kind. The only sound they heard was the muffled howl of the wind.

"How long will it last?" asked Jill, a few loose strands of blonde hair sticking to her forehead with perspiration.

"There's no telling," said Kate. "I was in a blizzard that lasted nearly two weeks on Dakota Prime."

"What was it like there?"

"Not unlike Earth. Deadly terrain, though; we lost a girl on the way back."

"No kidding. I guess you just can't imagine yourself being beaten by a bit of wind. Or snow."

"So why did you choose terrain scouting?"

"I needed a change. It sounded more exciting than shining an office seat with my derriere."

Kate had never thought of Jill as the thrill-seeking type, but she couldn't imagine her behind a desk either. "So, you like scouting?"

Jill quirked an eyebrow. "Don't you?"

"It's a living, I guess." And right now, worth no more than the shrug she gave. "Climbing, surveying, searching for minerals in the ass-cracks of beyond? Like you say, it's better than the alternatives. We go where they send us, but the rest is up to us. And we do get to be Neil Armstrong a hundred times over."

"How's that?"

"Well, we're usually the first to set foot on any new rock they find. 'Toeing-in', we used to call it—on alien ground, in the history books. That lottery they hold before each primary landing, to see who gets to be first; that's more than a game, it decides whose name is logged in the record books. After a while it adds up to quite the resume. Novelty soon wears off, though."

An awkward pause took root between them, and neither spoke another word on the subject. The shelter's taut fabric *thwumped,* bulged inward. Kate kept an eye on the tent cords behind Jill. As the wind assaulted from that side, those would be the first to snap. Maybe she should've double-pegged.

"Everyone sit tight; the pick-up's on its way," said the voice over the com-link. "Until I give the word, stay inside the shelters. Command says the entire hemisphere's about to white out. Wait for my signal."

Jill closed her eyes and, clasping Kate's hands, began mouthing a prayer.

Recalling the direst moments she herself had endured on Dakota Prime, Kate sighed. *A couple of minutes and already Hailing Mary. Save some for when it really gets rough, sweetheart.*

Another ten minutes passed. The tent cords held, but Kate didn't like the ferocious strain. Though she'd seen them hold a sky-limo suspended in mid-air, she was less sure of the shelter's fabric. The slightest rip and the canopy might open up like a crepe wrapper. And the thought of Remington trying to hold his together only made her more anxious.

But wouldn't he be the calm one?

The team leader finally broke silence: "Twenty seconds. I want everyone out and re—"

A double thump of dead air curtailed his order, quickly followed by a deafening overlap of crackling and staggered screams over the com-link. Kate didn't panic. Instead, she sprung to her feet, wrenching Jill up with her. As she unzipped the door, the entire tent caved in behind them. A hurtful force propelled Jill into her, knocking her flat. *Shit.* No sooner had Kate spun to see what had struck them than a boulder the size of a sky-cab crashed on top of Jill, crushing her completely, before spinning out into a blizzard of rock and ice. Another struck somewhere close behind. It shattered on impact, its huge jagged pieces careening by a few metres to her right. Kate scrabbled to stand upright, and glued her gaze ahead skyward, following the trajectory of the next falling boulders. As if swiped by the hand some unseen alien god, two rocks the size of houses hit the mountain side by side. They smashed square into the rock face and shook the entire ledge.

That's no avalanche!

Another torrent of massive rocks battered the ridge *sideways* on her left hand side—an angle from which there were no peaks, no slopes, just thin air. What wind could be so powerful? In Hailing Mary, had Jill instead hailed this unimaginable force from the heavens? Kate knew there was only one chance for survival. To jump!

She wiped the specks of bloodied snow from

her visor, blanking Jill from her mind. She leaned into the wind and inched toward the ledge. It wasn't until a torn orange tent flapped about her helmet that she noticed a body lying nearby on rock scraped clear by the force of the storm.

Another missile shook the ground, followed by another. One passed between her and the body, almost rolling in from the sky like the blades of an aerial harvester, not quite touching the ledge. Kate knelt over the body. *Remington.* He wasn't moving, but the instrumentation on his suit gauges showed he was still alive. Thank God. But how badly injured was he?

No time to think. With a tremendous effort she dragged him to the very edge of the cliff and pushed him over. A sheer drop. Without even gathering breath, she flung herself after him. It all occurred so quickly and matter-of-factly in her mind that the transition from climber to free-faller didn't register at first.

Jolts of wind torqued her this way and that. A few huge rocks flew by, missing her by inches. Kate sensed her chances of survival had just increased, but from zero to what? Her gaze remained fixed on Remington's spinning starfish form as he drew closer through the barrage of icy pellets. Her suit shielded her from the impact of this onslaught. But something wasn't right. She'd skydived before, but here it felt…different somehow. Directionless. As though she could hold out her arm and feel the same gravity pulling her every which way.

She struggled to remain streamlined in her dive posture. The chaotic air currents veered her off course again and again. She flung an outstretched arm toward Remington, almost reaching him. Two more attempts fell short. On the fourth lunge she grasped his ankle and pulled herself close.

Kate wanted to feel relieved. He was already married, but so what? She'd thrown the man of her dreams from a cliff and caught him on the way down. Yet, hope remained in her parachute, fastened to the back of her survival suit. All she could do now was hold him tight and wait...

Face to face, helmets chattering together, they fell through whirl after whirl of violet cloud. She'd clipped them both together by the waist, but also kept her arms and legs wrapped tightly around him. She could open his chute for him, but might never see him again; the winds would rip the canopy to shreds. Same for hers. If only she knew how high they'd been back on the mountain. If only she could spy the ground—a second was all it would take. If only she knew when it was time to open. If only...

It was the least romantic clinch of her life. Imperative to think of him only as an unconscious patient in her care. Nothing more. At a time when they'd never been closer, they were never farther apart. Twenty minutes lapsed. Ice no longer pelted them.

We've passed through the blizzard, at least. Kate checked her instrumentation again. Still no altitude reading. They must be getting close now, though. Still too much goddamn cloud to discern anything below. *Something* definitely wasn't right—she should've seen the ground by now. Soon she would just have to chance it, however high they really were. If the chute failed, it failed. Hell, they always had another.

She decided to set the next cloud layer as her parachute deployment point. After that, the wind speed would make or break their survival. If it was too harsh, the rig wouldn't hold. Even though they had a second chute, she knew this first would be the crucial one; the fate of number one would likely spell that of number two as well.

It remained tough to keep any kind of bearing. At times they seemed to plummet at an alarming rate, positive g's almost crucifying her elastically, then she'd flip upside down and her stomach would knot anew, yanked in some other direction. At least Remington's extra weight gave her a sense of being anchored, kept her view steady over his shoulder. A quick glance here, a fleeting glimpse during a barrel roll there, her knowledge of the world below snatched from a dizzying descent.

The violet sky streamed as colors in a fresco, running while still damp. Tremendous gas jets washed up from below—a sight she likened to lilac ink injected into a tank of bloody water. Elsewhere, the lilac gas plumed to giant mushrooms from tornado slivers.

"We're in for a rough ride down there," she said to Jason. "Whichever sadist chose Kratos for us to scout should be here instead, if you ask me. What goddamn mineral's worth all this? Pyrofluvium? A freaking energy catalyst? Like we need another one of those. Sheer profiteering; sheer waste. But who am I trying to blame—no one ordered me on this frozen rock. I've got what I came for. Ha! He's just in a coma, that's all. *Next time, next time, next time...*

Her clock read 15:34. The fall had lasted how

long? An hour and five minutes? That couldn't be right. They seemed no nearer to the swirling cloud below, her parachute deployment point. Another wicked thrust kicked them into a dizzying spin.

Kratos was a fairly large planet in terms of circumference, yet physicists knew very little of its topography. The range of corborilium mountains in the northern hemisphere, the peaks of which Kate's party had partially surveyed, suggested mind-boggling geography. Scans, however, had failed to penetrate successive cloud layers. Experts cited an electromagnetic anomaly in the atmosphere as the reason for this. As a result, estimates of the height of those peaks varied by many miles. The surface of Kratos was, as yet, an unexplored world.

After all their bullshit, I'm the one left praying to a parachute.

Kate tried to relax through a long, slow exhale. Her shoulders ached, so she tried to roll them loose. The fall now seemed smooth, consistent, almost gentle as they stopped spinning. Her throat, though, was dry and ready for cracking. A terrible hunger began to swell inside as she tasted inviting flavors in her saliva—apricot biscuit, Magmalava grill steak, Arinto liqueur—or at least thought she did. Remington never so much as twitched in her clutches.

18:51. Four and a half hours had brought them no nearer to her parachute deployment point. Kate's mind wandered back to her quarters on the ship, where a family photograph she stuffed in a drawer whenever anyone came in, now stood proudly on her bedside table; she always left it on display while she was away in the grind, while she wasn't there in person to have to explain it, to reminisce about things no one else had any right to know. Her mother and two sisters boasted sunflower grins on her graduation day, but Kate managed only half a smile. For some reason, that had always bothered her. Was she really that defensive, that morose? Was that why she'd never had a real boyfriend to speak of, when everyone else seemed to boast a directory of conquests?

"You're not one for shallow romance," her mother once told her. "You're a one-man girl, like me, and you'll win him over when you least expect to, just like I did."

Mum, I hope this isn't what you meant by that.

The air seemed to cushion them as Kate's mind drifted further away. Shades of purple and red in the sky blended as though brushed by a master dreamscape painter. In all her scouting experience as mineralogist, mountaineer and loner, Kate had never felt so ineffectual. Her reputation for an iron resolve now seemed almost coy, so utterly was she at the mercy of invisible forces. Her mindset, together with all notions of practicality, began to slip. Staring lovingly into Remington's face, she struggled to stay alert.

She remembered their first meeting well, well enough to cringe all over again. The *Fair Monique* had picked him up from one of the Saskatchewan moons en route to the Kratosian system, along with thirty-one geologists and mineral ore specialists, and one state-of-the-art Pyro refining platform designed to be transferred from planet to planet by the largest Pioneer vessels. Remington had been a career tool-push, a mining engineer without the schooling for the more lucrative administrative positions, until a few months before embarkation, when he'd qualified for ISPA's new All Environment Survival (On Planet) program, or AESOP, for deep space terrain scouts. Not a great training course to be honest—it required minimal actual field experience, and put too much emphasis on simulated virtual scenarios where the conditions were controlled, predictable. Scouting was not like that. Theory gave you the tools, but experience and improvisation kept you alive.

The first time they'd spoken had almost been the last. He was sitting on his own in the gymnasium cafe, unwashed, unshaven, and wolfing down high-carb food with shocking abandon—shocking to her because he'd been assigned to her scouting corps, and she, like all good scouts, watched her diet by the calorie. Not an auspicious start to his new career. On the other hand, he was a loner like her, and hot in a primal, natural way most of the preening men she'd met in deep space exploration—interstellar business heirs and university golden boys—could never be. He'd earned his cot on a starship the hard way, from the gutter.

Hi there Number 317. You've received an invitation to the Baccarat Commemoration dinner tomorrow evening in the Observation Restaurant on A deck. 1730 hrs. This message was sent by WITHHELD.

Kate sent the message via wrist text, having spotted the number on his unique ID tag and the absence of a wedding ring on his finger. A gutless invitation perhaps, withholding her name like that, but he was so cute and he didn't know her antisocial reputation and she didn't have a date for the dinner and anyway she couldn't—not in a million years—ask someone out face to face before they'd even been introduced.

To her astonishment he looked in her direction straightaway, even held up his beaker of lager. OhmyGod. She shivered, couldn't breathe, was on the verge of walking away when he typed a reply on his wrist text:

Thanks for the invite, WITHHELD. Unfortunately my wife and I already have a reservation. Sorry. Join us for a drink afterward. Jason Remington.

No sooner had she squeezed the circulation from her wrist, her gaze boring a shameful hole in the floor, than Mrs. Remington marched into the cafe and hit Kate with a full-on stink-eye. If she were in wifey's place she'd probably be fuming too; Kate was wearing her Lyrca cycling shorts and sports bra that left precious little to the imagination. But Mrs. Remington, the leech, had to have been on a joint text account with her husband, and had seen fit to nip this liaison in the bud before it even started. Blonde, willowy, not the most attractive woman on the ship, but she had a fierce, dynamite protective instinct that both impressed Kate and rubbed her the wrong way. More specifically, she had what Kate wanted, and promptly trundled him out of the cafe before he'd finished his meal, poor bloke.

As it turned out, their marriage had been an extraordinary one from the outset, and soon became the object of gossip and admiration for everyone on the *Fair Monique,* much to Kate's dismay. In his teens, Jason had been a political prisoner on Fourmyle Beta after the planet was invaded by the blockaded neighbouring colonists on Fourmyle Sigma. To help ensure the amnesty mediated by ISPA, hundreds of orphan girls from the Sigma Christian missions had volunteered to marry Beta political prisoners by lottery, and were given a dowry of sorts by ISPA to set up a new, cooperative colony on Fourmyle Epsilon. Thus, these couples became famous throughout occupied space as the peacemakers of one of the most volatile systems ever settled.

Humble celebrities, then, but Jason and Daniella Remington were admired wherever they went, not to mention inseparable.

Kate didn't attend the Baccarat Commemoration dinner that year, nor any other holiday function after that. But she watched for him at every fitness session, every Virtual Co-op (VCO) movie evening, every pre-drop briefing, pretty much any time she ventured out of her quarters.

"For chrissakes, how many times did I almost tell you how I felt? How many different futures have I mapped out for us? If I'd asked you outright, *would* you have turned me down flat? Not that I'm a home wrecker or anything, but it was an arranged marriage, a lottery marriage. Do you really love her, or is it just duty keeping you together? Hmm...one way or another, I'm going to get us through this. Just look how drop-dead han...I mean how handsome you are...do you even know I'm unattached? Unattached...ha! That's funny. Katie girl, you'll laugh at this whole thing one day. Mr. and

Mrs. Freefall—engaged for a matter of hours, inseparable, fell for each other on cloud nine, landed on their feet and lived happily ever after. Mum would be proud."

Kate traced her finger over his visor, following the contours of his face. Boyish but stern, Remington preferred the unkempt look. She found his heavy stubble and longish black hair incredibly enticing. Even unconscious, he exuded her ideal image of masculinity, and had in fact reinvented it for her in their past year on the *Fair Monique*.

Yes, we're going to get through this.

At around 20:05 a number of conspicuous dark streaks appeared in the sky. They'd climbed from below and now appeared to keep pace with Kate and Remington. Swirling in elegant patterns some distance away, they drew closer. Soon, the disparate streaks merged into a snake-like procession. She held onto her man tighter than ever. *Some kind of flying creatures? They'd better keep their distance. We can't exactly fend them off.*

Spinning to look once more at the aim of their descent, she felt again the pangs of despair as the lower cloud cover appeared not an inch nearer. They might as well have not been falling at all.

That notion woke Kate like a swill of ice water. "How can one tell if one is actually falling? Sky-diving training includes jet cushions a few feet off the ground; it sure feels like falling, only you're not. The force of air keeps you suspended. What if that same principle is at work here? Are those incredible updrafts keeping us aloft? All right, so what now? Do we have to tango up here forever?" She studied the flying creatures. "They flew up here. How do they get back down?"

She watched intently as the dark procession approached with funereal precision. Soon, their enormous wing spans were visible. Dark brown beaks came into view next, not long and slender but wide and half-conical. Tendrils flapped beneath them in the manner of braided beards. As they drew closer, she saw that their bodies were covered with fur instead of feathers. Their tails, the length of city blocks, were thin, streamlined. Kate made as little movement as possible. Were she to categorize the creatures at all, it would be as a cross between a stingray and a bat. Unearthly creations...heading straight for her!

The leader came to within ten feet. It eyed them for a moment before opening its massive beak. Kate embraced Remington one last time, and closed her eyes. "At least I tried," she whispered to him.

She felt her legs being gripped, and waited for the crunch. And waited. *Why's there no pain?* Opening her eyes, she was shocked to see the creature's great beak simply holding the two of them as it flew. It had no teeth. Its hold was firm, but hadn't pierced either of their suits. *Where the hell is it taking us?* Kate's head began to spin. *It must know a way down to the surface. Where there's life, there's a chance. Just get us down in one piece.*

She checked her oxygen gauge. Just over seven hours left. The monstrous bird flapped its wings once every few seconds; this hypnotic rhythm lulled Kate into a kind of querulous fascination just the right side of insomnia. The creatures moved so gracefully through the sky, it was hard to imagine them living up to their horrific aspect. "Likely they're the eagles of Kratos, Jason, or the condors. But if we're not food, then what does it want with us? Unless we're a meal for the nest. Right, well either way we'll be out of the sky—let's take it from there, shall we? One step at a time."

Despite not knowing for certain where the creature was taking them, Kate began to focus on ways of fending off an attack from the ground. She itemized, from memory, all the resources in her supply belt. Food for three days; plenty of rope and cams for climbing; mini-incendiaries for lighting fires; two flares; and best of all, a tasker, the multi-tasking climbing apparatus designed specifically for scaling difficult terrain. *But no real weapon, damn it. Time to play dead, Katie girl; surprise is all we've got.*

Her mind pin-wheeled out of faux nightmare scenarios for what seemed days on end. She struggled to stay limber in the beak of the giant bird. Her thighs, sandwiched between Remington's lifeless body and the tough, sinewy lining of the creature's jaw, grew very sore. A girl in a shell within her shell, she'd never felt as restricted or restless. Remington now seemed more distant than ever. Every so often she'd feel his arm pat against hers, nudging her from tenterhook thoughts, and each time her hopes rose. But he didn't wake.

00:30 came and went. Almost ten hours since the jump. Kate could think of nothing except how thirsty she'd become. Swallowing saliva now caused her physical pain; her throat was acrid dry. The sky did lighten, though. The winds eased. There remained only a slack updraft from beneath.

The creature suddenly veered to one side and began a dive that scythed through the air. Kate held her breath. The purple hues quickly converged into a jiving spiral, an enormous chimney into which the birds now flew. Downward, the whole flock spun and twisted into the spine of a tornado. The force sucking them in was quite unlike anything Kate had experienced. If she hadn't closed her eyes, she would've blacked out for sure.

We're in a gas jet. The wake of a huge gas jet. It's vanished and left a vacuum. So this is what happens in a vacuum...Christ!

Like a g-force simulation gone haywire, the descent inside the funnel racked her against the creature's beak with sickening pressure. Only a cycle of stubborn thoughts staved her panic. *You've trained for this. No one else could even survive it. You're the only one. Think of the story you'll be able to tell.*

The creature held them firm in its bite. Kate's stomach flexed and retracted as though it were a slinky on a never-ending spiral staircase. From the time they eventually left the vortex, her mind wheeled on for another fifteen minutes. She was one revolution away from throwing up when her legs lifted free. Without warning, the creature let go. They plummeted once more. Kate had to embrace her man all over again in freefall. Glancing up, she discerned two separate clusters of dark streaks, one chasing the other. Was her escort now embroiled in its own flight for survival? What titanic avian combat was underway above them in the skies of Kratos?

She regained her composure. The pins-and-needles in her lower legs hardly registered as she hurtled through a layer of settled clouds. Then, as if it had been there all along, waiting just beneath, the ground filled Kate's vision with the heart-stopping shine of an instantaneous sunrise. Pale yellow desert stretched as far as the eye could see. The roving shadows of clouds spilled faint blues and purples onto the landscape. Far away to the right, a long, dark ridge snaked across the desert. Kate deafened herself with a cry of joy inside her helmet. "We've made it!"

Though she hadn't parachuted for some time—with the abundance of landing craft, there simply wasn't any need—her training clicked into gear in an instant. Flipping the protective casing, she pressed the function on her wrist and assumed a taut position. In seconds, the canopy spread itself open and snapped them into a gentle float. Kate checked the time. 01:26. *An eleven-hour fall! That's definitely one for the history books.*

As the sherbet contours below drew nearer, she thought for a moment of the vast continents she'd encountered on a dozen different worlds, and of the crippled man in her arms. *Right, this is it now, Katie girl; playtime's over. Your life's back in your own hands. You've a home to make and a man to see to, married or not. You didn't hang on to him all this time for nothing.*

Maneuvering them toward a flat basin between two large, wrinkled yellow sand dunes, she braced herself for a painful touchdown. Despite trying for a skid landing, her knees buckled as a marionette's on impact. Crumpled and weary, she unclipped herself from Remington for the first time in eleven hours. She rested his lifeless body onto the sand, but could taste no affection for him. He seemed to blend easily with the pale dust and rocks of this alien valley. Kate wanted to cry, but couldn't.

Had he been her patient for too long? Was he ever going to wake up from his coma? And if he did, would he not be better off asleep? *I wish I could sleep. You've got a million things to do, Katie girl, and only a few hours to do them in. Get up, get up right now.*

Spindrift from a nearby dune curled high above the gold horizon. Kate struggled to her feet and took the first human steps on this hidden world. *First thing first,* she thought. Their mission briefing had identified oxygen around the mountain peaks, but not enough for them to breathe. Kate hoped the oxygen down here would be adequate, otherwise, in a few hours time, they'd suffocate. Their chances of being rescued were close to nil. What risk, then, was there in gambling with the air right now? She unfastened her helmet to taste the new atmosphere. Without the tint of her visor, her eyes squinted at the bright yellow sand and purple sky. Kate took in a massive breath...then exhaled...breathed in again...then out. She opened her eyes and managed a wry smile. *There's always a chance.*

The air was extremely humid, yet clear and held a slight hint of salt. Kate wasted no time in stripping down to her shorts and green vest. She thought for a moment Remington might be watching, or perhaps she wanted him to watch. Her long chestnut hair clung to her face and shoulders as perspiration glazed her pale, lightly freckled skin. She helped herself to a few bites of an apple-flavored biscuit from her supply belt. Forcing her dry throat to swallow even those few morsels of food proved painful. But it was worth the effort. Delicious.

Many miles to the right, there appeared to be a dark region of the desert. Kate made up her mind to reach it post haste. And Remington? She'd have to carry him, or drag him, until they found shelter.

If it occurred to her how hopeless her situation was, she didn't register the thought. Couldn't. Proactive thinking was the staple of every survival lesson she'd ever received. After half a day in a cocoon, she now stretched her limbs and felt surprisingly loose—ready to begin a survival cycle for two.

Chapter Two
The First Shelter

Fashioning her parachute rig into a harness for dragging such a heavy body as Remington's proved simple enough, and the yellow sand gave easily under their weight, but Kate, after cushioning her man for the journey, frowned as she took her first step. He weighed close to two hundred pounds. That, combined with the anchor of a pair of survival suits and belts, proved far heavier than she'd reckoned. She wouldn't get far like this.

Yet, what could be left behind? The entire desert panorama revealed no hint of precipitous obstacles, yet they'd just fallen from the highest peaks ever discovered by man. Kate wrestled with a quote from her first instructor, "Always doubt the horizon; it changes with each step, and each step is where your thoughts should be."

Hmm...but if Kratos was as big as they said, the planet's curvature ought to be almost negligible to the human eye. She'd be able to see a great deal farther than on Earth. On the other hand, the farther she could see, the smaller the topography would appear. It looked relatively flat, but so would the Himalayas viewed from a great enough distance. *All right, enough homework. I'm going to play it safe.*

Kate worked up a massive breath, gritted her

teeth and took the strain. She leaned forward and dug into the sand with her molded silver boots. Remington was heavier than she'd guessed, but she quickly found her rhythm and grew accustomed to her shadow on the yellow sand. It seemed to glide, the opposite of her lumbering travail. Focusing on this smoothed her temperament, and the more she concentrated on the next step, the easier the shadow seemed to achieve it.

It was through this simple meditation that Kate Borrowdale crossed miles of desert that first day, to reach the first brown rocks she'd seen upon landing.

There she collapsed, utterly exhausted, parched and famished. Rocks of every shape and size, up to thirty feet high, lay strewn for miles ahead. This darker terrain seemed to drain color from the sky itself, which now grew an ominous grey. The temperature dropped with it. Looking back, she could make out no sign of the helmets or the giant message she'd carved in the sand with her boot, BORROWDALE & REMINGTON LANDED SAFELY, HEADED EAST TO FIND WATER. COME & FIND US: markers she'd left behind for a lucky landing craft. Their trail arced through the sand but appeared somewhat jagged where they'd crossed uneven ground. It resembled a crescent zip through the desert. That Remington had still not made a peep troubled her, as his coma had now lasted almost a full day.

Come on, man, open those eyes. I can't do everything myself.

Kate left to find a suitable shelter but almost fainted as she rose. Her throat and stomach were dry, sculpted from inside. One particular rock caught her eye. It was too heavy to lift yet displayed a strange pattern. Neither carved nor painted, the anomaly was in the shape of a bizarre, fossilized creature in the rock. A closer inspection revealed a horned skull and six limbs protruding from a curved spine, rather like a scorpion without its tail. This evidence of life she found encouraging, but not its insect shape. *I hope they're extinct.*

She happened on a much larger boulder about the size of bungalow. Round the side was a hollow in the ground, more than deep enough for them to spend the night. A ring of piled sand around it suggested it hadn't been formed by natural forces but had rather been dug, yet they had no choice; it was getting too cold to stay outside. They'd just have to risk meeting tonight's tenant, if there was one. Pity she had no weapon. *Hmm...there's always fire.*

She dragged Remington and their supplies with considerable difficulty over the rocky obstacles, and hoped like hell she hadn't injured the poor guy. Though one hundred percent spent, she managed to roll everything into a tight bundle and let it slide down into the hollow, herself collapsing in after it.

As there was nothing to burn, she gave up the idea of lighting a fire for protection. The cave, scarcely high enough for her to stand upright, was black beyond the few feet in front of her. No telling how deep it actually went. Kate tried to sigh but managed only a bitter shiver. Unable to keep her eyes open, she barely had enough wherewithal to cover herself for the night, first with her survival suit, then with the canopy itself.

A smothered sound of creaking wood rising in pitch, almost to a groan, woke her with a start. If her eyes hadn't smarted, she'd have checked to see if they were open—the cave was utterly black. Not even the outline of the entrance remained. She felt for her hip torch, but it was not there. Ripped loose in the bird's beak? And Jason didn't have one either. *No bloody luck.* She felt high along the cave wall in an effort to locate the exit. Another groan of warping wood rose behind her—very close indeed. But what the hell was it? How could she find out if she couldn't see?

Her hands scraped across a smooth, hard surface, some kind of water-eroded rock? But no exit, not even the seams of one. That couldn't be. A chill breath of wind tickled the back of her neck—or *was* it wind? Her fingertips suddenly dug into something soft, damp. Thinking only of Remington helpless at the mercy of a creature she couldn't see, Kate tore away at the ceiling until daylight flickered in. The glimpse was brief but telling. A rock now partially covered the hole and, during the night, a mortar of wet sand had plugged the gaps. Either it was done deliberately, or she missed a helluva storm last night. *Right, Katie girl, on three; one...two...three!*

She forced the rock up on her back and shoulders, spitting wet sand. With an incredible push she tried to up-end it at arms' length. Her shoulders and biceps shook wildly as it teetered on the brink. She shifted her footing to secure the final leverage when, in an instant, it all came tumbling down as she slipped on a layer of sand. The rock gashed her leg. Kate winced. Another unnatural groan from behind spun her around. What in God's name...?

She almost threw up as she saw what had arrived.

The thing was so repulsive it beggared belief. Around three feet tall and four long, its slug-like body tapered to a quivering, forked tail. Its brown skin, oily at the sides and underbelly while tough as an elephant's on the head and back, was patterned with black streaks that splayed outward from the neck all the way down its spine. Worst of all, though, its front, with no eyes, two saber fangs curving upward from a large distending mouth, two slimy trunks protruding from its chest, and one as its snout, was a miracle of hideous design. Two more crept up behind.

Kate leapt in front of them, fists clenched, when she realized how close the things were to Remington and screamed, "Get away from him, bastards!" To her surprise, they recoiled in a shuddery wave from trunk to tail and, after a chorus of groans, slunk back into the shadows.

What did I do?

Not an experiment to repeat. She wrapped all the supplies with Remington in the canopy and wasted no time in hoisting the bundle up through the hole. A loose stone clattered into the hollow behind them. Its echo elicited further groans from inside. *So it was noise they were afraid of...loud noise? Without eyes, they must rely on other senses, possibly sound and touch? And subterranean creatures like those wouldn't be used to anything loud.*

Kate's heart lifted at this minor victory. But when she turned to scout the landscape, her hope sank again. The plateau she'd spent half a day reaching, while still dark, was now indistinguishable from the ten miles behind her. Most of the rocks were covered by a tide of wet earth. She was in the middle of a storm-swept terrain that appeared to stretch forever in all directions.

So much for dragging her man to safety.

The air was fresh, the sky clear and faintly purple. The majority of clouds huddled far behind them, in apology for what Kate described as "a mother of a hurricane." She'd deemed their landing site the centre of Kratos, and their initial heading north; the storm, therefore, was many leagues to the south.

The two suns appeared almost conjoined on that second day. She couldn't remember their names but knew their orbits were somewhat eccentric. Kratos itself spun slowly on its axis; the planet's day was around forty hours long. Yet, with binary stars to revolve around, daylight time on the surface elongated concurrently with the distance between suns. Kate pulled the bundle to a safe distance from the creatures' lair. She then feasted on a "pickled onion meatloaf" that tasted more like vinegar on rye. If there was any justice, the idiot who prepared it would be laid up with food poisoning right now. As if things weren't tough enough.

Remington's arm twitched at her side. She checked his breathing and his pupils. No change. "You're wanting to come round, aren't you. Well, now's the time, brother. I can't keep this up for much longer. It needs both of us."

Having climbed the tallest boulder she could find, Kate scrutinized the distance for signs of vegetation, water, or even animals. Nothing. The only shape she discerned was a rock wall roughly north-north-east, many miles away. "It's worth a try," she said aloud. "At this point, anything's worth a try."

Pockets of water on the various rocks were bitter to the taste, yet went a long way to revitalizing her. She managed to channel some into the fold-up water pouches which detached from the legs of her survival suit; from these she cupped a few handfuls into Remington's mouth, more in hope than anything. The rest she saved for the day's walk, pleased that the suit would keep it relatively cool for her. It was extra weight, but she'd rested, fed and taken on liquid. Not a bad way to start a hike.

The temperature remained constant for a while. By the time they stopped for their ninth rest, she gazed back over their path through the wet sand and quirked a smile. The canopy's trail had erased her footprints. She then stared ahead to the rock wall. Its contours were almost visible, and for the first time since landing, the terrain scout in her sensed they were finally making progress.

Chapter Three
Tenterhooks

"Toss me a cigarette; I think there's one in my raincoat...we smoked the last one an hour ago...so I looked at the scenery, she read her magazine...and the moon rose over an open field..."

The few hundred yards ahead were completely flat. The sand beneath her feet gave very little; it seemed almost concrete as Kate stopped to take in the grim grandeur of the cliff in her path.

"...counting the cars on the New Jersey turnpike—they've all come to look for Am-e-rica..."

Simon and Garfunkel had played in her head for the best part of seven hours. It faded in an instant when she looked up. The escarpment was well over fifteen hundred feet high. Dark brown and sheer, it looked nigh un-scalable for anyone with such a burden to carry. Kate tried to figure a possible route up: one, two, three decent ledges early on...hardly any foot holes at all. That would get her three hundred feet up, if that...after which it was another two hundred to anything remotely workable. Without the tasker, it would be touch and go. There had to be a better way up, or perhaps through...

After a brief stop for refreshment, she scouted the cliff base to the west, where she found no pores or depressions whatsoever. No way through.

Similarly, any easy route up the escarpment never reached all the way to the top; large, precipitous gaps ruined any chance at every conceivable point along the mile or so she studied. Unbelievable. She'd never seen odds stacked so high against anyone. Pursing her lips, she hurled a pebble at the cliff face and swore not to give up until her luck turned. This meant a sojourn to the east, which, to her dismay, met a similar result. *The bastard's been put here just to infuriate me. To hell with it. I'm not trying to walk around. We're giving it a shot right here.*

The moist air and damp sand conjured uneasy memories of Kate's sister burying her up to her neck mere inches from the incoming tide. That was at Southport beach; here, there was no one to bury her, not even if she fell, and no tide to rescue her either. If only Annie could see her now. *Hmm...shaking her head, telling me I've taken a dumb turn, as always...telling me I should get a new wardrobe...like nothing's changed. I hear you, Annie, and I totally agree.*

"But here goes," she said aloud, digging into her survival belt for a final inventory before she planned the ascent.

The crux of her climb was to be the tasker, an ingeniously compact grappling gun ISPA had started issuing to all terrain scouts shortly before the *Fair Monique's* latest embarkation. It fired a taut, thread-like cable with a harpoon at the end. Given that everything was miniaturized, the device, used by rock climbers for decades, had been perfected for ISPA by Martian science researchers into a truly amazing instrument. A sighting display on the gun contained a targeting lock; digital cross-hairs, fixed on a desired spot on the rock, relayed precise coordinates to the spearhead. Once the trigger was pressed a first time, the coordinates were set in stone, as it were, and the tasker would never miss.

Though she had two at her disposal, with five spearheads apiece, Kate decided to use the taskers only when all else failed. After a final sip of water and a nibble of her favored apple biscuit, she began the climb. Her plan was a simple one: reach half way, then hoist the bundle; reach the top, then hoist the bundle. There wouldn't be enough rope otherwise. At least this way she could concentrate on her own climb almost completely. *You've done this a hundred times, Katie girl; there's nothing to it. Let's see what we can find up top.*

She fastened one end of the first rope to her survival belt and the other to Remington's chute, which she'd folded into as tight a package as possible. Kate decided to save the spare rope for use with the cams. She looped it alongside the other on her belt, bent her knees and then leapt for the first hold. A sidestep to the right. The next, directly above, required every inch of her reach. After several uneasy grips, Kate soon hit her stride. She'd always maintained free climbing was the toughest of sports to master:

"Almost every muscle in the body is engaged," she'd written in the *Fair Monique's* Climber's Manual for New Recruits, as ISPA hadn't yet issued its official document, "and even then there's no guarantee of picking the correct route. It's problem-solving on the verge of exhaustion; the very best climbers operate more by intuition than science."

Kate made short work of the first few hundred feet. Each cam she used became her new anchor; this simply involved unthreading the rope from the previous cam and feeding it through the new. By this method, any fall would be saved by the loop of the rope, as the cams were strong enough to stay a weight many times greater than Kate's. She dubbed the cliff 'Babylon Wall', after the high perimeter of that ancient city, hoping that beyond it would be a feast for the eyes. *It's the least I'll deserve after this.*

Just before the half way mark—a bitch of an overhang far more pronounced than it appeared from the ground—a devilish wind scoured the cliff, forcing her to cling even closer to the rock. After almost missing her footing twice, she decided to wait it out. As soon as it died down, she'd begin the lift. Peering down to the ground, about seven hundred feet below, she couldn't see Remington at all. A cloud of sand had enveloped the base of the escarpment, which meant he was exposed to something potentially dangerous—drifting sand. Hell, he could easily be buried alive! The sickening thought forced her to wrench the tasker from her belt, affix both harpoons and take careful aim.

Click!

The cross-hairs locked on the wall around eight feet above her and three to the right.

Click!

The first harpoon shot straight out. She glimpsed it for a split-second in mid-air as it about-faced and belted magnetically toward the cliff, close to her knee. *Ping!* Nice shot. No time to wait.

Click!

The second harpoon hurled its cable much farther out, curled back like a whip and cracked into the rock above. *Ping!* Nice one. The lower projectile extended its shaft which splayed into a silver platform. Kate stepped on. She attached Remington's rope to a spool on the tasker and, pulling the harpoon cable taut, clicked a switch to hoist him up from the ground. It required no effort on her part; the upper harpoon and the tasker took all the strain. She decided to rest awhile on the fan-like shelf, pretty sure they had this thing licked.

A constant gust slashed about her ears and drowned the whir of the tasker. Kate began to shiver. The wind shot underneath her vest, chilling her to the bone. All she could do was sit and hold her knees to her chest. Minutes inched by. The rope swayed and jerked. When the bundle finally rose to within grabbing distance, it scraped against the rock for the umpteenth time, and she swung it onto the platform, checked Remington for signs of life. "Thank God," she whispered. "You nearly made her a widow."

She laid him flat against the wall and attached the tasker's cable to her belt as before. *Okay, I'll not get far in this weather. Tasker, it's all up to you. We might be fish on a hook, but don't let us down.* The great overhang was twenty feet to her left. Kate estimated another eight hundred feet to the top. With four harpoon pairs left in her belt—she loathed the idea of using those from the second supply—the calculation was a simple one. Two hundred feet a shot.

The next two spearheads bulleted out of sight.

Moments later, the cord pulled tight on her harness, and began lifting her at a speed that torqued her stomach. As soon as she reached this higher platform, the winching operation resumed. Remington, still oblivious, waited on each subsequent level a matter of minutes. The ascent continued like clockwork. Kate finally stood astride him on the final platform and looked up. Her heart leapt. She could almost reach the cliff roof.

The bitter cold now bit into her marrow. Pressing her teeth shut to stop them chattering, she kicked her right leg high into a foothold and sprang onto it. Heaved herself up. Crouched on the summit. Hoisting Remington the final few feet proved tough; her strenuous early climb had taken its toll. With one last biceps-killing effort, she dragged him up and over the jagged rim to safety, and there she lay exhausted beside him on the roof of Babylon Wall, a conqueror of height and of rock.

Alright, Katie girl, you'd better pray it's all downhill from here.

Chapter Four
The Nest

For a brief moment, the name she'd chosen for the wall took on a bizarre significance. The rock summit was relatively flat as far as she could see, yet never exceeded a few hundred feet in width. A crevasse around sixty feet wide bisected the rock. Kate was struck by the dimensions of this gap, which appeared so linear, so uniform as to have been hewn by a masterly hand. The Babylonian significance was in the parallel walls, famously erected around that great city, one on either side of its moat. "That's eerie."

The gap narrowed at only one point, a quarter mile away, but still left a space of over twenty feet. By now the canopy was in a sorry state, torn beyond repair. A constant, tinny rumbling rose from below. She peered into the crevasse and tried to determine how deep it went. Too dark. She lit a mini-incendiary and let it fall. The flame illuminated both sides as it fell, and fell... The walls were smoother than she'd imagined. Just before the light vanished altogether, she glimpsed an incredible dark blue sliver specked with white. It had to be a river.

She gazed at Remington's lifeless packaged form with contempt for the first time, as though he'd become the Sisyphean weight for her thankless travails, then puffed her cheeks, shook the notion out of her head. Or tried to. The farther she dragged him, the more urgent her quandary would become. He was sapping her energy, her own chances for survival.

She'd found what looked like a water source, yes, and had happened on two signs of life so far, indicating some kind of food chain, but it was so remote here, so unforgiving. There was a chance she could make a go of it if luck rewarded her, but Remington halved that chance in every way. She'd be doing everything for two. And what if he never woke up? Was she supposed to nurse him, feed him, protect him indefinitely? He *was* already married, though admittedly that meant little down here on the surface—who would ever know they'd survived the great fall, let alone how and where to rescue them.

"What if I..." Kate gave her face a slap, utterly ashamed at having even entertained such a selfish thought. Nonetheless, her lack of compassion for him left her perplexed. *You'd think that after all we've been through...*

The wind eased. The purple sky remained light, soft, pretty. "There are advantages to every environment," she reassured herself, as all terrain scouts were taught to do. Beyond the far edge of the cliff stretched another interminable desert, yet she caught a series of glints far away to the northeast. They appeared close together across a single latitude. Some kind of lake, or glacier? Perhaps just a reflective element in the rock. She'd give anything for a damn telescope.

She shrugged and switched her mind to the immediate problem—getting Remington across the crevasse. Though only twenty feet wide where she stood, the gap, while straightforward for her to cross using the tasker, posed a tricky problem for him and the bundle. She couldn't throw it, nor could she use the tasker without Remington smashing against the far wall. The solution hit her as though ripped from the pages of a survival manual, diagram and all, though it was technically an improvisation. Not that she'd ever boast about that to anyone.

To anchor a rope to both sides; then, suspending the bundle from it, pull Remington along the line, over the drop.

But the tasker was an instrument intended for vertical progress, not horizontal. She winced at having to use any further spearheads, so decided to use just one.

Ping!

It clamped firmly on the opposite wall. Kate tied one end of the rope to her belt and secured the other with a cam locked in the ground. *Here goes.* She pulled the tasker cable taut until she tiptoed on the edge, then let her weight fall into the crevasse. Her stomach heaved. The line swung her forcibly into the far wall. If her legs hadn't broken the impact, she'd have broken a great deal more. The tasker then hoisted her up for phase two.

Fixing her end of the rope to another cam on the flat roof, so it was now a taut line over the drop, Kate inched herself across, back to Remington. She lowered him onto the rope, tied another line between them, shimmied once more to the far side and then proceeded to pull him across. Her head wheeled to one side after all the to-ing and fro-ing. "That's another one you owe me," she whispered in his ear, "and I intend for you to make good."

She held her fist in quiet celebration after peering over the far edge of the summit. Instead of another precipice, she found an uneven but gradual decline in the rock, incredibly rugged but honeycombed with caves. A number of different routes to the ground appeared before her. The sun had baked patches of the desert dry, creating a striking contrast between the yellow sand and dark brown rock. After being cold for so long, Kate found herself looking to the desert with a delightful envy. *Never thought I'd be pleased to see yellow sand again.*

Perched with her legs dangling over the edge, she lay back, head on hands, and took a long, revitalizing breath of cool air. Sublime. The cloud layers she'd fallen through were little more than frivolous wisps in the sky. The binary suns thus reigned unhindered over the whole of Kratos. She held out her arm. It cast a double shadow, now a single—a rogue cloud had obscured the first sun, so the shadow acceded to the angle of the second. *Kind of like Kate and Remington.*

She imagined their ship, the *Fair Monique*, gliding on its orbital path, its great umbrella collecting energy particles for a return voyage to Earth.

It couldn't leave for about another month; there was always a chance a scouting craft might make it to the surface. Hmm, the atmosphere was almost clear for the first time in God knew how long—

they'd never let this opportunity for recon go begging. If only it could stay like this...

Wishful thinking perhaps, but it lifted her spirits all the same. Remington and the equipment seemed much lighter as she dragged them onto the first steep slope and lowered them down. A compacted sand drift cushioned their fall. Negotiating innumerable ledges and jagged declines, she eventually came to the first cave entrance. It was around fifteen feet high, seven wide and surprisingly light inside. The ground was moist, slippery. Her eyes widened as she noticed a faint undercurrent of noise, a low rumbling, though from which direction it came she couldn't tell. *Must be the elusive river.*

The passage curved westward into the rock. Javelins of daylight penetrated the wall diagonally from above. A slight breeze from behind tickled strands of Kate's hair across her cheeks. After the first right turn, the passageway opened into a bell-shaped inner sanctum, the sides of which appeared glazed by a layer of clear, hardened honey. Something like fossilized amber, but colourless. The hollow appeared to be about sixty feet high and eighty in diameter. A pleasant smell of sawdust and wood-shavings greeted her.

A number of other passages fed into this cave from various points around its walls. All of them were pitch black, except for one on the right. This led out to the rocky descent and smothered the chamber with a blanket of lilac sunlight. Kate decided here was the perfect place to leave Remington and explore on her own for a while. "Hold the fort for us, soldier."

Despite lighting her way with a mini-incendiary, she came to a dead end at each of the first three passages. They became too narrow for her negotiate without crawling or sliding horizontally, and potholing had never been her favourite activity—tight places were death traps waiting to happen.

The floor of the fourth passageway gave way to a fathomless drop after just a few feet. *Hmm...this was a good idea. So much for a Journey to the Centre of* this *Earth.* At that moment a horrid, withering cry rang out from behind. Kate sprinted back to the chamber, where she found Remington safe and unharmed. The piercing cry resumed, but this time fell to a smothered croak. *What the hell is that?* The sound came from outside, through the daylit passage. It was soon joined by a cacophony of rock scrapes and ear-splitting shrieks. Kate pulled her tasker to hand and affixed the leftover harpoon.

The sawdust smell was now pungent. Her heart rate ratcheted, while her steps toward the din remained slow and stout. A large shape scurried past the entrance. She couldn't quite see what it was. Another followed. Then, as if from nowhere, one of the slug creatures she'd encountered the previous night landed at the mouth of the passage. It sprang up again with amazing force. Twice the size of the others, its motion shocked Kate to the core. Contorting its body like a ripple in a whip, from the tail forward, it left the ground as though a grenade had exploded beneath it.

No sooner did she set foot outside than her disgust at these creatures hiked to a deep hatred. The slug had in its jaws a baby eaglet, whose shape was identical to those she'd encountered in the sky. While as tall as Kate, the infant was outmatched by the monster in every way. She spied the wreckage of a butchered nest behind: feathers, fur and grey foliage strewn across dark pools of blood. The bastard hadn't give them a chance.

Incensed, she tore after it along the blood-spattered ledge. Remembering the creatures' aversion to loud noise, she screamed. But if the cries and shrieks of the eaglets hadn't repulsed it, what could hers hope to accomplish?

Around the next corner she found the creature ready to pounce on the last remaining hatchling. *Right!* Taking quick aim, she fired the spearhead. The slug cracked its tail and jumped; in mid-air, it flopped to ground, dead.

She switched her attention to the poor, cornered eaglet. Its pathetic shrieks struck right to her heart. Thrashing its immature wings against the rocks, it was for all the world doomed to suffer the fate of its brethren. Only, it had survived. But what would that mean if it couldn't yet take flight? Surely there'd be more predators hereabouts. For a moment it stopped flapping. Its large, oval eyes looked Kate over from head to toe. What might it make of her? A new species? A new predator? Only she'd just saved its life. A nasty cut stretched down one side of its breast, but it seemed otherwise unharmed. Cream-colored down covered its body from head to tail, and its posture appeared magnificently regal. After glancing at the broken nest, then back at Kate, it turned and scurried away down the rocky decline.

"Poor thing. I hope it makes out okay."

She jogged back to the cave. Her plan was to drag Remington on until they found access to the elusive water source. But when she reached the chamber, he was gone! The canopy, already in bad shape, lay in tatters, unfurled. The rest of the equipment lay strewn about.

Kate sank to her knees, bitter despair clawing her into its dark abyss.

It's all been for nothing; they've got him. I'm sorry, Jason, it's all been for nothing. She blamed herself for everything that had happened: Jill's death, the fall, leading Remington to his end...everything. What did she think would happen anyway? There never was any hope of escape. She should've stayed there on the mountain to be crushed with the others. At least that would've been quick.

A sharp scrape of displaced gravel jolted her to her senses. Its origin…the dim passageway through which they'd first entered the chamber. *Right, that's it, these bastards are extinct as of right now.* Loading her tasker once more, she crept to the wall and shuffled along until she could almost peer around the corner. She gave no sound, nor did her enemy. Just before darting into attack, she glanced down at her feet. *Oh, hell.* Kate shivered as she saw her distorted shadow stretch across the passage in full view of her foe. The last thing she felt was her head crack against the rock wall.

Chapter Five
Not Alone

"Borrowdale! Can you hear me? Borrowdale!"

She recognised those words and their speaker but couldn't identify them, rather like a blurry spectator to a rider on a merry-go-round. Kate tried to turn onto her side, sure that she still had a few minutes left before final wake-up call, pre-drop. Her head throbbed. What had hit her so hard?

"Borrowdale?"

The voice stabbed through her dizziness. *This isn't on board the Fair Monique.* She blinked salt and vinegar from her eyes. Scrawled contours of the cave sharpened into focus. The pit-pat of dripping water seemed to blend with the dank taste suspended over her tongue. In a split-second, everything flooded back: Babylon Wall, the nest, the slug-creatures and...the empty canopy.

A warm, gentle hand touched her forehead. Kate jerked upright. "Who...?"

"It's me—Remington: the idiot who almost killed you just now. I'm so sorry."

A jackhammer went off in her chest. The man's face was pale and rough—he looked a fright, in fact—but it was really him. "Remington! What? That was you?"

"Guilty, I'm afraid."

She needed to throw her arms round him, but she was a professional...damnit. "You! Do you know what I've been through to keep you alive? And after all that, you nearly kill me." She nursed the cut on her head. "Thanks."

"Sorry. Where the hell are we, anyway?"

"Two days nor-nor-west of nowhere, on the far side of Babylon Wall, in the middle of a desert."

"I see. And how did we get here? Or is something telling me that's one for the memoirs...the memoirs I'll never get to write."

Kate looked him in the eyes and quirked a smirk. "You hit me like that again...and I'll see to that myself."

For the next half hour, as they drank and ate, and chose which supplies to take along, Kate relayed her tale, beginning with their remarkable eleven hour fall. Remington shook his head often, unable to comprehend how one woman had accomplished all this on her own.

"How on earth did you drag two-hundred-and-fifty pounds?" he asked.

"On Earth? Hmm...I'd have left your ass for the coyotes on earth. But on Kratos...well, I needed at least one guy to kick around, didn't I? A girl can't last long without that."

Remington rolled his eyes, cupped his black hair back behind his ears for the umpteenth time. Kate liked that particular quirk of his. It resembled a kind of cute preening.

"Whichever way you spin it, Borrowdale, no one else could've even dreamed of doing what you've done. It's above and beyond, and then some."

He reached across and kissed her cheek. Kate took it politely and no more, for that was all it was.

"Just one thing. Borrowdale and Remington?" She shook her head. "How about Kate and Jason?"

He held out his hand. "Pleased to meet you."

"Oh, the pleasure's all yours."

It was the first time they'd really spoken together non-professionally, or beyond the odd cordial remark, and it seemed to Jason that she found his company at least agreeable. That was a start. Important that their last days not be spent at each other's throat, accusing, blaming, despairing. Despite her formidable can-do attitude, Kate clearly couldn't see they had almost zero chance of surviving here long-term. Good. That would help him cope with the inevitable countdown to failure, keep his spirits up till the bitter end. A woman like Kate Borrowdale wasn't born to die; she'd probably never faced it, not really. He had, over long months rotting in his Sigma prison, watching others being escorted out of their cells at gunpoint for execution by instant cremation, wondering if today would be his turn, or tomorrow. He'd come to hate those shapes of tomorrow—those man-traps of hope, those land mines beneath the promise of home. No, he had no hope left in him. Daniella was the living, breathing embodiment of whatever hope had survived his incarceration. Without her—and he was well and truly without her now—he would be an indifferent host when death came calling. And that was all right. He ought never to have survived this long. But in the meantime he'd go along with

Kate's tenacious approach, help her stay alive as far as humanly possible; she'd done that for him, would continue to do so, and he in turn would give her the best possible chance of surviving.

Still weak from his long inertia, he asked for help getting out of his survival suit, the inner lining of which was suckered to his legs. He jumped to his feet, but his legs immediately buckled.

"So much for recovery." He uncrumpled to his knees after a sharp dizzy spell. "I'd better leave the rough stuff for a while, Kate, if it's all the same with you. *Agh*...if my head weren't empty already, I'd say the grey stuff's gonna spill out of my ears."

"Now you know how I feel," replied Kate, rubbing her head.

The utter absence of sympathy in her voice took Jason aback, but he accredited it to her dry sense of humor. And she had earned the right to be a little testy.

"Okay, about this river," she said; "I'm almost certain it runs between the two halves of the cliff, at the bottom of the crevasse. What do you say we try and find it further down?"

"But what about those slug things you mentioned? Doesn't sound like we'd have much chance if we came face to face with a couple. I'm no coward, but I'm betting this shelter, together with that water source, is a cornucopia for those things. Let's take another look at those glints you saw in the distance. I reckon we say San fairy Ann to this place."

Kate frowned, and didn't reply right away. He could hear the stubborn cogwheels grinding, and based on her tendency to domineer in the field, she might be thinking, *Who does this bozo reckon he is? He's been mollycoddled for two whole days, while I've been to hell and back keeping him alive. And now he wants to start giving his two cents. He'd better leave the thinking to me, before he goes and leaves a yellow streak all the way home.*

"Hmm...we'd be better off at least finding the water first," she insisted. "There isn't much left in my suit, and, who knows, it might be a while before we find any more. Even if the river is alive with God-knows-what, at least we'll have something definite to come back and fight for if needs be...if the glint in the desert turns out to be nothing."

Jason's gaze flicked to and from her a number of times before he finally assented. Kate despised these absurd little power games that men always seemed to bring to the table whenever a woman had the temerity to take charge. *No big deal. He'll soon get used to it. If he ever wants to see his wife again, he'll get used to it. Mark my words.*

"Okey doke," she continued, "you re-pack what's left of the canopy—we might need it if the weather turns—and I'll see to the rest."

Jason saluted. "You're more pushy than I remembered, Borrowdale...I mean Kate. But for the record, I've no problem whatsoever with a lady calling the shots. Honestly, I'm glad you're here."

She replied, "Well, that makes one of us, but thanks…" and, throwing him her synthetic pickled onion meatloaf ration, added, "I bet you're good at hunting. Am I right?"

"Depends what I'm hunting."

"Alien beasts?"

"Alien beasts, no. But women..."

Kate played coy, shook her head playfully. *I'm being too hard on him. He's sweet in a scruffy schoolboy sort of way. If he plays along, I'm sure we'll get along. Funny, though—if he'd have flirted with me like this on the Fair Monique, I'd have been his in a heartbeat. What's wrong with me? It's this situation. He's being nice because he has to be; there's no more to it than that. Yes, he'll always be very married...so be it.*

The sky remained clear as they picked their way down the rocky slope. It seemed to Kate that they traversed hundreds of feet in mere minutes, so light now was her load. The thought of her painstaking journey across the desert, to the top of Babylon Wall, made her snort a laugh; what a crazy effort it had been! Checking behind occasionally, she grinned at the sight of her companion, though never when he was looking. For all her stubborn jealousy regarding men and command, she now felt twice the woman, and doubly alive.

After peering into four separate caves that led nowhere, they reached the desert floor. Jason suggested they search for passages to the left. They went right. Kate pretended not to hear his wolf-whistle as she bent to adjust her boot. Luckily, their path through the lower boulders soon met a deep scar in the cliff. It was tough to reach; its entrance rested atop a thirty degree scree incline. They each sported numerous cuts after scrabbling like goats against a landslide.

Inside, the seven foot wide slit zigzagged as it narrowed. Kate lit an incendiary. A distinct rumbling assaulted their ears, and deepened as they walked. They soon found themselves shuffling sideways past sharp, slate-like edges. The lowest few feet, however, proved far less perilous, and Kate suggested they crawl.

This brought them out into a vast barrel-shaped tunnel, a hundred and twenty feet in diameter, cleft along the roof by the huge crevasse. No light reached here from the top of Babylon Wall. The noise was a tremendous, acoustical roar. Kate brought Jason alongside her in case they had to communicate quickly. The torrent shot by at a white-water clip. In times past, the deluge must have reached the full height and width of the tunnel, smoothing it, expanding it with millennia of incredible force.

Spray peppered their faces, while the rock surface became very slippery underfoot as they neared the river. Jason dipped his hand first. *Wow.* The current almost whisked it clean away. *Now that's what I call rapid.*

Kate didn't bother trying to cup any for a drink; instead, she held her outstretched palm as a dam across the water's edge and savored the ferocious spray on her face. It was just what she needed.

Jason tugged her vest, pointing her downstream. The flow remained at a similar level as far as it was lit, and so did the walk space they were on. Kate shook the incendiary in her hand as if to say, *We've only got so many of these, and we don't have a clue how far this thing goes.* Jason replied by motioning his hand as if to curve round a bend, then held up a single finger. She knew exactly what he meant: *Let's give it a try, but if we don't find anything round the next corner, we'll call it a day.* Kate nodded.

Though only in their shorts and vests, they delighted in the unceasing draught brought down by the river. It was surprisingly warm, unlike the chilly water, and she wondered what the source of this current might be.

A mind-boggling waterfall?

A reservoir the size of the Pacific?

Jason stopped them dead at a winding left turn. He pointed to a wet trail which led perpendicularly from the water's edge.

Kate found another just beyond, and another. She grabbed him by the shoulders and shook her head firmly. It was time to leave. No sooner had they turned than the horrific shapes of five full-sized slugs barred the way. A sixth dropped from the ceiling right in front of them. As it landed, a spurt of slime shot from its underbelly and dribbled down Jason's leg. Revolted, he sprang to one side, before kicking it back with interest.

Turning to flee, they ran into three more monsters. These bowed in unison, ready, as Kate well knew, to strike. She screamed until her larynx almost caught fire, and this had a slight effect; the slugs recoiled, but only for a moment. Loud noise obviously had little effect on these larger brutes. The posse behind crept closer. Kate's grip on the incendiary began to shake. As the two groups converged, she reached into her belt for the tasker. Jason stopped her and, pulling her by the arm, bolted for the river. With boiling surges of adrenaline and deep intakes of breath, she hurled herself after him into the rapids and they were swept away.

Chapter Six
When Hope Came Crashing Down

Devilish sub-currents yanked her this way and that like slipstreams in the wake of a supersonic jet. Kate gripped Jason's wrist, but this left her only one arm for buoyancy. The heavy belt around her waist kept pulling her under. The volume of water she gulped was enough to quench a year's thirst. No sign of life breached the darkness as the river wound its way for what might've been a hundred leagues through the tunnel. Kate snatched glimpses of a sublime sliver of daylight following their course from far above. *We're in the moat between two Babylon walls.*

She tried not to imagine hideous slugs clinging to the roof and walls of the tunnel, or other ghastly apparitions drinking the water inches away. Maybe they should've crossed the desert as Jason had said, and *then* come back if the glints turned out to be nothing. *Ah, but you have to go with your instincts, Katie girl; you can't depend on anyone else's. It was a risk worth taking…I hope…*

The violent flow hurled current against current, from bank to bank, and the soapy foam spat up from this rendered the river a torrential brew. It pulled Jason under at one point, Kate at another. That they never once let go of each other was something they later found hard to believe. Indeed, as the river widened to a slow drift, brightly lit from above, and they swam to safety on the right hand bank, the first thing they did after crawling ashore was hold hands. Neither of them said a word. They were too exhausted.

Dots and dashes of sunlight entered through cracks in the wall, as though communicating something in alien code. Kate and Jason followed them for a quarter mile by the river that was now a lagoon. Finally, to their immense relief, Babylon Wall discontinued, and they stepped out onto a twilight reef of ocean pools and green alien coral. The vista was more breathtaking than anything they'd imagined, but potentially more dangerous as well.

After dumping their belts and suits in a heap, they sat side by side, digesting every facet of this new landscape in harsh, pragmatic chunks. Kate recalled a passage she'd memorized from her mentor Boris Yeltsin's textbook. It seemed apropos. 'The art of survival is skilled, but a survivor is not much of an artist. The landscape is his canvas, the elements his tools, and his own life the work in progress. Yet, nowhere in this toiling is there room for an aesthetic, save the occasional glow after going stroke for stroke with Nature, and winning. Survival is little more than a sketch over death: faintly practiced, improvised, monochromatic and easily erased. There is no end result, because the only result is to stave off the end.'

To Kate, red glints swashing like bloodied buccaneer blades simply indicated the width of lakes barring her path. To Kate, aisles of plush green carpet were nothing more than possible routes through the tricky maze. The setting suns were harbingers of cold hours ahead, while metallic-violet clouds spelled unpleasant weather.

"A poet'd have a field day here," said Jason.

"A poet'd be hot lunch by now," replied Kate.

He laughed.

She paid him no mind, and began unfolding their suits. Jason appeared to notice her sudden frown of concentration. "What is it?"

"Those shimmers," she replied. "They're more than just sparkles on the water. Look how deep the red is; the pigment in the sky isn't that deep. Besides, the water here is blue, not red. Check it out. There's another element at play."

Jason focused hard on the flickering hue, gasped. "Pyrofluvium?"

"Exactly! That red…yes, there…see for yourself." She handed him a sleeve. "The cuff sensor says it all. It's still programmed to detect pyro. We located a few deposits in the peaks, if you remember, but nothing on this scale. Look. The gauge's turning cartwheels. I'd say we've hit the mother lode of Kratos!"

As if boasting, the coral betrayed its precious secret through a phantasmagoria of red glints, stretching as far as the eye could see. The import of this, for human science, or at least for human interstellar commerce, was beyond measure. Pyrofluvium promised an elixir of energy for eons of future space flight.

"The storm in the atmosphere passed long since," said Jason. "They must've seen this by now.

With any luck, they'll send the whole armada. Who says greed never pays? Send all the ships you've got, I say – send 'em all."

"We'll just hang around on Pyromere till then. You reckon?"

"You bet your sweet-shaped buns I reckon. Ha! Pyromere—right on." He clasped his hands behind his head and gazed in wonder over their new domain. "So this is what we came over a hundred zees for. There's no way they'll blow this chance. No way. We'll just wait it out. In the meantime, though, it wouldn't hurt to try and find some food. What do you say? Looks fairly lifeless, but what food ever advertised itself as food, right? Come on, Kate—on your feet—we've a Kratosian menu to write."

* * * *

"I don't like those shades of cloud." Kate hopped from dry rock to dry rock across Pyromere, trying hard to keep up with Jason.

"Yeah, nasty…very nasty," he replied. "I dare say we're about to be dowsed; and given what this atmosphere's capable of, so are our chances of rescue. Shit! Me and my big mouth. It would have to start up now, wouldn't it."

Waning sunlight skimmed across acres of shallow pools as they turned without saying a word to pick their way across the pocked coral, having not found a single fish or crustacean for supper. *Looks like we're in for a long wait*, thought Kate.

As they rushed back inside the shelter of

Babylon Wall, the first heavy drops hit. In moments, their vantage was reduced to a few grey feet of torrential downpour. The temperature dropped far too low for bare skin, so they wasted no time in climbing into their survival suits. The ground was soon awash, the water level climbing.

"How about there?" Kate pointed to a wide ledge bearded with stalactites fifteen feet up the inner wall. They reached it by clambering up several collapsed rocks. Once there, they made themselves comfortable.

Hours later, Jason woke to the gentle lap and swish of water. *Oh, great—still here.*

Kate was already up. Gnawing on an oat biscuit, she waded knee-deep into the temporary sea outside, and seemed so unfazed by the whole scenario that Jason wondered for a moment which species had reared her. Amphibian? Bird? Some kind of desert dweller?

She was something else, that much was for sure. If ever he had a chance of surviving at all, she was it. A pity she didn't trust him, though; even a Valkyrie needed someone to lean on now and then. It was best to play along, and just pull his weight till she really needed him.

I wonder what Daniella's up to…sweet Daniella…Wish she was with me now…just not in this place…God, no! She'd hate not knowing what happens next…and yeah, she really would hate Borrowdale. Not feminine enough. She is though, just not homemaker feminine.

He slid into the water beside Kate, and they

scanned the sky together. "At least it's settled," she said.

"Clear enough to give the *Monique* a chance, even if the pyro has been swamped for a while."

Only a few green coral fingertips were visible above the surface. No glimmers of pyrofluvium remained. "They should be able to make it; my gauge can," he added, showing her the pulsing dial on his cuff. The sky was pale, almost translucent. Diffused light from the suns washed the atmosphere in a murky maroon, rendering objects on the surface ill-defined, ghostly.

They tramped on, hoping for signs of marine life, but none appeared. An hour passed. Two. Still nothing. "What do those slugs fee—" she began.

Jason cut her off with a cry of, "Look. Coming from the sun. What *is* that?"

She stared upward and held her breath. The larger sun, slightly higher in the sky than its sister, spat a fiery tongue from its equator. It whipped this way and that, dancing like a live cable. The show lasted over a minute.

"Solar flares?" said Jason.

"I didn't know they could be that violent. Nor that visible to the naked eye."

"Stars are confoundedly unpredictable," he replied, "twins even more so. They can pull at each other in subtle ways."

"You're kidding…a bull in a lasso has more subtlety."

"Indeed. Um, you were about to ask what the slugs feed on." Jason touched her shoulder; it had a warm marshmallowing effect.

"Yeah."

"That would be us. Babylon Wall, six o'clock."

Kate spun to see a dozen black creatures drop onto the archipelago and converge in the water in blatant tracking formation. "Not those bastards again."

After becoming one creeping, writhing blob in the distance, the alien hunters began to pick up speed across the flooded reef. A flush of adrenaline shot Kate into action. "They're not messing about." She stopped wading and stepped onto the higher levels of coral. Jason joined her, and they bolted like pond skippers, using coarse rims and submerged ledges as stepping stones. Despite the occasional slip, they felt safe enough to rest after a few miles.

"I can hardly make 'em out." Kate panted, hands on knees. "They'll only follow us so far…right?"

"Not if it's a territorial thing. Rama Core sidewinders hold dominion over hundreds of square miles on their home world. They kill any rivals for their supremacy without hesitation, and will track them inside their domain until they catch them or die trying, even from exhaustion. It's Darwinian, even out here. More so out here because there's no morality to muddy the waters. You said they can leap through the air? Well, they move slow enough through water, but I'd rather be out of sight by the time they reach dry land."

Kate agreed. They resumed their flight, at a more venerable pace this time, and before long the black posse was indeed out of sight.

Jason stopped her. He glanced behind them,

then to the right, then high behind them, high to the right.

"What's wrong?" asked Kate.

His mouth gaped but no sound emerged. So she followed his gaze to the sky. There, cutting through a spindly joint between two clouds, was a fiery streak, hurtling horizontally to ground. "What do you think it is?"

"For God's sake! Look!"

She'd never seen Jason this frightened. Petrified. The sheer urgency in his voice forced her to focus. *Okay, I can hear the rumble now. He must think it's more than a meteorite. There's definitely something dark and solid at the head. Alright, what else could it be? It's more or less directly above Pyromere…no, it couldn't be...that. What else? Oh, my God, it is. It is!*

"The *Fair Monique*?" Fear fisted her entire body.

"The *Fair Monique*," he replied. "She's going to crash."

Kate's knees began to buckle. The roar overhead grew to a staggered thunderclap. But she had to look. The inverted umbrella—the giant particle collection dish attached to the nose of the vessel—had completely melted away, leaving only the thin, oblong trunk to blaze. Giant sparks burst from the projectile as though it welded its way through the atmosphere. It fell and fell. Kate and Jason covered their ears as it tore past above them. Its steep trajectory began to flatten. *They're attempting an emergency landing.* A horrid trail of smoke blotted the suns. Random chunks of the ship's exterior splashed into the sea; a large panel cut vertically into the coral not fifty feet away.

"Pull up! Pull up!" they both shouted as the *Fair Monique* nose-dived toward the horizon. For a split second it vanished completely, before a mushrooming column of flames and putrid smoke leapt high into the air. The muffled boom hit seconds later. Neither of them said a word. Utterly alone, Kate shut her eyes and let her head drop. Finding Pyromere had raised their hopes. Those hopes had just come crashing down.

Chapter Seven
Dolphin Reef

Clusters of brown, Yucca-like plants, the roots of which reached many meters below thin layers of water and sand, proved extremely useful. Kate was the first to discover a colony of little crustaceans, similar to the fossilized scorpions she'd found that first night. They thrived on the outskirts of Pyromere, inches before a sandy incline that rose a few meters above sea level. The creatures, even with their pincers, were harmless to Kate and Jason, but revealed a stunning animosity toward one another. Whenever two crossed paths, they would fight for the right of way. The death toll was so high Jason wondered how the species could last a single day. "Good eating, though." He cracked one last shell open—his twenty-third—before lowering the succulent meat onto his tongue.

The fire was down to demonic black nostrils spitting the odd spark or flame. Kate threw on a few more Yucca leaves. The heat curled them inward. Their skins ignited as a coil of white firecrackers, before settling into a slow burn. Jason arrayed a few dozen crustaceans inside the ash, to cook in their shells for future meals. They both then lay back on the rim overlooking the reef. There was still no sign of the pursuing slugs.

"They've given up on us, Jason." Kate yawned. "Even the slugs have left us. I feel like we're a gazillion miles from a friendly face, I'm telling you." She realized how insensitive that sounded. After all, Jason had just lost his Daniella. She wanted to say something profound to make amends, but a grim, absurd chuckle was all that escaped her lips.

And he didn't chastise her for snatching any desperate humor. For all he knew, she'd lost someone close to her as well, and this was her way of coping with it.

In point of fact, Kate cared for only one citizen of the *Fair Monique*, and he lay right beside her. The crash had hit her hard, yes, as it would anyone with a heartbeat; but the greater tragedy was what it now meant for her own future.

"We're not leaving Kratos, are we?"

"No," replied Jason. "No, we're not. We never were."

"Fourteen thousand people…gone…just like that," she clicked her fingers, "and only two survivors. We owe it to them in a way, I reckon, to live on as long as we can."

She closed her eyes in shame. That sounded so false. *My God, you haven't got the smarts for it, so don't even try for anything meaningful. Just keep quiet from now on, Katie girl. If he wants to talk, he will.*

The suns overhead reached aphelion. Though it was close to mid-day, Kate's double shadow trailed her like a forked tail as she walked. The sky was clear and virtually colorless. Every now and then she swore a huge shadow followed them over the terrain, but it was never more than a glimpse, easily dismissed.

In the distance—exactly how far they couldn't tell—a continuous exhaust pumped smoke high into the atmosphere. The Fair Monique's funeral pyre. Jason insisted they reach it, if only to dispel any uncertainty from his mind. And to say a farewell prayer for Daniella. It turned out neither Kate nor Jason had ever prayed before, but Daniella had, in the old way, every night before bed. Incomplete memories of watching the two of them arm in arm on the Fair Monique, the hurtful jealousy, and the bitter self-loathing that accompanied it, ground through her mind. She realized it was still shock she felt, not any kind of loss. She was self-absorbed. The reality still hadn't hit.

An eight hour uphill hike met cool gusts and the odd cluster of Yuccas. After climbing a particularly steep dune, Kate and Jason stopped in their tracks. There they beheld a magnificent sight—an endless sea that swept out to the west from a crescent headland. The water was flat as a duck pond as far as the horizon. Patches of green and blue alternated across its surface in the manner of painted marble, suggesting hidden goings-on beneath. Closer to shore, a strong current pushed and pulled the shoreline as if it belonged to a different sea altogether. The coastline tapered to a narrow cove a hundred feet below them, and it was here that they forgot, at least for a moment, their terrible ordeal.

"It's magical," she whispered. A slick grass-covered shelf just beneath the surface partitioned the cove around seventy feet from shore. This orange grass swayed with the tide and provided a slippery cushion for the most remarkable water sport either of them had ever seen. The practitioners were white fish about the size of a man. Longer than a dolphin but bearing a resemblance in both snout and head shape, they glided across the grass as though it was their entire raison d'être. Two slender canals flanked the shelf, allowing them to swim back for more. Kate counted twenty-nine surfers.

"It's magical," she repeated.

"No," answered Jason, tears filling his eyes. "It isn't magic…it's paradise." And to himself, "It's paradise, Daniella…"

There, overlooking the most perfect yellow beach, listening to purrs of dolphin delight of a frequency almost too low for the human ear, they embraced. Jason cried and wouldn't stop. The seawater arced, thumped ashore, then hissed a retreat—an impossible siege. The white dolphins merely swayed on its shoulders, gliding over the spongy reef, truly going with the flow.

Are we somewhere between the two? thought Kate. *Stubborn yet graceful? We'd have to be; the odds of us having made it so far are astronomical, but it's more than luck that's got us here. More than luck.*

"We've been going hard at it for days now," she said softly, "and we're pretty sure those slugs have given in. I think we're due some R&R. What do you say we try a little reef surfing ourselves?"

Jason palmed his tears across his temples, sniffled a few times, then nodded. "Sounds good."

"I was gonna say we should've brought our bathing suits, but we're already in them."

"Hmm…that's what you think." Jason removed his vest and dropped his shorts before running stark naked down to the beach.

Kate savored her eyeful for a moment. "What the hell," she said, trembling with excitement as she stripped. "Who's watching anyway?"

* * * *

The fish kept their distance at first. They slid in two groups, one on each edge of the reef, leaving the centre open for their strange new acquaintances. Kate and Jason were wary, too. The water proved surprisingly warm, much warmer than Pyromere or the river tunnel. As they reached waist depth, a sudden swell lifted them from their feet and dragged them like writhing flotsam over twenty feet. They had to tread water. A few moments later, it rose again and heaved them onto the shelf. The grass was slick as wet plastic, tough as leather. The slide across was fast, juvenile and thrilling.

Kate gave the okay signal to Jason's suggestion of another run. They needed strong strokes to swim the cliff-side channel back to the starting point. The second drag proved even more exhilarating. Each wanting to burst out with glee, each fiercely attracted to the other, they nonetheless kept to an intense, private excitement. The perception was tacit, Kate knew. Anything further, considering the recent tragedy, would be inappropriate. Stolen glances had to suffice.

After two more runs, the dolphins mingled freely with Kate and Jason, buffeting them about on the grass, nudging them impatiently along the channels. The creatures' skins were coarse but fleshy to the touch. They had no teeth. Instead, their mouths were lined with barbs all the way down their throats. These, together with the ability to suck water in with great force—often jetted out through their tails for propulsion—rendered them lithe and efficient hunters, according to Jason.

"I could do this forever," she yelled.

"Let's!"

"Don't tempt me." And she performed a three-sixty slide over the grass on her stomach.

* * * *

Jason hadn't quite swum the channel in time for that particular surge. Those few moments alone allowed his thoughts to drift back ashore. Actually, he was getting a little tired. They'd been at it for hours, and it was time for a rest. Soon as she swam round again, he'd tell her.

But Kate didn't show right away. A few minutes passed. He thought about either swimming back up the channel or surfing the shelf to find out. And no dolphins either? *What's happened?* Just then, Kate appeared at the far end of the channel. She clung to the rock face with one hand, while jabbing toward the shore with her other. Jason spun round, looked up, and felt the cold inescapable grasp of death. "Hell. They tracked us all this way."

Atop the sand bank, a dozen black slugs rummaged through their clothes and equipment. *That's some sense of smell they have.*

Kate waved for him to join her at once. He didn't hesitate.

"Well," he whispered, "what do we do now?"

"We wait."

"For what? You think hiding here'll dissuade them? They've tracked us across water and desert for God-knows-how-long. What's a few more feet?"

"Alright then, let's go back and see if they'll mind not eating our heads first. That about right for an alternative? Hmm?"

"I say we just swim for it," said Jason, "like those dolphins did."

"Where to? There's nowhere to climb up."

"There might be along there." He pointed across the cove to the coastline that stretched perpendicularly from the cliff.

"Alright then. They are slow swimmers," she thought aloud. "As soon as they make a move, so will we."

There they waited, in stalemate, warm as the sea heaved beneath them, their pruned fingers soon aching as they clung to insufficient grooves in the rock. The posse didn't budge. Had they had the same idea—to wait for their prey to make a move? Despite a beastly appearance, how smart were they?

The strange war of attrition continued. A lonely shadow roved across the cove. *Not more rain*, thought Jason. Then another sped by, and another. *What? No cloud moves that fast.* A deafening shriek pierced the air. The slugs cowered, while Kate and Jason tilted their heads skyward once more.

Chapter Eight
The Wings of Change

"Dive under!" The enormous swooping wings filled her with terror. Kate and Jason each sucked in a deep breath, plunged beneath the surface and waited there, on the sea bed, until their chests were ready to implode.

They resurfaced together, gasping. The entire beach erupted into a chaos of *thwapping* sounds, flying sand, and vicious alien combat. Seven slugs lay disemboweled atop the slope. The rest were engaged at various points on the yellow sand by five giant birds—exactly like those Kate had encountered during her eleven hour fall.

"Keep low, keep still," she said.

The wings flapped and thudded like sail-sheets flexing taut. They kicked up clouds of sand that masked much of the slaughter. The birds' stingray tails slashed through the water. Bat-like fur bristled on their bodies. All that identified the slugs was a smothered, stuttery groan. This sound finally ceased, and the birds folded their wings to peck, side by side, at their victims' corpses.

"So that's the end of the posse," Kate said.

"Yeah, and let's hope these new predators haven't—"As the creatures turned to face the sea, Jason shook her gently by the shoulder. "They're communicating," he whispered. "Can you hear it?"

Kate spied the tendrils suspended beneath their beaks. They appeared to quiver where there was no wind. Their heads, even more horrific than she'd remembered from her hours-long side view, swiveled in languid motions, not bird-like at all. "They're searching for us," she said, "but they can't see us." Grabbing Jason by the arm, she motioned for them to hide behind the shelf. No sooner did they start than one of the creatures lifted its beak, appeared to sense them by means of its tendrils, then leapt vertically into the air and dove after them.

"No! Under again!" cried Jason.

Mid-way to the bottom, two enormous beaks snatched them from the water and carried them kicking and thumping to shore. The struggle was futile. The birds soon dropped them, still naked, on top of the sand bank. The horrific black carcasses lay strewn about, guts half exposed, half eaten. Kate threw her arms around Jason and shut her eyes. He held her just as tight. Not a single thought pierced her bitter sense of failure, of defeat, except one—that she'd never told him how she felt.

Something hard and blunt hit her back. It made her squeeze Jason even tighter. Again the same blunt impact, only higher up between her shoulders. The monsters were toying with them? After enduring a further four blows, she unhooked Jason's arms and whipped around to end it quickly. The spin left her flat on her face, and she looked up, perplexed. "What? You?"

There, in front of them, stood a six-foot tall bird, a hatchling, with a survival helmet gripped in its beak. Jason pulled Kate back. "Is this the one…?"

"Yes," she replied in disbelief. "This is the guy I saved yesterday. Look at the scar across his chest. He must've made it to safety after all."

With a face as hideous as its seniors, the eaglet nonetheless retained a regal pose, its wings tucked diagonally upward against its sides, head and breast held high and straight, its gaze at Kate unblinking. It hopped forward and pressed the helmet against her face. She took it. And immediately the eaglet hopped back to the feet of its parent, where it was scooped up by a giant beak. Without sound, the entire flock lifted high into the air, before gliding off toward the horizon, toward the smoke rising from the *Fair Monique*.

"What the hell just happened?" Coughing with relief, Jason slumped onto the sand.

"It seems to me…reciprocity." Her eyes widened as she watched the eagle dynasty disappear into the distance. "I saved the baby's life; they've returned the favor. Those shadows I thought I saw following us over the lake: the wings of Kratos fly for us after all."

"Allies? Who'd have thought it on this godforsaken rock?"

"Yeah. We might not be the most intelligent species, after all."

"Well, that's a given where you're concerned, Borrowdale, but as of right now, you might as well crown me King of Kratos. I'm feeling that lucky."

"Actually," she replied, "I'm thinking we just met him."

"Who? That guy with the scar?"

"Uh-huh."

"Well, he'd get my vote, too, but he's just left us in the middle of nowhere without directions, and a heck of a hike to anywhere safe."

Kate smiled, looking him over. "Some survivalist you are."

* * * *

Now in shorts and vest again, with his belt and suit (partially filled with water) slung over his shoulder, Jason threw Dolphin Cove a grateful salute. "So far, it's the only place I wouldn't mind seeing again. Who knows…maybe one day…"

Kate shielded the sun from her eyes as she looked out over the ocean for signs of their aquatic friends. Not so much as a foam bubble disrupted the calm beyond the coastal current. Would she and Jason ever return? The cove itself, having not long since teemed with the creatures of Kratos, disappeared beneath the cliff. For chrissakes, on such a huge world, there had to be at least one safe hiding place.

Their destination, the Fair Monique's crash site, was about forty miles away by her reckoning; the black fumes continued to column as though an oil well had been set ablaze.

"More like forty-one." Jason seemed to be trying his best to wind her up. Though the atmosphere was still gloomy, the suns' glares grew livid. A close stifling heat labored their breaths and halved their pace. They trudged for a few hours, hardly a word passing between them.

Jason exhausted his seafood reserves in a single meal, proclaiming them "tasty, but an insult to nouveau cuisine."

Kate devoured a synthetic gammon paste, followed by a handful of her completely crumbled apple biscuit. They each finished with a few swigs of fine Kratosian water, a kingly beverage on a day of such hot travails.

Far to the west, the light green ocean was still visible, though seemed on the verge of a wicked change. Deep violet clouds lay crouched on the horizon, ready to pounce at any moment.

"Looks volatile over there," she observed.

"And we'll be exposed when it hits."

"Not if I've got anything to do with it."

Jason thumbed his forehead—an old-fashioned ISPA salute—which Kate saw from the corner of her eye. "I'm serious," she added. "You don't know how quickly this atmosphere turns. When we were falling, the updraft was enough to hold us in mid-air for hours. Just imagine meeting that kind of force on the surface." She stopped to look back. "And we've already seen what the rain can do."

"I agree. We need some shelter, pronto."

"Let me know if you see anything: a rock formation, a hollow in the ground, anything we might be able to use."

"Affirm."

"Good. The fliers went this way, so that's good enough for me," she replied.

"Perhaps."

"It's slender, I know, but you've heard of a

woman's intuition?"

"Yeah, never contest a dog for its bone, or a woman's intuition."

She gave a playful growl and motioned to slap him, which he mockingly sidestepped. The quick shuffle, however, lost him his footing, and he soon spat sand from where he lay. "See," he groaned, "Hell hath no fury…"

Kate grinned as she helped him up. The inclement clouds piled across the sea, and in minutes the temperature dropped below anything they'd experienced so far on the surface. They emptied the water from their suits and hopped inside. Days' worth of dried sweat and the sodden inner lining threw up sickly smells of plastic and old rubber. The suns vanished behind a burgundy veil. A strong wind picked up. Loose rocks rolled and bounced by Kate and Jason, toward the coast. Swiping sand stung their cheeks and eyes. Each step they tried became one half forward, two to the left; the gust quickly turned into a hurricane.

"It's no use," she shouted, but Jason didn't hear her. She gritted her teeth, grabbed him by the arm and, spying a rock firmly embedded in the ground, let the wind carry them to it. The current began to lilt in a peculiar manner. It scooped rocks and sand diagonally into the air, whisked them off at tangents as though they were on the outskirts of a tornado. They made the thirty feet in a single bound. A few seconds more and the power of the updraft would never have brought them back to ground. The rock was around four feet high and ten wide, yet shielded them well for the time it took to program the taskers. Kate saw Jason's lips move and his face contort, but what was he trying to say? The wind screeched by at ground level and roared up overhead. Not a single syllable met her ears. It didn't matter. She knew exactly what to do.

Jason fired first. The harpoon burrowed deep into the rock, pulling his cable taut.

Right, my turn.

About to take aim, she felt something tugging at her shoulders. Her lower back lifted as she struggled to kneel. Jason looked her in the eyes from his crouched position, as if to say, *Come on, what are you waiting for?* But the gentle pull erupted. A terrific jerk wrenched her into the wind. The ground hurtled past like the tail of a comet; sand and gravel and grey rocks sublimed from the surface as a gushing river. Higher and higher. Her survival suit pressed even tighter to her chest.

It's the parachute. It's opened!

Kate knew her only chance was to anchor herself to the ground. In their haste, she and Jason had accidentally switched suits. It made her furious. Her own parachute had saved both their lives at the end of an eleven hour fall; *his* had just ripped loose for no apparent reason, hurling *her* into the wind instead. She held the tasker at arm's length but struggled to keep her eyes open long enough to aim. The current lifted her higher still, and was stronger than ever. On the verge of firing blindly to ground, she glimpsed a smooth bedrock below.

And fired.

As soon as the cable began to un-spool, she clipped the gun onto her belt and waited. It'd better have enough line. At the rate she flew, the harpoon might not have time to burrow sufficiently into the rock, if it even reached or hit the rock.

Kate ground her teeth together, willing it to have enough line. *Ugh!* An electrifying jolt almost ripped her in two. If both harnesses had not been attached to her sturdy suit, her spine would have snapped like a wish-bone.

It was anchored. Now to cut the bastard chute loose. *C'mon, Katie girl...think. What cuts? What cuts? What...*

The solution was so atypical, so ironic, she had to run it through her mind three times. *That's it.* Squeezing her hand into the taut belt, she managed to pull out a single flare.

One...two...three...go!

In a single motion, she struck it alight, flung her arms behind her head and gripped the parachute cord. With this in one hand, she burned through it using the flame held in her other. Kate melted away her wings in no time. She then reeled herself in with the tasker. An endless stream of sand and rocks met her head-on. A single cable was all that defied the hurricane. She'd fired blind, and was still unable to look at her anchor. Shielding her face, Kate didn't realize she'd reached ground until something hard pressed her knee.

The tasker had reeled her in completely. She kissed the harpoon, curled up into a ball and concentrated on breathing rhythmically, thankfully.

All the while she whispered, "Hang on, Jason...hang on!"

Chapter Nine
Finding the Fair Monique

We'd like to help you learn to help yourself...look around you...all you see are sympathetic eyes...and here's to you, Mrs. Robinson; Jesus loves you more than you will know...

A tranquil ring in her ears muffled the raging wind. Simon and Garfunkel once again filled that blank sheet in her mind. Kate couldn't remember all the words. Those she did were set in stone before the storm passed, carved in the bones of memory.

The rhythm comforted her like one of her grandpa's old cardigans—venerable, familiar, tobacco-stained. She wrapped herself in the playful guitar twangs and quaint melody of *Mrs. Robinson*, shutting out even the stings from rocks pelting her back. This was her meditation, her bridge between sanities, her secret survival formula...and it had never failed. Others rattled off lists from A-Z; some imagined themselves in idyllic places, or building elaborate structures one brick at a time; Kate played her grandpa's jukebox, 1960's style.

When the winds finally passed, she burst into tears. Days of constant shock and release now eroded even the toughest barriers of her mind. A dire loneliness flooded in. Though she stayed put long enough to finish her Beach Boys concert—*Wouldn't It Be Nice* and *Surfin' USA*—the lyrics stuttered, and she didn't listen to a word. If the thought of Jason hadn't hoisted her up, she might never have moved again.

Some survivor. C'mon, Katie girl, you've failed completely at everything you were taught; how about changing a few things from now on. Right, first rule—listen to Jason. Second rule—listen to Jason. Third rule—you don't live for survival, you survive in order to live. Now get up and go find him.

What seemed like an age passed before they met. Jason had simply followed the wind direction. He appeared to the north, miles and miles away. If the afternoon had been any gloomier, they might have missed each other altogether.

Up close, he noticed the dried tear streams on her dusty cheeks. "Next time there's so much as a breeze, I'm roping us together. Agreed?"

"Agreed."

They embraced. After a deep breath, Kate settled against his chest with a strange new frame of mind. It was hard to describe. A sensation of, for the first time, belonging? The Fair Monique had never given her that; nor had a career of countless scouting expeditions in the company of faceless colleagues. Was it just the extreme situation? Or did some part of a lonely professional need to feel this, despite what she'd maintained? She snuggled closer.

Or should I be asking at all? The thought gave her comfort. *Maybe I should just let go. Remember…you don't live for survival, you survive in order to live.*

Those words seemed designed for Kate Borrowdale, and that she'd coined them suggested a strong subconscious cry had been answered. Repressed longing? She'd delved so far into her nomadic profession that even hugging a man now opened a can of neurotic worms.

"We need to stop meeting like this," he said, letting go.

"How do you mean?"

"Relief after finding each other alive. It's damn well bordering on traumatic. Look at me; do you really think I'd be able to last here on my own, ma'am?"

"Hmm, you are rather pathetic," she replied.

"Thank you. The feeling's mutual."

She chuckled even though it wasn't funny in the least. Kate described the sky through which they'd fallen days before, pointing out current similarities.

"It's layered, do you see? We're not beneath it any more, so you can make out the slow, swirling motion. And there, look—those huge slivers: gas jets or something, stretching right to the top of the updraft. We must've danced up there for hours without knowing it. Well, you didn't know anything anyway, but I sure as hell did. The whole thing's like a blanket of air."

Jason whistled. "Perhaps it's a gargantuan tornado of some kind. Maybe those slivers are its funnels, and the forces combine to create this general updraft phenomenon. Each mini tornado feeds off the others, like a cluster of twisters."

"Not bad."

"Not good either."

The violet storm covered one-hundred-and-thirty degrees of their vista to the west. The remainder of the sky remained gloomy with dull and purple hues, affording the suns only translucent admission.

Kate and Jason started once again for the Fair Monique. The smoke columned to the west, owing to the strong wind in that direction. The air was now fresh and cool. They walked at a relaxed pace. The warm, fidgety breeze reminded her of balmy summer days in California, where she'd spent three pre-adolescent years living on the road in Granddad's Winnebago while Mum started life again in Los Angeles after the divorce. Lots of travelling to and from the city, lots of bad kiosk food, and lots of dreaming...of off-world adventures. None remotely like this one.

It wasn't until Jason found an entire seventy-foot section of the ship buried in the sand that he struck up conversation. "I was going to suggest we try to salvage supplies, but it's not looking good." He gestured at the horrifically-melted exterior.

"Yeah, it's been burning for a long time now. I'll be surprised if there's anything but shells and cinders."

"We'll see."

"I still can't believe that solar flare, though," she said. "How could it have knocked her out of orbit like that? She had safety precautions up the proverbial."

"Hmm, those solar flares, though, don't take kindly to anything man-made. The one we saw must've been a real sonofabitch."

"And we were saved by the planet's EM shield? Whereas anything outside must've caught a broadside?"

"Sounds that way."

They fell silent. The landscape grew softer underfoot, more powdery, given to hiding sharp rocks just beneath the surface. As they approached the smoke, it blotted out the suns. The atmosphere thickened with a putrid, noxious smell.

"So much for the Fair Monique." Kate lowered to one knee as she stared out over the wreckage.

The scale of devastation dwarfed any emotion she could conjure. Not a hint of silver remained on the mangled metal segments that lay crumpled, torn from one another, like the remains of a giant frazzled centipede. Its impact had raked a shallow crater about three hundred yards wide. The separate segments lay at crazy angles: one was split apart down its centre; most were flat inside the crater, while two, having somehow spun off on their own, were twisted and upended as a croquet hoop.

The storm had blown tonnes of sand across the crash site. This partially buried the black remains. Here and there molten swamps mixed sand with rocket fuel. These bubbled and gurgled, coughing up awful grey smoke.

Jason rubbed the acrid smoke from his eyes. Grim. Beaten. The entire area resembled a hellish, aborted funeral. Half cremated, half buried, the wreckage bore no resemblance whatever to the graceful Fair Monique.

Daniella isn't here, he thought. *She died up there. This is an empty grave. There's nothing here.*

Not that that was any consolation. Why should he survive this end and Daniella not, when everything he was, everything he'd accomplished since Fourmyle would not exist if she hadn't put her name forward on that missionary petition. Saved him when no one else would. An orphan girl who'd shamed the entire ISPA establishment with a gesture of peace, of sacrifice unheard of in these empty, impersonal times. He owed her his *life*. But how, God, how could he repay her now? If he could swap places he'd do it without a second thought, but...

She wasn't the only one he owed his life to.

He'd known two guardian angels in his lifetime, and both were with him now: one in spirit, one in short shorts and a green tank top. Both were women the likes of which he'd never met anywhere else in the galaxy. And suddenly the idea of his wife never falling to ground, somehow remaining in the heavens, brought bittersweet tears to his eyes. "There's nothing here," he repeated aloud. "Let's go...all of us."

"Yes, let's."

He clasped Kate's hand and began the long walk around the wreckage—hundreds of acres—while trying to disavow all memory of life aboard the *Fair Monique*. This was his life now, his third life, and for Daniella, for Kate, he'd make the most of it for as long as he possibly could. He focused on the horizon. It blended with an endless clear sky, resembling a uniform beach with an infinite sherry ocean. He now felt lucky, not ashamed; hopeful, not glum; neither alive nor a ghost; something forgotten. That was all there was to it. He and Kate had simply slipped by, sugar-stealers in the breeze. They weren't meant to see such sights. They were

accidents, and death had somehow miscounted.
   Well, at least for the time being.

Chapter Ten
The Heart of Kratos

"It's up to you." Kate spat the noxious taste from her mouth. "I've led us this far, and it's not exactly improved our situation, let's face it. For all I know, south might've taken us to the garden spot of the whole planet. I think it's your turn to pick a path, Jason."

"No pressure, then."

"Ha! Nope. No pressure."

"Well, see if you can follow my reasoning." He cleared his throat and concentrated on the panorama. "West leads to the ocean, which has its possibilities—food, maybe water from tributaries. On the other hand, we don't know what predators live there. It'd just be my luck to run straight into a giant squid or some damn thing. East looks about as inviting as a Fourmyle prison—long, hot and miserable. South is out, obviously. I'm intrigued by this 'horizon' ahead; it's getting closer with every step, almost like we're approaching the edge of the world. North, I say, Ms. Borrowdale. I'm sticking with your plan. Now…aren't you glad you asked?"

"Oh, tickled pink."

The smoke column had shrunk to no more than that of a small bonfire when she glanced behind. They'd walked for some four hours since bidding the *Fair Monique* farewell. The declining desert stretched a mile ahead, after which there was nothing, just as Jason had said. The edge of the world? *Not unless you're standing at the prow of a longship, with a name like Olaf.* It was a bizarre phenomenon, but one with a scientific explanation. Of that much she was certain.

But if this was the desert *and* sea level, how could there be a sheer drop?

"It's the scale of this place," Jason answered her puzzled expression. "We're thinking in terms of Earth and the colonies, the topography there. This is through the looking glass the other way. If something appears to make no physical sense, it's only because we haven't seen the whole picture. Take our fall from the mountain. You thought we were plummeting to ground like we would on Earth, but there were bigger forces at work, air currents on a far larger scale. And something tells me we'll kick ourselves up ahead, when we solve this 'ere mystery."

"And if it turns out to be the edge of the world, I'm kicking you over it."

"So it's like that, is it?" he said. "I get to make the choice, but I get the boot if it goes belly-up?"

"Yup."

"I'm so glad you're finally starting to trust me."

"Don't mention it. I told you I couldn't manage without a guy to kick around."

"Ouch! You're all heart, Borrowdale."

The sand became rock-solid underfoot, and incredibly flat. The shallow decline to the precipice grew unusually smooth the closer they got. Two hundred yards from the edge, Jason stopped to make a bare patch in the sand with his boot.

What the...? Kate scowled as she crouched to inspect it.

"It looks metallic," she said. After widening the uncovered area, they looked at one another, eyes pin-wheeling.

"Crafted metal?" said Jason. "But what's it doing buried at the end of the world?"

Their final steps toward the horizon were delicate, apprehensive, precarious. Hundreds of light-purple clouds roamed the sky as dreamy jellyfish. The depth of their number increased with each forward step. The sensation, as if spinning slowly upside down, tickled the hairs on Kate's neck. She held Jason's arm for fear of losing her balance at any moment. Each reverent step might've been down the aisle of a church, so close together were they, and so quiet. A faint lime rose from the edge, followed by streaks of dark blue. The colors were wispy, pastel, ethereal. Another step brought a swath of reddish-brown into view. *A rainbow through the clouds?* The next area of dark blue, however, covered a significant area, and was far deeper than the sky above. Outlines of random shapes were now distinct, along with scrawled borders and boundaries. A three-dimensional grey area reminded her of...a mountain? *Yes, it's a mountain range...far below.* Her perception shifted. No longer wheeling on the verge of nothingness, she looked down to a distant valley thousands of feet below.

Jason tugged at her vest and pointed straight down. She leaned over, steadying herself on him. It was an overhang, a metallic overhang, below which she made out grooves and straight edges as far as the eye could see. An enormous cylindrical shape jutted out hundreds of feet from the vertical grey surface.

A ship?

Peering right and left across the precipice, Kate perceived the full dimensions of the phenomenon. She gripped Jason by the shoulder and then fell to her knees, dizzy.

"Take a minute," he said. "You'll be all right." In the meantime, he leaned over the edge once more and counted, "Three, four, five more cylinders, at least, half a mile apart. He whipped round to face the desert. "My God. Our whole route?" He muttered to himself, appeared to be calculating something in his mind. "Kate, you want to hear something mind-blowing?"

"Hmm."

"I think every step we've taken, ever since we landed, has been on the roof of this thing."

"Excuse me?"

"Think about it. A craft as big as a continent…crashed millions of years ago…buried by countless sand storms and geological upheavals…and we've been exploring its surface for four days."

She stared at him, shaking her head. "How do you account for Babylon Wall, the river tunnel, the ocean? How do you get rocks to grow from a spaceship? Or enough water—"

"How do you get rocks on top of a spaceship? We should know that better than anyone. Remember that day on the mountain…the storm that started this whole misadventure…boulders the size of houses hurled through the sky like pellets in a blizzard?"

"That doesn't explain Babylon Wall, or the tunnel," she insisted.

"I think those might actually be part of the craft. That would explain the circular tunnel and the sheer cliff you climbed. Maybe the rock is really just a crust on the shell of the ship, formed by millions of years of violent atmospheric conditions. Maybe the sand was congealed by super-hot temperatures. Who's to say? Each of those cylinders is about the size of the Titanic, and I've counted five already. And we're standing on the rim of the thing, thousands of feet from the valley floor."

"The ocean might just be rainwater collected in a dip in the surface…a dent the size of the Atlantic…over millions of years," suggested Kate, now coming to grips with the awesome implications.

"And the *Fair Monique* crashed on top of a crashed ship."

A sudden gust blew sand in a spindrift over the edge. Kate cast her mind back to the snowy mountain pass—days, years, worlds ago—with infinite curiosity. What was she like back then? What was Kate Borrowdale really doing on Kratos in the first place? As she glanced back over the desert, her moods and past secrets seemed buried, out of reach in the sandy trail behind her. The floor of one world, the ceiling of another. Was the alien ship hollow? If so, what magnitude of emptiness had she walked over? What might this discovery be like if she was alone?

She shuffled over to Jason and, tilting his head toward her with both hands, kissed him slowly. Her cheeks flamed red.

His hands roved across her shoulders and back. It felt beyond perfect. She knew he wanted it, too.

Jason had to steady them. "We're on a roll," he said. "How about we find somewhere a little safer?"

"After you."

They rose together, overlooking a valley of vague colors and incredible possibilities. Hand in hand, neither of them had the faintest idea of how to reach it. What seemed like tiny trickles of water from the precipice to the west Kate knew were massive waterfalls plunging from the ocean rim. She saw scores of giant birds circling the landscape far below. The pastel greens and blues under the clouds suddenly reminded her of Earth. The reddish-brown swath appeared to snake toward the mountain range, as though it was an enormous, migrating herd. Whatever might happen, the valley was where they needed to be.

"It's not unlike home, is it?" he said.

"No," she replied, looking up at the twin suns drawing closer together. "It is home."

* * * *

BOOK TWO
THE ELEMENTAL CROSSING

Chapter Eleven
A New Mode of Travel

"Keep that line taut." Jason yanked his own rope back to straighten the sail.

As the wind picked up, they skimmed over shallow sand drifts, the keel of their craft barely touching the ground. The faster they went, the farther back Jason had to lean in order to keep them upright. His control of the 'sand yacht' was by two ropes, one in each hand, which tilted the sail accordingly. It required not only every muscle, but an incredible concentration at all times.

"I said keep that line taut!" he snarled.

"Shout at me one more time, I dare you," Kate screamed back. But he didn't seem to hear, so wholeheartedly was he at the reins of his contraption.

Boys and their toys. And it had been his dumbass idea…

The wind speed had grown almost cyclonic since those first kick-starting gusts. Jason's ingenious creation—the beak and rigor-mortised wing of a dead giant eagle, lashed together, rigged with ropes—shot across the desert. Kate's whole body now shook with the strain and the bitter cold.

"How long has it been now? Half an hour?" he shouted, teeth bared in the throes of exhilaration. "I'm telling you…this is amazing, bloody amazing."

Her daredevil partner had adapted so quickly to the steering that Kate wondered if there really was genius at work, or whether he'd simply done this before…maybe on Fourmyle?

Either way, he was too damn reckless.

"That's it," he yelled down to her through the wind. "You've got it, Kate. Hold that line. Now is this awesome or what? I'm telling you."

She shifted position to raise her butt for the next big impact. *Thud!* The keel slammed into a steep dune, gouged its way up and then ricocheted over a bed of pebbles down the other side.

He's out of control. If he crashes us, it won't be the impact that kills him…so help me.

The giant stiff wing dragged them across a mile-long, level plateau, scraping their keel over a bed of tiny, sharp rocks, all the while picking up speed. Its ragged skin caught every gust; Jason seemed to tilt the rig intuitively for optimal propulsion.

How fast now? Thirty, forty miles-an-hour? *Crazy*.

They hurtled toward a sandy incline at the far edge of the plain. It was only shallow but continued to rise and rise—exactly how high, she couldn't tell. Its peak obscured the entire desert beyond.

"Alright, you can stop us any time now," she yelled up.

No answer. Jason leaned farther back, wrapping the two ropes around his white knuckles. The yacht slowed for a moment, before a punch of wind hit diagonally from behind, flexing the sail's leathery skin. Kate elbowed his shin and screamed, "Stop. Now. What the hell are you doing?"

Leaning forward, she made ready to jump off, but something held her back. *He* needed her, damn it. If she could hold on just a bit longer...

Kate's stomach did its elastic catapult thing as they accelerated up the slope. The ground fell away without warning, revealing a wind-whipped, rolling surface fifty feet below. No time to prepare. Rocketing through mid-air caused her to grip the ropes with every ounce of strength. The two halves of the giant beak chattered. The sail dipped sharply, jerking them forward, and then shot up, wrenching them back. Kate's heart floundered as she realised her man had no control at all over the sand yacht.

After so long without reprieve, Jason's right arm went spastic under the strain. The wind eased momentarily, causing them to plummet. At about twenty feet, however, a powerful gust wheeled the sail through forty-five degrees, tipping the yacht. The tendrils holding Jason's feet tore loose. He had to let go of his left-hand rope. Now flapping through the air at the end of a single line, his whole body creased under sickening shockwaves, as though he was the tip of a whip enduring crack after crack.

"Let go! Jesus!" She tried to figure out a way to work him loose, cut him loose, but the mad hombre *chose* to cling.

At that moment the sand yacht rolled over into a final diving spin.

We're going...going...shit. Jason!

Letting go of the stay rope, she wrenched her feet free from the tendril straps and flung herself at him. The impact knocked the wind out of her, but was enough to break Jason's hold on the wild line. They landed in a tangle ten feet below, on the crest of a windswept dune. Jason watched in horror as his great invention veered sharply, corkscrewed, and then crash-landed into a nearby trough. The wingtip stabbed the sand again and again. Its beak stood upended at its side, lashed jaws pointing skyward, and looked remarkably like a bird corpse half buried in the desert.

"That could've easily been us." She gave Jason's arm a firm punch. "I hope you're satisfied."

"Too right," he replied, still shaking with adrenaline. "That was unbelievable. Un-fricking-believable! How about another go?"

Kate let herself collapse into a slide down the dune, and saw in his sparkling gaze watching her that he meant it. She shook her head.

"Men."

* * * *

While they dragged the sand yacht to the summit of a large slope, another sandstorm hit from the east. Visibility shrank to just a few metres, but the wind wasn't especially fierce. Kate tromped on for the ocean.

"The longer we wait for this thing to clear, the more dehydrated we'll be," she said, stepping into her survival suit for the umpteenth time on Kratos.

Jason had stopped trying to second-guess her. Though she offered him the democratic veto on most decisions, Kate Borrowdale was the most qualified, the fittest, the most intuitive terrain scout he'd ever come across.

That's a decent marker, he thought, glancing back to their giant wing wedged high on the peak. *Good thinking, Kate.* They'd be able to find it again in no time.

Their belts tied together with a twenty-foot rope, they shielded their faces to trudge through a swirling semi-dusk. The desert surface morphed all about them. The occasional coarse gust stung his ears and tried to unstitch a wound on his chin; by the time the winds eased, both were red raw. The sky, too, bled reddish purple between blue clouds.

Bruised in the aftermath.

Jason suddenly scooped her off her feet from behind and, holding her close, pressed his cheek against hers.

"We've made it," he said. "The only sand from now on is beachfront property."

Swept up by the man of her dreams, her lift was physical, spiritual, vital. A week ago, in the desert, Kate had started a survival cycle for two; here, on the mysterious shore of a green-blue ocean, the cycle had come full circle. *Jason Remington…Jason and I.* Though fate had raised its skull and crossbones more than once on Kratos—most tragically to destroy the *Fair Monique*—Kate had in fact won everything she'd wanted: her man, her life, and a chance to explore a hidden world. But in the bargain, just as many questions, if not more. Their journey to the ocean was now complete…

But in a survival *cycle,* nothing was ever complete.

The seascape tantrumed into an elemental brew, a dark green wilderness unable to settle after a hurricane upheaval. The wind tossed manes of spray from the crests of swells. Waves danced, merged like feverish loners in an icy rave. Two miles to the north, the giant precipice curtailed the ocean for as far as the eye could see. This straight line amid the chaos haunted Kate. The idea of an entire ocean being little more than a puddle on the surface of a giant craft made her dizzy again.

"If you had to guess," said Jason, "how far would you say it stretches?"

"Well, how far can we see to the horizon?"

"Say about twice as far as on Earth."

"That's conservative," she replied. "Kratos is proportionally a lot bigger than that."

"Yes, but our eyes can't see infinitely through this erratic atmosphere," added Jason.

"You mean the electromagnetic anomaly we were told about? Something to do with gravitational distortion?"

"Let's just say if there wasn't an anomaly, we'd never have made it through the EM shield. One of the biggest solid planets ever explored, in terms of circumference; I can't even imagine the gravitational forces we *should* be experiencing right now."

"We're miraculous survivors on a miraculous world," she said. "And you can make a note of that for our epitaph."

Jason kissed her on the cheek, before setting her down on the sand.

"So what's the plan?" He resumed his walk.

"I thought this was the plan," she replied.

"I mean what now? Say we can make a go of it here for a while—if there's a permanent food supply—what next, Mrs. Miraculous Survivor on a miraculous world? Where do we go from here?"

Kate tossed her hair in a playful haughty gesture as she overtook him. "Haven't the foggiest."

But it was a fair question. That they couldn't even see a way around the ocean yet didn't matter a great deal; there was so much exploring to be done. And the injection of hope she'd felt at finally escaping the sandstorm and the desert buoyed her optimism for some time. Survival, as ever, was a finite problem with a finite solution, begging to be solved by rational minds.

It was when they traversed the last steep dune on their way to the sea that Kate heard a series of strange, barely audible staccato clicks. Training her ears on the motion of their suits, she decided it had to be something else. Something farther away.

"Jason, stop a minute. Can you hear that?"

"What?"

"Listen...click, click-click, click...then a rash of clicks. I don't know, I can hardly make it out. But there's definitely something—"

He whipped his head to the south and began to creep with measured strides. "I heard it, too. There's something alive over here."

Kate wanted to grab his collar and yank him on toward the ocean, but each and every discovery might prove crucial to their chances of survival, of sustaining survival in one place.

Like the old man had said—referring to her Mars mentor, Yuri Yeltsin—real survival was ten percent planning, ninety percent improvisation.

Though she personally thought preparation was a better word than planning; without that training, that knowhow, anyone could improvise a thousand ways to not make it through the night.

The clicks grew higher in pitch and more syncopated as Kate and Jason approached a long, hidden trough in the lower sand drifts. Though they had a tasker apiece, only three harpoons remained between them.

One each, at least.

Attaching spear-tip to tasker produced a click not unlike those coming from the trough, and each sound of the loading mechanism provoked an agitated reply.

"It's definitely alive," said Kate, "whatever it is. It's communicating."

The tip of something long and slender spiralled high in the air and struck down like a lash. They jumped back with a start. Sand tossed from the trough curled high into the breeze. Kate pointed her tasker. As she inched around the incline, two massive rubbery tentacles rose out of the sand. Coiled in midair ready to strike. Taut, quivering, they snapped forward to the ground. Three more rose and followed a similar projection, a few feet apart. All appeared to aim for the same target. Kate and Jason stepped out into the trough to see the full horrific nature of what they'd discovered.

It was not a single monster like a hydra or a squid. The tentacles appeared sentient, in competition. Their coarse skin appeared grey but for a crimson tip and sandy veins at the root. Two banks of these monstrosities faced one another in the trough, about twenty feet apart. The way they whipped the sand reminded Jason of regimental beatings he used to witness as an ISPA cadet, when an offender would have his bare back lashed by ranks of towel-wielding colleagues. He'd suffered one such beating, and it made his blood simmer even now.

"Cruel bastards."

Click-click, cli-cli-click-click

"What *is* that?" Kate craned her neck trying to see inside the tossed sand. "Am I seeing things or is there something there? Looks almost like…like a hologram, or a ghost."

"There's definitely something," he replied. "Definitely…something."

Jason crept toward the plant-like tentacles, his tasker aimed at the nearest root.

"What are you doing? Jason. *Jason.*"

Kate called futilely as he stalked the deadliest-looking sand creatures he'd ever seen. Why? What possible advantage could it serve? They'd be at the water's edge in a matter of minutes. Easy, no obstacles. But this…this was going out of his way to find trouble.

Some things you couldn't just ignore.

The apparition, the victim in the sand became no more visible as he approached than it had from where Kate stood. Just a phantom shape struggling, clicking to break free. Memories of scratching at the mortar in his cell in Fourmyle—with a spoon handle, a sharp piece of brick, his fingernails—desperate to loosen a brick or a rock and somehow communicate with someone, anyone in the next cell, wounded him in tender places he'd mentally bandaged, deep inside. No, he'd never spoken to another soul in all that time. Over thirteen Earth months. Not until an orphan girl had risked her future to set him free, sight unseen.

He owed Daniella this much.

"Because no one should have to suffer like that. No one. Nothing." And he took aim.

"For chrissakes, don't do anything stupid." Kate, probably the voice of reason but who gave a shit about reason? This was justice. His tasker's cross-hairs locked on the tentacle root.

Cli-click, cliiiick, cli-click

Jason answered the poor creature's distress call with a satisfying shot. The harpoon buried deep into the rubbery tentacle, and with it came a loud pop, rather like a bursting inner-tube. The horrid thing flailed for a few seconds before snapping backward, writhing, and slowly furled into a sandy grave. The victim still wasn't free, however. Two tentacles must have taken turns anchoring it to the ground, because when the first died, the second clamped itself horizontally over the ghost-like creature.

"Okay, try this." And Kate fired her own harpoon at the monstrosity.

Bullseye. The tentacle shot straight up to its extremity, almost tearing itself out of its own inflating roots, then popped. It withered to the same violent end as its brethren. Jason kicked out, threw his fist in celebration.

Jesus, it meant more to him than he'd realised.

A form neither of them expected scurried out from the cloud of sand. Jason leapt in front of Kate to shield her, but he needn't have. The thing had six legs, four close together at the front, two, thick and muscular, at the back. It was about eight feet long and resembled a large salamander. Instead of scales, it had smooth, oily, chameleonic skin that adapted to the colours and contours of the desert. But it was clearly a solid shape. What shocked him, however, was not the creature itself, but what preceded it.

A spectral twin?

He rubbed his eyes to make sure he wasn't seeing double. As the salamander ran, a phantom extension of itself seemed to predict its every turn and movement. The actions were not simultaneous, though, like those of shadow and host; no, the holographic ghost moved *before* the body, leading it over the sand as a kind of precognitive double.

"What the hell is that?" He knew full well he wouldn't receive an answer. "Looks like it's chasing itself."

It was dizzying just watching the thing. It stayed low to ground as it ran, its head wide and quite flat around the edges, resembling a stingray's, especially at the mouth. From what he could tell, a black, throbbing dome forming the crown of its head had some kind of sensory function. A three-hundred-and-sixty-degree blink occurred, in a wave of skin around the reflective dome, every twenty seconds or so, releasing a halo of dark particles, a kind of momentary Saturnian ring that dissipated in the air. Some kind of alien sonar? A hyper-sensitive mapping ability? Or another secret altogether? The creature had no nose or ears, but three eyes, each as black as the halo, in the middle of its head. He could only guess at the complexity of alien biology inside.

Just before it stopped on the next slope, its spectral twin retracted. The clicking ceased. The salamander waited there, fifty yards ahead on the way to the ocean, just staring at Kate and Jason.

"What's it thinking?" she asked.

"Curiously," he replied. "It's never seen people before."

The tentacles' thumps eased, too, behind them, and Jason wondered whether the creature might be waiting for something. Or someone? Glancing round, he swallowed a lump in his throat. Four or five large mounds emerged as the sand cloud vanished in the centre of the trough. The giant tentacles coiled backward, perhaps waiting for their next unsuspecting prey. Or had they fed enough for one day?

"He wasn't the only one." Jason pointed Kate to the mounds. "That was probably his family. Poor lad, he's really suffered."

He gazed into the eyes of the salamander. Beaten down, stripped of its family, saved by strangers from certain death, whatever language it spoke from now on, it was Jason's language.

"Poor boy," he whispered.

As they approached it, the creature's ghost turned sharply away, but the creature itself only flinched.

Was it rebelling against something? Against instinct? Was that what the phantom extension was—instinct?

He hoped his new friend would stay with them a while. To his relief, it waited. And when he bent to touch its oily skin turning pink and bronzed like his own, and saw its three deep, inquisitive eyes looking right back, he hoped it wouldn't leave him any time soon.

Chapter Twelve
Beyond the Dunes

It wasn't the shoreline they'd expected. Pale sand, yes, and greenish water; but there was a dull, antiseptic feel about the place, like a class field trip to a sterile industrial plant. Apart from three or four clusters of white seaweed, there was no evidence of life. Kate immediately thought back to Dolphin Cove and the sublime atmosphere shared by the creatures there. She shuddered. This was as far removed from that joy as a funeral from a wedding. A cold gust brought with it a sickly smell, rather like rancid dairy products.

"Zombie beach," she said. "No other way to describe it."

"None," agreed Jason.

Even the salamander looked the other way as it came to rest between them.

"Ladies first," invited Jason with a courteous sweep of his arm.

Dark green water bobbed as a million dancing shoulders. It would take a while to settle after the storm. So inhospitable was the view that Kate gazed southwest across the coast, back over their original route.

Anything was better than this. Maybe they should try for Dolphin Cove again. The slug posse was wiped out, but how many more were there? They couldn't risk another manhunt. But that spot *was* paradise. This was more like the anti-paradise.

Jason crouched to rub the salamander's back often. It loved that. In return, it kept at least one of its three eyes on him at all times.

"You'd better think of a name." Kate tickled their new companion behind the gills.

"I like Mandy," he replied. "Mandy the salamander."

The creature's black dome blinked in its swift circumferential motion. They had no clue what the gesture meant, but it seemed benign. And as the salamander had displayed nothing but affection for Jason, Kate perceived the bond as instinctive.

Gratitude? Loyalty? They'd saved its life and now it was bound to save theirs? Like the eagles? There was an evolved intelligence here, a social curiosity—they'd seen it already in a few species: the eagles, the dolphins, and now Mandy. It wasn't like Nature to repay good deeds, though, unless it benefitted the species in a practical Darwinian sense. Or perhaps making friends as opposed to enemies *did* make good survival sense. *Best face it, Katie girl, this eco-system is playing by a whole new set of rules.*

"But not all," she said aloud, rubbing her empty stomach.

"Not all what?"

"Um…not all bad news. Mandy might know where to find food. Of the three of us, she's the only one who lives here, after all."

"So he's a she now, is he?"

Kate laughed. "Hey, sexist pig, you came up with Mandy."

"So that's how it is, huh? What say we let the salamander decide whether it's a boy or a girl."

"How do we do that exactly?"

"We each throw a boot in the same direction, and whosever boot Mandy fetches determines the gender."

"Okay, that's dumb on so many levels," she replied, "but here goes."

They each removed a boot and, after counting down from three, hurled it across the beach. Mandy looked up at Jason, then across to Kate, paying no mind at all to the flying footwear.

"Go on, Mandy. Go fetch." He waved both arms at the boots. "Go on, boy."

The bemused salamander dropped its head and slinked over to Kate, who hadn't given a word or gesture of encouragement.

"I think that's settled," she said.

Mandy lay motionless at her side, watching Jason as though he'd just scolded them both. As Kate bent to stroke her, the gentle creature turned a light purple colour, mirroring that of the sky. She seemed utterly content.

"It's the beginning of the end," he said with a sigh. "Two, I repeat two, females to contend with."

* * * *

While mammoth cloud swirls gathered high in the atmosphere, the weather on the surface remained fine. Rather like the day they'd landed, Kratos seemed to consist of separate realms—realms dictated by altitude. What happened high above them often had no bearing on the surface, and vice versa. A hurricane in the heavens might stay in the heavens; a desert storm might have its ceiling well under the main cloud strata. It was a world of many layers.

"Underwater?" asked Jason. "How are you underwater?"

"I hold six ISPA records. Why?"

"What's your longest dive?"

"Free dive—four minutes and five seconds. Yours?"

He cleared his throat, adopted a gruff tone. "Yes, well, four-o-five, huh? Not bad, not bad, Borrowdale. Let's see how you do, then."

"I'm first?"

"You're first."

"Um, groovy." She dipped a toe in the green water, pulled her face as she tried to see under the surface. Nothing. It was translucent, but no signs of life or even flotsam were evident. She waded out until submerged to her thighs. Warm, viscous, reeking water. An oily film covered the surface a little farther out.

"It's a toxic pond," she shouted.

"What can you see underwater?"

Bugger all. But you'll never know till you...

She took the plunge before she had the opportunity to dwell on it—an old tactic she'd learned from Yeltsin. A warm rush fogged her brain. Being fully submerged was pleasant, soothing. All the mechanics of underwater exhalation returned, as if she were still in the training pool ten years ago, a thousand light years away. *Step by step, Katie girl…step by step.*

While the sea bed was mostly sand, the occasional bare spot revealed smooth metal. A breathtaking shift in perception. The awesome implications of an ocean on the hull of a giant craft would not let her relax. And as she found nothing but seaweed and a few shrimp-sized organisms over the next half hour, she returned to the beach dejected, her eyes aching and bloodshot.

"Nothing?" asked Jason.

She shook her head.

"Maybe she'll have better luck."

"What?"

"Yeah, Mandy went out shortly after you. Whether she'll come back or not…well, I hope she does. If not, I don't know what we're going to do for food."

Kate plonked herself on the beach next to him, her tatty vest and shorts dripping wet. He caressed, then began to massage her shoulders. A disarming, unknotting sensation that made her feel alternately sleepy, sensual, and like so much cookie dough. All the while they watched the artificial ocean, waiting, hoping for Mandy's return.

* * * *

A grim swath of cloud threw a rain cloak over the binary suns on the horizon, casting an immediate, premature darkness over Kratos. Kate stopped watching. Instead she lay back, arms folded under her head on the sand. But Jason remained transfixed by the desolation, the enormity of what lay ahead for them.

What were they trying to achieve here? What was their ultimate goal in this place? To reach the lowland at the base of the giant craft—then what? Existing, surviving would be an achievement. But was survival itself ever reward enough, reason enough to try? Perhaps not, but Kate was. *Correction, Kate and Jason.*

Daniella's face appeared more vivid than ever over the twilit ocean. It didn't take much imagination; she was with him still, reminding him not to despair. To hope. Always. High cheekbones and small, narrow brown eyes; hair dyed strawberry red, something he'd never really liked but it had helped her forget those dark years on Fourmyle; pale skin, and soft, almost sad features that only really came to vibrant life when he was around: she wasn't someone he'd have picked out of a crowd in terms of looks, but she was the most purely feminine woman he'd ever encountered. With a heart big enough for the both of them—and he'd needed that for a long time after Fourmyle. As he imagined her in the twilight embers, tears streamed down her cheeks, as when he'd asked her to marry him a second time—but for love, not merely peace—on a bench on the *Fair Monique's* C-deck observatory. It had seemed more romantic at the time.

Moments after her tears fell, a violent spark shot up from the ocean. Jason squinted to identify it, couldn't, leapt onto his knees.

Violet and violent. What the hell?

"Kate, look at this. Quick."

"What is it?"

The spark plumed as a spectacular firework. A purple tree that blazed for at least thirty seconds before dying to leave the surrounding sea glowing violet. A few seconds later, another firework lit to its left, just as impressive. When that burned out, another erupted, and so on until half the horizon was illuminated. Almost as if the sunset were being churned and recycled up through the sea in a sequence of blazing smithereens.

"Ideas?" Jason rubbed his bearded chin.

Kate stared on without a word as the millions of sparks spread to form a burgundy blanket over miles and miles of water. She looked down across their inhospitable shoreline. No signs of life. But *this*. Yes, this was something new—something full of mystery—and possibilities. Good and bad.

"We have to go out there," she said.

"And fry?"

"And try…try to find out what intelligence is behind it. Those aren't naturally occurring geysers."

"And they're not exactly friendly geysers either."

"Listen," she said, "that sequence was set at perfect intervals. Perfect. It might be a form of communication, or part of some machine, or some kind of celebration—like New Year's Eve—for all we know. The point is there's someone, or something, causing it. And we need to make contact. As soon as possible. Jason, we're dying."

The notion hit him hard and in tender places. Her matter-of-fact delivery doubled its impact.

We're dying, and we've no choice but to attempt a crossing…while we've still got enough strength. This is it then; this is where it all ends. On a goddamn alien sea.

"The sand yacht." She looked him square in the eyes. "Now we'll see what you can really do with that thing."

"But it probably won't float."

"No, but we'll have to figure out a way to make it float, or find something else that will."

"Like what?"

"Beats me, but it's either that or walk round—and risk being stalked by those slugs we love so much."

"Kate, that thing won't float without some serious buoyancy."

"So get thinking."

"Yes, ma'am."

An hour after the fireworks, Mandy returned with two eel-like creatures in her mouth. When she dropped them on the sand, one at Kate's feet, one at Jason's, it was obvious that even with the salamander's best efforts, there wasn't enough food to sustain them here. Mandy had been gone half a day for this one meal. Plus the eels were disgusting, and a long way from filling.

"Thank you anyway, girl." Jason gave her pale-yellow back a good rub. "You did good."

"Good girl, Mandy," Kate managed between coughs—the slimy tail didn't go down well. "But cooking-wise, not so good."

That evening, the twin suns vanished simultaneously and didn't reappear until Kate and Jason had retrieved the sand yacht. Their suits defeated the night's bitter chill. Despite its crash landing, the rig was in decent shape. And as the storm had drifted sand over any rocks between yacht and ocean, they decided to drag it by the beak, letting the wing-sail simply trail behind.

Navigating by the purple glow over the ocean, they reached the coast full of hope...and trepidation. The yacht barely floated as it filled with water. Just as they'd guessed, it was nowhere near seaworthy. While they pulled it back ashore, Mandy rushed into the sea.

She was amphibian after all. Not like their clunky sand-surfer.

That was Jason's last thought before he collapsed next to Kate on the sand and saw her pull the giant, leathery wing over them.

The following afternoon, she woke alone. Jason wasn't there. Nor was he on the beach nearby or in the sea, or even behind her in the dunes. But two sets of tracks led away to the southwest, along the coast.

It was another dour, overcast day. The horizon's mysterious purple glow had disappeared, leaving a pastel, green-blue expanse of calm water. Kate scanned the coastline until she came across two tiny shapes at the water's edge. One she recognised immediately as Jason, the second, long and slender, lay on the sand. What the heck was it? Something he'd found in the water? Mandy's camouflaged (sand-coloured) form ran in front of the object as, curiously, Jason appeared to lift its end and drag it along the beach.

Something to eat? A piece of flotsam they could use for the yacht?

Ten minutes later, Jason heaved his catch off his shoulder and plonked it down next to the yacht.

"A tentacle?" she observed. "You've brought us…a tentacle? How nice."

"Hey, I walked all morning to find this, while you had a lie-in."

Thick rubber, scaly, over twenty feet long, the thing was identical to the creatures responsible for killing Mandy's family in the dunes. The salamander herself scurried along at Jason's side, paying the dead beast no mind.

"Let me show you something." He dragged it into the water, left it to float in the green shallows.

"Yes?" she asked.

"Yes."

"Yes what?"

"There, on the water," he said. "Floating on the water. Kate, it floats."

"I can see that."

"Kate, the tentacle's dead and it's floating."

"Good for the tentacle."

He laughed. "You really don't see it do you."

"I might if you had something for me to see."

"All right, remember when we shot them with harpoons, to save Mandy? Remember the sound they made?"

"A tiny explosion. Like something burst…"

He clicked his fingers. "There you go."

Ah. So the tentacles were buoyant, and from the effort Jason had to put in to hold this one underwater, extremely buoyant. "Remind me not to lie-in so long in future." She shook her head. "So…how many of these for the sand yacht?"

"I'd say a couple more."

She whistled. "I guess we know where to look, then."

By dusk, they had the vessel fully rigged for the voyage. Mandy wouldn't go near the nest of tentacles where her family lay buried. Kate and Jason managed to detach the two they'd already killed by tying ropes around the roots and wrenching them free. It proved easier than they'd expected, as the other vines appeared unresponsive, perhaps asleep.

Jason discovered the tentacle's body was segmented, rather like a worm's; even with a puncture, there was still more than enough buoyancy in the other sections to keep it afloat. Without life, it had contracted to become a taut, rubbery flotation tube, and it floated exceedingly well.

Next, they wrapped the three tentacles around the giant beak, experimenting with buoyancy and the waterline. A top-heavy yacht would be disastrous, as would one constantly submerging. The deck measured about fifteen feet from port to starboard, and near twelve from bow to stern, owing to the odd shape of the beak—not a good one for a sailing vessel. But with the strong buoyancy aids, and so long as the crew minded their positions on deck, it had a decent enough balance.

Jason had to use far more rope for the next part. As the voyage would be stop-start, perhaps for weeks, the sail now had to be rigged as part of the boat itself. No less than eight lines secured the wing mast at various heights, again making any movement by the crew across the deck a tricky affair.

A heavy, low sky threatened the sea with the dangling tails of dark twisters. Kate and Jason racked their brains to cover each and every contingency. The prospect was daunting, yet unavoidable. The danger of risking their lives to the temper of an alien sea only upped their concentration. They focused on the minutiae. Worked toward the safest. Planned for the unseen. Prepared for the worst.

"I think we're good." Kate adjusted the collar of her suit with one hand, stroked Mandy's back with the other.

Jason scooped up a handful of dry sand and let it run though his fist. The wind wasn't strong but flew in the same direction, as always—east to west. His boots squelched into the sand as surf pooled about them. In his beard and battered survival suit, he resembled Robinson Crusoe on Mars.

"Okay, here goes," he whispered.

One, two, three!

His huge effort slid the yacht from sand to gentle waves. The vessel bobbed, groaned and nodded as he pulled himself up onto the stern. Mandy settled beside him, her black dome giving a slow, three-sixty halo blink. Quite why the ocean was so restful they didn't care to question as the yacht inched outward, ever outward. The name scratched across its starboard side read, *Elemental*.

Chapter Thirteen
Maiden Voyage of the Elemental

Day 1

At thirty-one, Kate Borrowdale was in peak physical shape. Months of circuit training, practice on the climbing wall's steepest overhang, low-g and high-g cycling in the velodrome, aerobics, swimming, and other habitual exertions aboard the *Fair Monique* had put her at the forefront of competitors, both male and female. Even Jason, himself no slouch, remained a distant second in all areas of physical fitness. And as she'd proved over the past two weeks, very few obstacles perturbed Kate. She could think, push, pull, run, jump, climb or fight to beat anything in her way. But drifting on the ocean was a different matter entirely. Those myriad attributes she boasted, and which she relied on, counted for nothing. Absolutely nothing.

The smooth, bone-hard deck was a bitch to sit on for long periods, but what else could she do? Taut lines holding the mast in place resembled webbing all about her. The odd breeze nudged the *Elemental* forward but Kate, parched, famished and miserable, felt like dead weight.

"I can still make out the shore," she said. "How long's it been, do you reckon?"

"Couple of hours or so." Jason adjusted the last spearhead onto the line of his tasker.

"How's that thing coming?"

"Well, the theory's sound, but it all depends."

"On what?"

"On how dumb these fishes are," he said.

The idea was all Jason's. As they'd banked on edible life existing at a manageable size in the deep, this was to be the crux of their voyage—fishing with the tasker. If it failed, they would probably die.

"Talk me through it again," said Kate. "I felt a bit dizzy the first time."

"What's wrong?"

"Just hungry, I think…I hope."

"Okay, but if you feel anything else, let me know right away," he insisted. "We'll get through this thing, but we'll have to do it together."

She blushed.

"Right, tasker fishing 101," he said. "It's a highly scientific and laborious exercise involving dangling a line with a hook at the end into the water. And sitting there like a cold cadaver until you snag dinner. Any questions?"

"Yes, what if you snag Moby Dick?"

"Then it's bon appetite…for Moby Dick."

The green ocean settled further that afternoon, but Kate sensed they were still drifting, despite there being no wind. Mandy observed Jason's antics with intent curiosity, eyeing the fishing line and responding with a low click whenever it jerked in the water.

"I bet she's thinking 'How the heck did you two last a day on Kratos?'" Sarcasm—Kate's only contribution to the first day's sailing.

By late evening, they'd caught nothing. Worse still, there'd been no signs of fish of any size, no vegetation floating by, and no rainwater for them to collect. She watched Jason's tireless concentration, then glanced at the dark, twister-heavy blanket hanging from the heavens.

Time's not the only thing in short supply.

Day 2

"You want to play rough?"

Jason had knelt upright for the best part of an hour to keep a firm grip on the tasker, his sore back buckling under the strain. Whatever the catch was, it was momentous but, with each passing minute, proportionately outweighed by his ego. Clearly he'd never let go until one end of the line out-pulled the other.

"Why don't you give it up?" she groaned at last. "You're hungry, it's not obliging. Can't you try for something else? Come on, let it go."

"Shut it!"

She yawned, rubbed her eyes. "Aye, aye, Cap'n…Ahab."

The tasker did winch something up that afternoon, but it wasn't what Jason expected. Around two hundred feet of white, elastic slime, dredged from the sea bed, spilled from his hands as he gathered it up like a spaghetti fathom line. His excitement slipped as he pulled and pulled, hoping to see a creature attached at the other end. Nothing. Only slime—endless coils of slime. When he finally gave up, sinking onto his back, Kate shook her head and grinned a superior grin over him.

"Bolognese with that?"

Through all the commotion, neither of them had noticed the third crew member, the sedentary salamander, slink over the side and disappear into the toxic-looking depths. Mandy had deserted them, but why and for how long?

"She did find food last time," said Kate.

"And we found it barely edible."

"Who are we to grumble, though? If it stays down, it goes down with thanks—that's my motto."

"Hmm…what was that you used to love? Orange biscuits?"

"Wow, apple biscuits," she corrected, pleased he'd remembered that from their time in the gymnasium cafe. "Crumbly apple biscuits. I'd die happy if I only had a few packs of those. I'm telling you, the space gods eat those wherever space gods go to eat. Divine, I'm telling you."

She closed her eyes and recalled the first meal she'd selected after being rescued from the barren planet Dakota Prime, years ago. In the field, astronaut and terrain scout provisions were always synthetic, non-decomposing food squares; back on board her ship at the time, the *Santa Maria,* Kate had been given free reign to choose her next week's diet from the organic orchards—her reward for a job well done. Mangos, bananas, pears, strawberries, grapes and apples: she'd never forgotten those tastes, not even after years of synthetic diluting.

She hadn't been scheduled to take part in this particular scouting mission in the peaks of Kratos. They were saving her strength and expertise for a subsequent, even more hazardous drop in the southern hemisphere. But she'd volunteered for this one as well, much to the surprise of her superiors. Itching to get out there, they'd said. *Itching to be near him,* she'd thought. The request wasn't unprecedented, but it was unorthodox. As was the last thing on her pre-drop itinerary—a sneak sojourn to the *Fair Monique's* orchards on G-deck, specifically the apple orchard. G-deck was off-limits, but she'd tiptoed in wonderment through the verdant greens and ankle-high grass, reminding herself of what Nature *should* look like, while the constant whirring of fans provided a soothing breeze. Like Eve, she took a single apple, half of her anticipating the taste, the other half anticipating what it would be like to kiss Jason Remington.

She diced that apple minutely. Her friend on the catering staff, Alice Bevan, agreed to prepare a dozen "extra special" biscuits using Kate's fruity contraband. Those smuggled treats had sustained Kate for days on Kratos. But the *Fair Monique* was long gone, Alice was long gone, and the apple biscuits and orchards were long gone. Yet each was now vivid in her mind. The Spartan comfort of her quarters, the smell of popcorn as she and Alice would queue for the movie theatre on B-deck, the eerie, magical silence of the orchard. Whenever she swallowed, that organic apple flavour fizzed with juicy acid over her tonsils. It was a remnant taste of a past life, the residue of Earth. And it was hers.

Jason checked the buoyant vines wrapping the *Elemental* every hour or so. He found no signs of decomposition, corrosion or other defects. The vessel itself wasn't much of a seafarer—the shape resembled a half-flattened egg—but it stayed afloat, took its jabs of wind, and nodded politely toward the great horizon.

"You going to try again?" She pointed to the fishing tackle.

A puff of the cheeks. "Let's wait and see if Mandy brings us anything. I don't fancy wrestling with any more gloop today."

"You want me to have a bash?"

"In a while," he replied. "Something's telling me we're still not out far enough to catch anything worth eating."

All guesswork. As they waited, the twin suns tag-teamed through roving clouds in the western sky, lightening the green ocean and offering a clearer view of what lay in store. Endless, endless water. Kate thought she spied a few notch-like shadows on the horizon, but nothing she could pinpoint. The northern precipice glimmered every now and then—the edge of the world, as Jason liked to call it. Its metallic rim was perhaps millions of years old, yet still managed to sparkle through the shallow troughs between swells. Such durable metal didn't belong on any periodic table known to man, and the only other alien structure she'd ever heard of to match it was the abandoned giant receptor dish, Altimere, which over the eons had collected enough rainwater to become a sea in its own right. ISPA had built its Outer Colonies Command Hub there (at 65z), on the surface of the sea, without knowing a thing about the creatures who'd erected the dish in the first place. Might those original builders belong to the same alien race behind this colossal crashed vessel? Engineers operating on a scale large enough to turn Earth's starships into matchbox toys and her colony moons into corky balls.

The *Elemental* began to rock, a series of clicks announcing Mandy's return as she clambered aboard. Water cascaded from her glassy-green back and streamed across the deck. Hanging from her mouth were five limp stems of an undersea plant, a foot-long orange bulb attached to each.

"What's this, Mandy?" asked Jason in his softest voice.

The salamander gazed at him, her head tilted up, her stingray-like mouth gasping for air as she dropped the plants.

"This is what you've brought us to eat?" asked Kate.

The sensory dome on top of Mandy's head blinked rapidly; she appeared to be spent.

The lack of conviction in Jason's expression as he picked up an orange bulb made Kate snort a laugh. She imagined him as a food taster at a Borgia soiree.

"It feels…like an egg without the shell," he said.

"See if you can pierce it."

A runny red liquid streamed out as Jason pricked the soft surface with his fingernail.

"Okay, it's bleeding now." He scrunched his face with disgust. "I think you should—"

"Oh no you don't. This one's all yours, Bub."

An ironic lick of the lips. He then tore the bulb open. Inside was a honeycomb of brown, papery skin, with a red filling rather like watermelon. He inspected it closely, took a deep breath and…

"Not…not inedible." He tentatively chewed a small chunk of the watermelon. "Hardly any taste.

In fact, no taste whatsoever." He paused to manoeuvre his tongue around a piece of the brown skin.

"I've found it. Okay, the fruity part is bland but the skin itself is sweet. Bizarre. See what you think," and he handed her half a bulb.

"It'll do," she agreed, sucking on a piece, "until we die or find something better." And, nibbling the celery-like plant stem, "But we need a refund on that."

They chose to save two bulbs for the next day, in case Mandy couldn't find any. Then they finished their one apiece and gave the last to their loyal huntress, who lay between them on the hard deck giving measured, contented blinks.

"If only she could speak," said Kate. "We'd have a lot to talk about."

"Yeah, and if I know women, it's a good thing she can't."

Day 5

Sunrise. Heavy waxwork clouds loomed over the most brilliant burgundy dawn Kate had ever seen. The almost flat calm didn't inspire much confidence in their progress, but it did allow them to relax, be lazy for perhaps the first time on Kratos. The gentle squeak of vine against keel whenever a gentle swell nudged them westward was the only sound for miles around. Kate and Jason snuggled together in front of the mast, their knees tucked up to their chests, wondering, imagining what might have been had things happened differently.

"It's strange having so much time to think," said Kate. "There's always been something there to distract me—exercise, reading, movies, what I've got planned for tomorrow. It's quite frightening, really. I don't know why it hasn't sunk in before. There's no one…*no one* else coming. Ever. Jason, we'll never see another person as long as we live. You know, survival training can teach you everything, but it always has the same objective, the same goal—to keep you alive so that you can be with people again. It's a means to an end. The tools to bring you back to civilisation, I guess. Only I've never been what you'd call the sociable sort, not unless I've no other choice. Always done things on my own, you know; never liked to rely on anyone if I could help it. I suppose that's what made me so good at survival. Except now I've found someone I want to rely on and, as it happens, I need to rely on. Strange. All very strange."

Jason remained silent for a moment before answering, "Yeah, I see what you mean. You've just given up more information about yourself in two minutes than I've learned in two weeks. I'm liking it."

He pecked her once on the cheek, then quickly on her lips, before settling into a sublime, hungry-yet-patient, dizzying kiss that for a moment freed her of the long yesterday and of tomorrow, and Kate gave herself completely to the man of her dreams. *This is all there'll ever be*, she thought.

"Mm." *This is all there'll ever be!*

The *Elemental* drifted for two more days. Mandy's diligent hunting kept them stocked with ocean vegetation. Liquid from the orange bulbs slaked their thirst, though Kate often grumbled over the lack of real water. For exercise, regular swimming to and from the yacht proved invaluable. Mandy would often dive with them, her magnificent agility through the water a constant source of awe for Kate and Jason. Their routine was one of companionship—friends, lovers, colleagues in survival. And that they relied so much on Mandy kept them ever appreciative of what they had.

On the evening of the eighth day, Kate swore she saw notch-like shadows on the horizon ahead, silhouetted against the last of the two suns to set.

"I don't see anything." Jason squinted, shrugged.

"Well then, I've got better eyes than you. I can see a whole line of thin notches."

"How far away, if you had to guess?"

"Next dumb question. The horizon could be a continent away, and you can't even see them."

"Then we'll just wait."

Kate looked at him, avoided his return glance, then grinned. "Don't mind if I do."

Chapter Fourteen
Nemo's Menu

Day 10

Spectacular! The underwater visibility improved dramatically, as if they'd crossed a purifying meridian. The partition between pale, murky green and glassy emerald stood out a mile, as clearly defined as night and day. Kate dipped her hand in the new water. "It's balmy."

"Shall we try it out?" asked Jason.

"Immediately."

She lowered herself over the starboard side, Jason over the port. Both clung to the buoyant tentacles. They submerged to view the secrets of the transparent ocean. From between clouds, capes of sunlight wavered across the deep, highlighting minute formations of sea life no bigger than fingernails, and introducing enormous, roving shapes that spread and contracted like bloating submarines. Slender white shoots stretched up to within fifty feet of the surface; these were identical to the spaghetti slime-line Jason had snagged during his fishing debacle. Quite where they originated from he still couldn't fathom.

The further they drifted across this new ocean realm, the more it teemed with life. Jason lifted his head to breathe every couple of minutes, Kate every few. The sunlight intensified over the next hour, penetrating deeper into the aquatic. Enormous mandibles clasped shut far below, sending whirls of plankton up toward them. Kate even spied a dolphin, identical to those they'd befriended back at the reef. It dodged between a school of tiny lights and a spinning starfish.

Amazing, she thought, *what evolution, unchecked, can produce.*

After taking another breath, she pressed a hand to her stomach. Something wasn't right. A sharp, sickening jab of pain. She waited a minute without moving. The pain didn't return. In its place, only mild discomfort.

"It's just a slight stomach ache," she said, doubling up on the hard deck.

"We understand the word 'slight' differently," he replied. "Either you've got stomach cramp or it's something you ate. Right, no more exercise for you today."

"Does this mean I need a sick—"

She immediately winced and clutched her lower torso. According to Jason, her face had lost all colour. The pain seemed to twist inside as a jagged, rusty blade, tightening, lacerating. All her senses merged into one and surrendered on the spot. Her world shrunk to the throb of this agonising epicentre. All she wanted to do was rip into her flesh and purge her innards. The pain was relentless. Her fingertips stung like brittle icicles whenever she lifted them free. Jason held her as dearly as she'd ever been held while she trembled, screamed, convulsed, cried and cried in his arms.

The *Elemental's* sail caught a few jabs of wind. Kate, no longer able to stand the pain, finally passed out after what had seemed like hours of extreme pain. Jason had never witnessed suffering like it, not even at the Fourmyle prison, even with those fellow cadets, officers, teachers dragged kicking and screaming to their executions.

"Thank God." He inhaled, exhaled with juddery looseness, giving his own sore diaphragm a reprieve. "She's not feeling it any more, at least. Thank God."

Bitter realisation welled inside him.

He was alone on Kratos? What if this was it? What if she never came to? God, there was no…*No, don't even think that. Take what happens if and when it happens. Anything else is poison. Alone has no meaning while there's two of you. Keep talking to her; keep talking to Kate.*

"So it's the sunniest day we've had so far," he said. "The *Elemental's* moving at a fair clip, and…"

The words hardened like sun-baked cement in his throat. He sank to his knees and sobbed against the mast. The flexing sail thrummed in his ear. He gazed down at Kate. Her small, lovely face was chalk white. Her perennial frown of concentration had lightened, and she lay peaceful, unaware—the tepid core of a raging flame.

He guessed it was food poisoning. Inevitable. Earthly biology digesting an alien diet. How soon would it be before *his* illness kicked in? Which element in the vegetation was the cause? Not that it mattered if Kate died. Not a jot. He'd end the voyage then and there and be happy to do it. Drown, probably, or swim for the goddamn precipice and throw himself over, just for the hell of it.

"Some survivalist you are, Remington." He recalled the words exactly as Kate had spoken them. "There's time yet."

He sat by her side for hours that dragged like millennia. The wind picked up, blowing them steadily on toward their vague westward destination. An uneven rhythm crept into the boat's rocking when, early that evening, Mandy returned from her hunt.

Cli-click, cliiick, click, cli-click

A phantom head and neck preceded the salamander as she scrambled aboard at the stern, not pausing for breath. Pale pink skin, a human hue, covered every inch of her body. What did that mean? She wanted to be near her human friends? She was afraid and she needed them? As Mandy scurried the short distance to him, her ghostly twin protracted more then ever. It preceded her by half a second. The poor creature was, quite literally, beside herself.

"Come here, girl." He rubbed her sides as she gave Kate a close inspection. "You can calm down now. At least now I have an inkling of what that remarkable instinct of yours is all about. Coping with fear, some kind of adrenaline? It's for survival, isn't it? I wish mine could dodge danger in advance like that."

He held Kate's hand as he spoke. Just then, Mandy spun to face the spot where she'd climbed up. Like a watchdog sensing an intruder, she sprang from side to side on the deck, clicking madly.

"What the hell is it, girl? What's there?"

Jason ducked under one rope and strode over another, before peering past the buoyant vines, into the ocean. Transparent, shimmering, dark green and…He jerked back as if something cold and sharp had prodded his bowels. A heavy dread pressed him low to the deck and the *Elemental* to the water. He dared to look again. No mistake. The shadow passing under the keel was at least five times the size of the biggest whale on Earth. He stared not in horror but in frozen, floating disbelief, as though his brain had reached its capacity for processing reality and saw only an absurd fantasy. Specks of white light spangled its edges like diamond studs. As a mass, it propelled in thrusts, similar to the dome of a jellyfish. The force and scale of each movement conducted straight to his heartbeat. The behemoth's shape was elliptical—a shadow hundreds of feet below the surface.

Christ. How big would it be at close quarters?

Mandy's panic now made perfect sense. With snappy head pivots Jason quested for inspiration around the deck. The tasker came to mind, but what effect could a harpoon have on *this*? Kate shivered under the survival suit he'd covered her with. Three bulbs on their stalks hung from the starboard stay rope. Apart from that, the *Elemental* was a bare vessel, and the way it bobbed in the water more closely resembled a buoy than a boat. If the leviathan decided to attack, he could do nothing to stop it. Their fate now rested with the appetite and curiosity of the beast.

Day 11

The giant stalker wandered now and then but always returned, territorially, to the shadow of the *Elemental's* drift. Inconstant breezes staggered their westward progress. Jason spent a full day resting at Kate's side, with only Mandy for company. The salamander moved the least of the three, so petrified was she at the thought of entering the water.

So that's that for food, until the bastard lets us be.

Kate sweated pounds in the grip of her fever. Her chestnut hair remained as soaked near the roots as if it had been underwater, and Jason habitually dabbed her forehead with his vest. A long day with no beginning, no middle and no end in sight.

Day 12

Two more behemoths! A hunting party of three now circled the yacht, always at the same distance beneath the surface.

"What do they want? Are they even going to attack? They sure gave you the heebie-jeebies, didn't they, Mandy. Two days without touching water; I'm no biologist, but for an amphibian, that can't be good. What do you say, Mandy? Are you as dehydrated as we are? Don't answer that...I'd rather not know. Just let me know when...I don't know...when the coast is clear. Put that precognition to some use for once. It didn't exactly do you much good ashore."

He realised he was talking nonsense. His mind felt as starved as his stomach, and the constant, barbed fear of the last two days began to swell inside. Edgy, frustrated, Jason carved another notch into the mast with the tip of his harpoon—number twelve—before exploding into a series of star-jumps on the deck. It was the first real exercise he'd had since Kate's ordeal, and he found the vigorous pace exhilarating. At the three-hundred-and-twenty count, however, he stopped, mid-crouch.

Fizzzzzzzzz...

The quick, zap-like noise, low as a mosquito's buzz, rose past his left ear. Another sounded behind him, then one more again to the left. He saw only a flicker in the corner of his eye. There! The next one blazed into full view on the starboard side. But what the hell was it?

A streak of light?

Rising from the sea at some speed, the thing shot up like a spark from a bonfire. It didn't dissipate, though. Its trajectory altered mid-flight to home in on the *Elemental*. No bigger than a human thumb, the bizarre creature bounced off the wing-sail, changed direction and headed straight for Mandy. She'd already leapt up as per her precognitive instruction, but even that wasn't enough. The tiny spark veered and struck her on the back. *Cli-cliiick!* Mandy raced over to Jason and cowered between his legs.

"What the hell?"

The entire ocean around them illuminated. Peering over the side, Jason froze at the sight of a leviathan, its diamond areas brilliant white, ablaze in the deep. If he hadn't wrenched his head back a dozen sparks would have hit him. He rushed straight for Kate. The survival suit covered her body but not her head, so he adjusted it accordingly. A volley of streaking lights fizzed upward on all sides of the *Elemental*. In moments brilliant white light enveloped the vessel. Jason tried to reach his own suit in time, but the first barrage of incandescent creatures hit him with a hailstorm of static shocks.

"Shit!"

His entire skeleton clenched. The things were electrically charged. Two more struck his neck and he bit his tongue. A cavalcade of blazes scorched its way down the sail, heading straight for him. "Shit!" He grabbed his suit and swung it up, knocking dozens of sparks into the sea. Countless more got through; his scalp burned amid a blizzard of spinal jolts. Ducking under the sail, thrashing wildly with his suit, Jason could only glimpse the blitzkrieg poor Mandy was enduring.

Each hit was comparable to the stinging thump when touching an electrified fence. Shockwaves ripped through him from ears to toes and vice versa. In an act of sheer instinct, he dived to ground and, lying on his back, held the suit over his crouched posture to deflect the cascade. It worked.

"This is insane. Oh my God, Mandy!"

Hit with enough volts to fry an elephant, she crawled in agony toward Jason, who willed her on with every inch of his tensed frame. The salamander jumped and jolted with each strike, and there were now dozens per second.

"Mandy, come on. Please."

Jason wanted to cry as he looked into her wounded, pleading eyes. Her dome blinked several times a second—a rapid lighthouse beacon pulsing shadow through light instead of vice versa—but she couldn't move. The hailstorm pinned her, grew even more intense. Sparks shattered on top of her as molten monsoon rain. He watched her mouth quiver open for the last time before light seemed to blanket her from existence.

"Mandy!"

All three behemoths at once?

He closed his eyes and wanted to die. *All three at once.* But the thought woke something inside him, his own spark...of defiance.

"Not like this." He rolled forward onto his feet while still shielding his head with the suit. He sidestepped over to Mandy, the smell of the electrical charge heightening his every sense. The heavy fizz, fizz, buzz of creatures bouncing off his umbrella rose above the tidal downpour all around. The illumination grew so intense he could barely see the deck. Mandy lay flat on her stomach. A noxious, gaseous discharge revolted Jason as he tucked her tail in and slowly stretched himself, and the suit, over the rest of her.

No pulse, no heartbeat, nothing. Mandy?

He blew as hard as he could over her sensory dome. Coughed. The loyal salamander didn't even twitch. Jason found it tough to inhale through the heat, but managed to endure the electrical blitz for a further five minutes. When it finally ceased, he stayed undercover with her in case of another eruption.

"Never heard of anything like this, Mandy. Disabling prey with an electrical volley. The hot springs on Ireton Four are teeming with fish that disable their prey with electromagnetic pulses, and some eels on Earth give off a charge, but this...this is insane. Must be even more lethal in the water, though. That's why you were so afraid to go back in, Mandy. I see it now. These giants must be the wreckers of the deep, swimming low and shooting their load up, killing everything above. And if there's a few of them, it'll be like a fishing trawler, only upside down, where nothing can escape the electrical barrage.

"They mustn't have known what to make of the *Elemental,* Mandy. They followed us for ages without making a move, didn't they? Must have decided we were a big new fish after all. The joke's on them, though, if they try to swallow—"

He cursed himself for being so logical. It was like any trapper: kill first, come to collect later.

The thought spurred him up. On wobbly legs, he shook with his own type of fever—the electrical kind. He ran a hand through his upended hair. Yes, Einstein without the smarts. Thousands of tiny white organisms littered the deck. No longer lit, they resembled spinning jennies piled on a forest floor. Boomerang-shaped oddities.

"So that's how they were able to change direction in flight."

The notion that they might still be alive incensed him. Not keen on touching them, he shovelled them over the side with his boot.

Kate's shins were exposed but, luckily for her, they lay directly under one of the stay ropes. Most of the parasites had made for her body, which was shielded to the millimetre. Jason kissed her forehead, suffering for his love with a slight static shock. He managed her into her suit and clipped her belt to the stay rope. This last part was a precaution should the boat be tipped. To his great relief and surprise, the sail itself remained undamaged but for a plethora of scorch marks.

A potent, sickly smell of burnt blubber lingered over the *Elemental*. Imagining what he might have to face should the behemoths come to claim their meal, he laid one hand on his breast, the other on his solar plexus, set on calming himself. "Bastards, and cowards to boot." Yet, shuffling about the deck in a hyperactive daze, he was hardly in a fit state to fight for composure.

"To hell with it. I'll have to go out swinging." He kicked into his suit and snapped the final harpoon to the tasker. Glancing back to Kate and Mandy lying motionless on the giant beak, he wiped his mouth with a white knuckle fist. "They'll have to come through me first."

The ocean seemed unaffected by the onslaught. The tiny organisms had sunk back to the depths. All appeared as it had been during the first leg of the voyage—the maiden voyage of the *Elemental*.

Jason perched in anticipation in the manner of a Viking at the prow of his long-ship. In Norse mythology, the Kraken was a feared leviathan of the deep. With three such beasts to contend with, each of a scale to dwarf even that monster of legend, reality sucked hard at his resolve. Seriously, what could he do against those? His knees began to shake, not with adrenaline but diminishment. An absolute fear bled his will to stand. Nothing in his training had prepared him for this.

The dark shapes heaved by below. Rhythmic, tectonic masses. The shadow grew bigger still. He mistook the fabric of his suit for his own skin, itching a thick seam over his elbow. The vessel was now in a lake of shadow. He swallowed a mouthful of saliva down the wrong pipe, almost coughed his guts up. His heartbeat thumped the drums in his ears.

Squeak!

The stern lifted slightly, a few feet in the water. The buoyant vines scraped against the hull. Jason steadied himself as the whole vessel now rose and fell with a splash.

They're feeling us out. They still don't know what to make of us.

The bow leapt into the air to a forty-five degree angle. His stomach trampolined and he barely clung to the nearest stay rope. Thank God Kate was still attached.

But Mandy?

Mandy was gone. The tilt had tipped her into the sea, where she now descended to a deep, watery grave. Jason had no time to mourn her. Another jolt wrenched them sharply anticlockwise, throwing foamy wash from all sides of the vessel. He saw the giant beast up close for the first time as it eased out of the water, its tough, sinuous membrane almost black.

He froze.

The giant mouth opened a few metres wide directly beneath him. He peered inside but couldn't see very far. Black, cavernous, with an awful decaying smell. No way to survive this. The stern vines squeaked again. A low scrape followed. The deck began to vibrate. He had to close his eyes tight or his mind wouldn't be able to take any more. Another scrape woke him with a jolt.

His crooked spine tingled with dread as he instinctively made his way toward a hideous sentinel stalking Kate. Four feet tall, wrapped with seaweed, it appeared as the chewed-up spokes of a bicycle wheel, without the wheel. Its limbs dripped slime onto the deck as it rolled toward sleeping Kate. Jason wanted to throw up. The thing was offensive, a starfish unlike any he'd ever seen, able to 'walk' upright.

"Get away from her."

He pounced in front of it and crouched, unleashing a haymaker to the eye between its limbs. The thing flew overboard like a cartwheel from a cliff.

"Have some of that."

No sooner had he thrown a fist in victory than six more crept up from the stern, using the vines. He stepped back. They'd seemingly learned from the first encounter, as their motion across the deck was quicker, more supple through the ropes, more purposeful. Jason stood over his beloved Kate and gripped the tasker for all its worth. Last harpoon. Last chance. He waited until the left hand sentinel was almost upon them.

Crack!

The harpoon shot straight through its middle, showering the deck with black liquid, and stuck into the deck behind. Jason then ran across the next two creatures, snagging them in the tasker's cable, and sprinted to the stern, yanking the line with him. This momentum launched them powerfully over the side. Two more down.

"Kate!"

Three of the remaining four made a beeline for her. Throwing all strategy aside, he flew into them in a frenzied bloodlust. He lifted one by the legs and tore it apart. Another wrapped itself around him, its spiny feelers digging into his back, mandibles gouging from its central mouth. He screamed and jumped backward to the deck. As it tried to crawl from under his weight, he unleashed a reverse headbutt. The thing scurried away, a flattened crab.

One pulled at Kate's arm with frightening force, the last helping it by yanking at her leg. The stay rope holding her buckled and snapped loose. They had Kate. Dragging her through the rigging, they left behind a trail of colourless slime. With a torrent of barbaric threats he tore after them, but tripped on a line. The sentinels slid their prey over the side before he could get to his feet.

"Kate!"

Fully ready to leap after her into the massive mouth, he stopped at the port edge of his vessel. Kate lay directly beneath, just a few feet away. The sentinels rolled hell for leather toward the gaping crevasse. Jason, so relieved to see his girl unharmed, couldn't believe his eyes when he saw a dark, lithe shape race after the horrific predators.

"Mandy? It *is* Mandy. She made it!"

Heaving Kate back aboard, he gritted his teeth at the thought that all his efforts had been in vain. The battle won, but what of extinction? The behemoth still had them in its clutches. How many more acolytes did it command? Or what if it simply bit down…hard? Retrieving his last harpoon from the deck, he waited for Mandy to return. And waited.

Jason sighed a shivery sigh. As he did, the giant mouth twitched, rocking the *Elemental*. He held Kate tight in his arms, combed her hair with his rigid fingers. She still breathed but showed no signs of consciousness. A warm, bitter spray showered out from the creature's lips, soaking them both with a fine sea rain. Another tremor, this time more violent, rattled the vessel onto the ocean once again.

"What's happening?" he yelled in sheer, blank frustration.

Without warning the colossal creature vanished back into the sea. For what, and why, he couldn't guess. No more prayers. No more tears. Just wait and see what happens, then overcome it—the pure survival instinct. Jason knew that whatever else happened, he'd proven himself worthy to stand alongside Kate Borrowdale. His Valkyrie. And as the last part of the leviathan submerged, he thought he saw a small, lithe shape ram it head-on.

The boat bobbed for a while on the clear emerald water. The suns were still bright, the air still warm, their destination in the west no nearer. Jason traced the lovely curves of Kate's face with his fingertips, before cupping her hair back from her forehead. He was dying to tell her everything that had happened.

"Now I know how you fe—"

Before he knew it, he was underwater. A mind-boggling surge sucked him down. Like a serviette in the Titanic's wake, he was wrenched, powerless, into the deep. His lungs almost exploded as he fought for the surface. A faint kernel of light the only thing keeping him conscious. *A hard nudge.*

Moving fast. Pushed…from below. Must breathe…no air…must…

Purple erupted all around him. He swallowed the sky in a single gulp, before spitting the ocean in exchange. He wasn't sure what kept him afloat. He glanced down to see two dolphins—just like those from the cove—holding him safely on the surface, one under each arm. But why? What were they doing there? What had happened?

Where's Kate?

He struggled free, desperate to find her. The frothy sea raged. He regained his bearings by looking for the glimmers of metal on the northern rim. There, just as he'd thought, a few miles away through the troughs of waves. At that moment a leviathan surfaced two hundred yards to the south, pushing a large swell toward him. And another, away to the east, slightly closer. He dizzied, hated himself for it. A third surfaced, this time to the west. Enough to wrench his heart in two. For ahead, sailing away, driven faster by the wind than he'd ever imagined, his very own invention, the *Elemental,* raced.

"Fly, Kate. Fly."

A half dozen dolphins circled him in concentric formation. He was too exhausted to imagine why. His closed his eyes, maybe with fatigue, maybe because he'd transmitted every synapse of hope he had left to Kate and the *Elemental*. She had to be on board, and that was all he wanted in his time left.

"Kate."

When he opened his eyes, the half dozen dolphins had become twenty. In less than a minute, the twenty became two hundred. And by the time

Mandy leapt out of the water, corkscrewing through the air to splash down at his side, the sea between Jason and the leviathans held ranks of aquatic allies numbering in the thousands.

"We're at war," he whispered, spinning slowly in the water to see dolphins completely encircling him. "They've started a war…for us?"

Mandy brushed up against him, arching her back for Jason to climb on.

"Okay, girl, I'm in your world now." He rubbed her neck. "I've done all I can."

Chapter Fifteen
Irony in a Storm

It was like something from a Lovecraftian fever dream. The megalithic bullies of the deep had Jason in a triangulated trap. Their widening mouths pushed skin ripples across their black, fleshy bulks. Each monster was, in effect, nothing but a giant mouth. And as the three of them had stalked him for two days, they could never let him flee the pot, not in *their* ocean.

Mandy paddled strongly with Jason on her back. The miniature circle she repeated was concentric to those created by the dolphin ranks. He recalled the choreography in those old Busby Berkley musicals—elaborate dance numbers, often shot from overhead. For an eagle of Kratos, it had to be quite a show.

Neither Mandy nor the dolphins made a sound apart from wave-making rushes. Jason nonetheless sensed they had a strange repartee. Whenever the salamander flicked her head to one side, the nearest dolphin repeated the gesture.

Is she orchestrating all this?

A few minutes into the bizarre standoff, as if lit by a fuse, the northern behemoth shot its first volley of sparks at the dolphin lines. Only a dozen projectiles to start. A test of the army's defence?

Whoosh!

Twenty dolphins flung their powerful tails from the water, throwing up a shower to dowse and knock the sparks off course. First round to the allies.

Next, mirroring the attack on the *Elemental,* the leviathan erupted its entire electrical arsenal. The other two followed suit. Jason went dizzy once more as he looked up to see the sky splinter into a million blazing particles. Mandy reared up, forcing him to cling tight, before she entered a strong, muscular dive. Her ghost shot out ahead. He kept his eyes open. All around him dolphin brothers submerged, U-turned underwater, raced for the surface and unleashed powerful jets from their tails, before breaking the surface again like dive-bombers coming to re-arm. The sky above dimmed quickly before a few limp sparks hit the sea. Whatever the dolphins' tactic was, it seemed to negate the electric volley.

Mandy swam deeper and deeper. Jason hung on, his arms clasped around her neck, his head wedged behind her halo dome. Deeper still. The pressure stabbed iron chisels into his ears and hammered. He remembered to equalize. *Pinch your nose and try to exhale.* His skull clicked through a grim, pulsing cloud. He prodded her flesh with his fingertips. Mandy levelled and started to rise. The pressure squeeze dissipated. His ears still hurt like hell, though, even with the chisels removed.

They breached the surface and waited a few seconds. Mandy's dome blinked. Jason didn't dare to look anywhere but straight down at her light-green skin. She reared up once more—the signal to dive. *So soon?* He took three quick breaths in preparation for the biggest he could muster. Down they went. Much warmer underwater than on the now-chilly surface. For a minute he forgot all about the oceanic battle being waged behind them. He closed his eyes, entrusting himself completely to the extraordinary salamander.

Fast, graceful, her motion through the water lulled him into a peaceful yet blank state of mind. They surfaced whenever he pressed his fingers against her skin. How many breaths, he didn't care to count. Hours' worth? He barely managed a coherent thought, and by the time Mandy tipped him off her back for a rest, he panicked, not knowing where he was.

"Help. What's happening?"

He saw Mandy floating upside down on the rough sea, stretching her two rear legs into the air. His own lower back ached after hours in the same posture.

Okay, now I remember. But where the hell are we?

A strong wind whipped him with heavy rain from behind. A constant, bitter flogging. Burgundy veins bled through the grey clouds above them so low that Jason felt he could touch the open wounds if only he could reach up. The ocean itself appeared desolate. Three-hundred-and-sixty degrees of bare water waiting for the brunt of the storm. Gone were the leviathans and the dolphins. And there was no sign of the *Elemental*.

"It's just you and me, girl," he shouted through the wind.

Mandy kicked her six legs and flipped over onto her stomach.

"Ready." He resumed his jockey position on her back.

She waited until the trough of a huge swell dipped under them before nodding once more into the sea. As she propelled them with her tail and her six legs, Mandy watched the surface as it rolled above them. The waves were now thirty feet high. If the storm continued to grow worse, how big might they get?

But Jason could think of nothing except Kate and the *Elemental*.

It's never been tested in severe weather. No reason why it shouldn't stay afloat, but in this *storm…come on, Kate, just a little longer. I'll find you…somehow.*

* * * *

The wind braced Kate's back and made her think the eleven hour fall had never ended, that everything she'd endured on Kratos was in her mind. The desert, Jason's survival, the air being fit to breathe, discovering the giant craft, the sand yacht, even Mandy: it was all too far-fetched to be real.

She rolled from her side onto her back. Pins and needles tickled her right arm as she took her weight off it. Rain lashed her face.

This isn't falling.

Her brain had double-crossed her. The whole ordeal was real. As it flooded in, soapy seawater washed onto the deck, hurling her onto her side against the mast. The impact knocked the wind out of her. She doubled up, inadvertently tightening a loose rope that had snagged her belt.

Did Jason tie that?

His face blazed into her mind and seemed to imprint on the backs of her eyelids. Rubbing her eyes, she looked carefully over the *Elemental* for signs of him. White foam, dark water, but no Jason. And no Mandy.

"Without something to float on, he's dead," she decided, curling up against the billowed wing-sail, utterly alone. "How long was I out?"

The ocean seemed to forge mountains as the *Elemental* rose high for a few seconds, then sank the same distance, again and again. And with the wind pushing her onward, Kate repeated the boat's name over and over in her mind. Though its honorary captain, she felt subordinate to each and every element.

The vessel itself was no seafarer. With the sail low to the deck and firmly secured—Jason had done a marvellous job rigging the stay ropes—it was not top-heavy, but nonetheless leaned forward from the wind. It also spun occasionally due to its wacky shape.

What kept the *Elemental* afloat, though, were the buoyant tentacles. Tough, fastened tight, extraordinarily difficult to submerge, they maintained the boat's equilibrium as well as resisting the toppling effect of both waves and the wind. Such deadly creatures ashore, they had proven themselves lifesavers at sea.

The wind held Kate tight against the bony mast. She had no intention of moving anyway.

If I'm still heading west, I might get to see what the notches are. If not, you might as well sink me here and now.

Thirsty. So damn thirsty. Bloody saltwater—the wetter it gets, the drier you end up.

That irony capsized in her mind. She held her hands high, shaping her palms and pruned fingers into a cup.

"Well, well," she said, now on her knees to sip the rainwater she'd collected. "Trying to sink me *and* keeping me alive. How careless."

<u>Day 13</u>

Waves towered a hundred feet. Whenever Jason tapped on Mandy's neck, it was with trepidation. He needed oxygen, yes, but not between collapsing skyscrapers, and not if it was simply to prolong the inevitable. Yet the salamander proved herself a canny creature. Rather than dash up straight away at Jason's signal, she waited for the next significant trough between the aquatic peaks. Jason adapted to this by tapping while he still had air to spare. Thus, more frequent trips were needed, but Mandy's instincts now played a crucial role, too.

Tired, sore, dazed most of the time, Jason trusted his companion more than he'd ever trusted anything or anyone. Survival by the frayed end of a thread. Life pared down to the snatching of breaths—nothing more.

He hardly noticed when the storm began to subside. His eyes weren't open anyway. Waves calmed in the manner of blips on a heart monitor, but he was only attuned to Mandy's constant pulse. At last his arms fell from around her neck as she surfaced. The salamander wriggled to wake him. No energy for a response. His head rested on hers, his legs straddling her back. No matter how bizarre the bed, it had been the longest day of his life.

Mandy simply lifted her chin, fastened her three eyes on the horizon, and paddled—in dogged pursuit of the *Elemental*.

Chapter Sixteen
Jason's Ordeal

<u>Day 14</u>

Jason cursed himself for missing the opportunity to collect rainwater. He was parched. Saltwater sores appeared on his legs for the first time. He'd clung tightly to Mandy for two days, and his thighs in particular had rubbed against her skin whenever she'd made a sudden move.

"I'm not hurting you am I?" He sculled for a bit on his own while she rested.

Her adoring eyes—three dark gems embedded side by side—couldn't blink. She had the sort of stare that would unnerve anyone until they knew the love behind it, at which point it became sweet and loyal. Her underside was softer, not as chameleonic as her hide. Jason considered for a second how vulnerable she looked.

Non-threatening mouth, tiny teeth, no claws that I can see—she doesn't look much of a predator. Doesn't have to be, I suppose, with camouflage like that. And smart, too.

The grim weather lifted mid-afternoon. Jason scanned the horizon and held his breath. A cocktail of excitement and dread effervesced inside him. On his belt, a depleted tasker; a few miles ahead, a series of massive, dark chimneys set equidistantly apart in the ocean.

"The black notches," he exclaimed, remembering Kate's discovery.

He tried to remain composed. Each was the size of the Washington Monument. And there were hundreds. Dark brown, metallic, surprisingly smooth given the ferocious elements to which they were exposed, the towers also appeared deserted, defunct.

No signs of life.

"There goes *that* theory," he said. "But they are still standing, and we did see fireworks. Maybe someone is operating a machine after all? What do you think, girl, is this one big wild goose chase or not?"

As they swam closer, he saw erratically-carved pores in the metal—a strange, unnatural design stretching right to the tops.

Some sort of ladder? What the hell kind of creature had limbs like that? Was it climbable?

But Mandy steered clear of the chimneys.

"Come on, girl, let's have a closer look." He tried prodding her to the nearest one.

She declined with a bucking tantrum, even sped up to get past.

"Have it your way," he said.

He slipped off her back and swam on his own, smirking as he heard the salamander click and follow him after all.

Sunlight seeped through the clouds as Jason hung from the first pore above the waterline. It didn't penetrate the chimney. "Ah, bugger." He'd underestimated the gaps between handholds, as well as the size of the pores. The ladder was obviously not built for human limbs.

"They don't make things easy on Kratos, do they?" He programmed the tasker at full magnification, took aim.

Ping!

The harpoon bulleted up, entered the chimney funnel high above and grappled the rim as the line pulled it taut. "Okay, Mandy, I can either tie a rope around you and hoist you up later, or you can cling onto me. I'm pretty sure it'll hold us both."

The salamander looked up at the tasker cable then straight at Jason. She hesitated for a split second before leaping onto the metal face. And in the most amazing display of agility he'd ever seen, she began to run—not climb, run—up the chimney.

"How the hell?"

All of a sudden his advanced technological toy seemed pitiful as he winched himself up, at half Mandy's speed, to the summit of the alien tower. A slight gust nudged him as he clambered onto the square, thick rim. Looking inside, he was disappointed by what he found. Warm, black nothing. The ocean painted a desolate picture. An eternity of translucent green now left him nauseous, parched, famished. No sign of Kate or the *Elemental*. Enormous shadows roved beneath him—those restless harbingers of death.

He'd never felt so alone in his life. Kratos was inhuman in all directions. Teeming with life, yes, but inhuman.

"There's nothing left to do, Mandy." He knocked on the chimney rim with his knuckles. "Nothing."

The salamander blinked. She turned and scurried down into the darkness, waiting twenty feet below for Jason to follow. He looked again. There was nothing there.

But then again, nothing could mean anything.

Down, down…like a bucket into a well. The seat of his survival suit pressed uncomfortably into his crotch, but he daren't adjust—the grappler was not embedded in anything above. It merely clung, and might scrape loose if he wasn't careful. The purple sky shrank to the size of a pen nib. Warm, balmy air teased sweat from his palms and brow. The chimney interior remained utterly black. As the warning beep sounded on his tasker, he swallowed hard. Wiped salty perspiration from his eyes. He was running out of cable.

How deep is this thing?

Click! Automatic lockdown. He now dangled in total darkness at the very end of his line. The tasker wouldn't risk another inch. For all he knew, the ground might indeed be an inch away, but it could just as easily be a mile.

"Right, what now, genius?"

The walls were too far apart for him to climb down the old-fashioned way—brace and shimmy. And too dark to see any footholds. He could winch back up, but then what? This was what the voyage had been for in the first place…these goddamn chimneys. *Alright, Remington, think. What's the best way to find out how deep something goes…drop something? But what?*

Rummaging in his belt, he found a handful of wet sand and a shard from the splintered wing. He'd used the latter to make the *Elemental.*

"I'd rather not lose that," he said. "The only weapon I've got left."

Okay, how about something even more basic.

He gathered a squall of phlegm in his throat and spat it into the void. Several seconds later, he thought he heard a small pat. But it was far from conclusive.

Okay, what else? Boots? Not ideal. Something I can do without…like…the vest. Hmm, what'll that accomplish—it's too light to make an impact. Okay, how to weight it…handful of sand…probably not enough. What about tying it into a bundle and then soaking it? *The best way is either saliva—which would take ages—or what else? Urine? Worth a try.*

The delicate operation took a few minutes: he removed his vest after peeling the survival suit from his shoulders. Next, he peed onto the vest he'd stuffed down his front, added the handful of sand, and then tied the bundle as tightly as he could. It reeked. He retched.

"It's not exactly in the manual, but here goes."

He didn't let it fall, he *threw* it down. The greater the impact, the more chance he'd have of hearing it.

The urine bomb he'd designed but never seen plummeted into the abyss. Jason gaped in anticipation. His head poised, his ears the booms to record *any* sound, he waited…and waited…and…

Splash!

He jerked upright in the harness. The watery echo swilled about in his mind.

Right, dilemma time. It had sounded a helluva fall, but it was solid proof of water below. How deep, though? And how wide? The bundle might've hit lucky, while he might not. *Oh, Christ.* It was a leap of faith. *Hang on while I send for the minister. Remington, make a decision...right now. Empty ocean...or the abyss?*

A smothered, tinny click came from far below. It didn't repeat, however.

"Mandy, is that you? Mandy?"

No reply. He waited a while, then called her name again.

"Mandy, I need to know if it's safe to jump."

Once more, no reply. Then he heard the echo of a big splash. It sounded remarkably like the salamander breaching a watery surface.

"That's good enough for me." And he shoved his arms back into his survival suit.

Right, this is it. Three...two...one...

He closed his eyes, clicked the safety catch to OFF and unclipped the cable. *Ugh!* Falling slid a cold pulse right through him. His brain spilled upwards in a narrow streak of colours. The sensation elasticised his stomach and flittered the life from his limbs. He wanted to scream but couldn't. Now regretted the decision to jump a million different ways all at once. Down, down, down...had he missed the water and found an endless drop? On the verge of opening his eyes, he despaired unlike anything he'd known.

Thud!

He thought he'd hit concrete. His legs collapsed beneath him and his right arm smashed into his side. Excruciating pain. He wanted to cry out but instinct forced his breath to hold. Underwater? He'd splashed down from far higher than he'd reckoned. Now he spat saltwater as he groaned in agony on the surface.

Cli-click, click.

Mandy eased herself under him like a wetsuit full of air. Though there was no light at all, she seemed to know where she was going.

"Sonofabitch. That hurts."

Jason knew he'd cracked a few ribs. Whenever he touched his side, a sharp pain lanced him. He couldn't raise his right arm and had to hold it, as still as possible, as though it was in a sling.

"I've gone and done it now," he groaned, meek as a Borodin calf, resting on Mandy's back as she paddled through the dark.

A warm air current wafted across his face. He looked up. Not even a jab of daylight pierced the void.

I'm past the chimney, he thought. *But where to now?*

Chapter Seventeen
Pyro Requiem

Day 15

"Gray Lady Down, Crimson Tide, Ice Station Zebra, The Enemy Below, 20,000 Leagues, Hunt for the Red October…um, U-571, The Poseidon Adventure…"

Kate knew the last one wasn't a submarine movie, but it was one of her granddad's favourites—they'd watched it together a dozen times in VVE (Vicarious Virtual Experience)—and it did take place underwater. Upside down underwater.

"You and your old submarine movies." She smiled, remembering his old brown cardigan and his fondness for the genre.

Colossal shadows roamed beneath her keel. They took on odd shapes through the surface haze. Sea creatures of every appearance prowled out of reach, oblivious, or maybe not, to the *Elemental's* clumsy drift. Kate followed them with curiosity. Whenever a shape appeared more than once, she gave it a nickname, no matter how tenuous the connection.

"Run Silent…Run Deep…ah, another Enemy Below…two Crimson Tides…a goddamn school of Das Boots…monsters, packed together like sardines. What's that one...a Widowmaker? Hmm, how droll."

The sentiment stuck in her throat. She couldn't get Jason out of her mind. A widow? He'd gone and made her something much more than that.

The last human within a hundred light-years...still in love.

His troubled brown eyes scarred her vision as though she'd stared directly at the twin suns. Whichever way she looked, he was there. Every daydream brought an awful moment of hope, when she snapped to at the sound of vine on beak or the leathery sail flexing taut, only to find Jason was *not* there. Not ever. No matter how much she wanted it. No matter how vivid he seemed. The way a spouse turns to speak to a partner of many years, forgetting he or she has passed, Kate couldn't imagine him not being there. Not after all they'd been through. Two weeks spanned the rugged straits of a lifetime; she had loved him long before Kratos. Unrequited at first, perhaps, but since when did that matter? Real in the mind was as real in the body...as far as love was concerned. And cast adrift, which had greater import: the body or the mind?

The ocean had made her a widow. The very last of her kind.

"An endangered species."

A quick swish of her hand through the water felt good. Warm. She repeated it a few times, each one slower. Relaxing. She shifted position to submerge her full forearm. The gentle current tickled her skin, and if a tiny shrimp-sized fish hadn't nibbled at her finger, she might have stayed there all day.

"Yow." She leapt up. "I said hot damn, it's a...goldfish. Katie girl, you used to be tough. What the hell happened? What next, hiding from your own shadow?"

The thought festered in her mind. Since when was succumbing to fear, giving up, in a terrain scout's vocabulary? A hundred ordeals on a dozen different worlds had not perturbed her. Indeed, they'd given her a reputation. So what was so special about this one?

But there's nothing to aim for. No goal. Even if I cross the ocean, I'm still the last human being within a hundred light years. Yeah, and? Since when is survival about the horizon? That's right…

Yuri Yeltsin's infamous words of advice:

The horizon changes with each step, and each step is where your thoughts should be.

"That's all well and good," she said, "but how exactly does one make steps on a ten-foot goddamn buoy beak? I've been trying to catch fish for two days, and all I've caught is…well, it just caught me."

She sucked a speck of blood from the bite wound on her finger.

"Nibbled…nibbled? That's it. That is *it*."

From something so innocuous, the idea exploded in her mind. How to stay alive on a boat with no real hunting weapon, no fishing line, no way on earth to catch food? Bait. The kind that even the tiniest Kratosian fish couldn't resist. But that would be too dangerous. No, she couldn't. It would have to be a last resort.

"Katie girl, you're kidding yourself. The last resort has been the only resort for weeks. And it ain't ever going to be five-star."

She eased herself into the water, clung with one arm to the starboard tentacle. Kicking like crazy, she imagined the bizarre ecosystem of creatures noseying beneath her in the deep. The suit was watertight. A rush of warm water entered through the neck, however. She shivered as it ran over her breasts and pooled at her stomach, soaking her vest. A tingle of excitement rang from head to toe.

Fear and necessity. A pretty crazy combination.

Kate made as much commotion as she could in the water. Her goal, to attract food. She was the bait, the fish would come to take her, and that would be the end of the fish, or so she hoped. The titles of a hundred submarine movies surfaced beneath her, but she forgot their names. Danger. And shadow. Her left arm clutching the boat began to shake. Kate gritted her teeth. She kicked even harder as the horrors of the deep swirled into action. Snake-like monsters, shoals of darting fish, a yellow streak whirling ominously. She gripped the jagged splinter of wing-frame firmly in her fist. A meagre weapon.

"*This* was a bright idea."

She'd never seen anything pierce a survival suit, though. And that included some pretty major accidents. Hell, hers should be in tatters after the grinding it had had. Fingers crossed. *Here we go.*

The first taker rammed her thigh with surprising force. She struggled to maintain her grip on the vine. A brown tail-fin thrashed the water a few feet away, while something blunt and hard pinned her against the boat.

"Jesus, that's strong."

She pulled her knees tight against her chest. The predator struck repeatedly. Its mouth, a miniature sucker, gripped her calf and rammed it against the vine. Kate knew she had little time to spare. She hacked and sliced the creature's neck with all her might. *Slam!* Another one smashed her left leg against the hull.

"Oh, hell."

She kicked, hammered, stabbed. Time tightened, constricted her like a boa. Either kill a snake now or climb back aboard before the heavy duty monsters arrive.

"Come on, bastard. Die!"

A powerful stab caught the nearest snake square in the side of its head. It flew into a mad frenzy, squirmed to get free, but Kate held onto her weapon. She ripped the creature's mouth loose from her suit. Holding it at arm's length, she saw it was the size of a moray eel; the way it thrashed, though, was more like a shark caught in a fishing net. The second creature now attacked from beneath. It lifted her legs, tilted her backward, headlong into the water. She felt her grip on the vine going, going…and…

"No."

She hurled her right arm—knife, snake and all—across her body and fully onto the *Elemental*. A desperate effort. She focused on gaining crucial footing, gritted her teeth and mashed her arm and side against the buoyant vine. The first snake flapped about on deck; she left it be. The second had her in its bite and wouldn't relent.

As she tried to kick the thing loose, a dark mass the size of a galleon rose beneath. Kate's mind froze, but she kicked on. The ocean appeared ready to swallow her *and* her vessel. Last chance. She threw both legs onto the deck and, using a lucky high swell, somehow found the momentum to heave her entire body aboard.

"Right, my turn," she snarled, stamping her foot on the throat of the first snake. Each gouge of her weapon ripped life from its head. After a half dozen stabs, it stopped flapping. The second creature lasted twice as long. At last she knelt between them. Her blood thumped, coursed like battery acid. Her chest seemed five sizes too small for each breath.

I'll never do that again. Ever.

There was no blood. Seawater streamed from the deck. The ocean lapped against the *Elemental* with an easy, soothing rhythm, as if nothing at all had happened.

I hope these things are edible after all this.

A sudden jerk pushed the boat a few metres through the water. It bobbed a little more than usual. Kate looked over the side and, seeing the enormous creature hurtle beneath her, crouched to the deck and buried her head in her knees.

"Run Silent, Run Deep…Crimson Tide…The Poseidon Adventure…"

She waited alone, cut off, subsisting. With her hands pressed hard over her ears, hardly any sound got through. Superstitious or not, she daren't lift her head. Why *not* accredit her survival to her impenetrable, private cocoon? A world within a world, it was her own—the only place she had left. She waited for the best part of an hour, remembering the old submarine movies and the actors who played in them. Nothing happened to

Kate or the *Elemental*. Her first attempt at fishing ended with an almighty sigh as she looked up…followed by a reflex lick of her lips.

Day 16

"U-571 and U-572…not bad eating." She tongued a stubborn piece of meat stuck between her teeth. "If only I could stomach more of you."

The U-snakes split easily into three parts. The outer layer was tough, sinuous, almost impossible to chew. Kate did swallow a few small chunks but couldn't discern any taste.

"Only if there's nothing else."

The inner membrane or core of the snake resembled a spine of pickled onions. Only they proved as tough to bite as elastic rubber. Instead of bones, the creature's skeletal strength was provided by a peculiar DNA-like configuration of this same material which spiralled through the body from head to tail. She guessed the elastic element must alternate between firm and flaccid states to enable such powerful locomotion.

Lastly, a brown meat constituted the remainder of the U-snake. While stringy, it was very succulent indeed. Kate spent a great deal of time picking it from the spiral 'skeleton'. All told, she had enough food for weeks.

"Two on normal rations, four to be safe."

That night a cool breeze tickled the wing-sail. Only a few thin rashes of cloud obscured her view to the stars. She lay at the bow where Jason had joined her every night during the first leg of their journey. Her insides sponged whenever she thought of him. A cold sponge, bursting with memory. The constellations seemed to wheel over a few degrees when she realised his hand didn't clasp hers. So where was he?

Maybe it was best she didn't know what happened. Then again, there was nothing worse than false hope. What if he'd gone diving with Mandy…and the boat had drifted too fast for him to make it back. He might have gotten cramp. Or maybe they were attacked and he was thrown overboard, unable to reach her. *Ah, hell, you've been over all this a hundred times, Katie girl. Face it, he's gone.*

But what if he'd made for the precipice, swam for it, and he was there right now, looking for a way down? Hmm, false hope, no hope, there was nothing she could do about it. The further she drifted, the less chance she would see him again.

The 'edge of the world', an ever-present in her mind, hung fast as an imaginary trailing anchor on the jagged sea bottom. She knew that if the boat drifted just a little northward, a new bank of stars would rise from that horizon. The notion that Jason, in desperation, would either have to swim for the precipice or drown would not leave her. Had he found a way down to the valley? In numerous *carpe diem* moments of clarity, she'd risen to her feet and contemplated the swim herself.

There was no way to manoeuvre the Elemental. Instead of drifting forever, maybe she should just rip the sail down and use it for a goddamn parachute.

Suicide. Something always held her back. Even staring ahead to a lifetime of loneliness…that was what her whole life had been about anyway…the keystone of her genetic architecture—survival. To take that away when it mattered most was more alien to Kate than anything lurking beneath her hull.

The night exploded before her thoughts could settle. Behind. To the east. A spectacular purple detonation lit the entire Kratosian sky. She spun round. There. There it was—the firework display.

"I couldn't have drifted *that* far, could I? How long was I out? What if Jason—"

A second eruption plumed and showered the ocean next to the first. Purple sparks glittered the darkness, spreading over the water as far-reaching invitations.

"*That's* why he got off. To investigate those notches. But he never made it back…or the boat drifted away too fast."

The third up-welling hit her in the gut.

"If he was anywhere near there, then that's that." She folding her arms in cold resignation. "Purple element. Looks like Pyrofluvium. As if I care. There's no way he could survive that. No. Way."

The chimneys lit in sequence. An amazing New Year's display she couldn't bear to watch. Every purple pulse over the dark sea rained a million bitter smithereens of her brief, aborted happiness. She knew it was the end her hopes. Of even false hopes.

"He's gone."

An image of the crashed *Fair Monique* haunted her. Crumpled, charred, nothing left but a funeral pyre of smoke and burning fuel. And no more Daniella. That had been the moment fate had gifted her the man of her dreams. Cruelly, but hers nonetheless. Jason Remington. A man to need, worth fighting for. Worth crossing a deadly world for.

"Some funeral pyre."

Kate immediately thought of the *Elemental*. His invention, his pride and joy. Running her hand up and down the nearest stay rope, she sank to her knees and cried like she'd never cried in her life.

Chapter Eighteen
Jason & Mandy

The solid ground gave nothing as Jason crept through the dark. An adamant metal in absolute blackness, the floor was grooved and level. Mandy had led him from the water channel into a realm of the imagination. Liquid with a smell he couldn't identify dripped from a ceiling he couldn't see to a floor he could only feel. Each droplet echoed acoustically. Thousands of them. Near or far. High or low. A chaos in his mind. Were it not for the feel of Mandy's soft tail in his grip, he knew his sanity would crumble.

The belly of the craft reeked. Rotten vegetables in a sweaty plastic bag. Short, shallow breaths were all he could afford; his cracked ribs stabbed at anything deeper. The salamander kept a steady pace. Whenever Jason needed to rest, he tugged on her tail. But he never let go. Not even to sneeze—the most excruciatingly painful sneezes he'd ever experienced.

The question of how Mandy was able to see in the dark fascinated him.

Another part of the spectrum? Infrared, ultraviolet, or something we haven't even discovered yet? And she seems to know exactly where she's going.

He guessed they'd walked for over a day. Instinct. A gut chronometer. His thighs ached and his feet hurt, which usually meant off-the-scale fatigue, as Jason liked to think he was at the peak of fitness.

Hmm, but you are undernourished…and dehydrated, among other things.

Whether a million acres wide or fifty feet, the black sanctum shrank to a narrow corridor in Jason's mind. He tried to visualise a wall on either side—as plain and nondescript as possible, partitioning him from all prying eyes.

He closed his own eyes until they ached. Every time he stumbled, or his boots scuffed a groove in the metal, his blood chilled to minus forty. What if the floor fell away? What if the next step was a fathomless hole? What if the ceiling suddenly lowered and his face struck solid metal? The salamander might not think of that; she was much shorter than him.

Christ, I can't go much longer without water. Come one, Mandy, where the hell's water?

His knees collapsed from under him. He stumbled back to his feet but decided rest was a better option. It actually made him giddy. Easing his tired limbs felt sublime, as if a warm fog seeped over those bones, blanketing him. His whole body chuckled. His ribs hurt like hell, but he couldn't stop. The ordeal seemed absurd—one long cosmic joke he'd just found the punch-line for. Lying on his back, he laughed maniacally. Pain bore into his side, a remorseless pneumatic drill. The sanctum's myriad drips disappeared in a cavalcade of gut hysterics.

Even when he stopped, the echoes lingered. And he couldn't get over how great it made him feel.

"Man, oh man, what a week. I mean is this insane or is it? All right, Remington, you've felt bad for the last time in this place. From here on in, it's brollies and margaritas. Savvy? If you can't laugh at this, you might as well say San fairy Ann right now. Come on, Mandy; best feet forward. There's a good girl."

He knew full well it was nothing more than his body releasing endorphins to lighten his demeanour, to avert fear. A defence mechanism. Human biology taking charge in the direst alien scenario. But what did he care? He was Jason Remington again, not some wilting weed dragged over concrete to a nook of a grave. As Mandy resumed her trek, he walked tall. Still favouring his right side, he nonetheless found a rhythm in his steps and in his breathing.

Then the darkness lifted. It was faint at first—a trace of a distant hue. Jason mistook it for a trick of the mind.

Purple. Thank God, it might be a way out.

"You hear that, Mandy? It might be the way out."

The salamander wriggled for a moment and started to click wildly.

"What is it? What is it, girl?"

The purple light now blazed with blinding brilliance, though it was still a long distance away. Jason had to squint. He let go of Mandy's tail for the first time as he rubbed his eyes. It was the only light he'd seen since entering the chimney. His loyal companion gazed up at him with three black, adoring eyes. Her ebony skin slowly adopted a smidgen of violet.

"Nice to see you again." He winced as he bent to rub her back.

The inside of the craft was cavernous. Fifty feet from floor to ceiling, the full dimensions of the place remained unknown. After two hundred feet ahead, shadow masked the view. Likewise behind him. The metal ground was perfectly grooved without a rivet, seam or bolt. The transparent liquid droplets appeared to fall through tiny pores in the ceiling and reflect the purple light.

"What is it with this planet and purple?"

He recoiled from the light ahead, shielded his face.

"Wow."

The intensity grew in increments as though someone was playing with flash shutters and light filters. Now as bright as the sun, it also seemed much larger in size.

They're like sparks igniting closer and closer. What the hell? Purple sparks?

"Purple sparks—*fireworks*."

The realisation jerked him into action. He scanned the now well-lit surroundings in a hurry. Nothing different. Just longer, wider.

Ah, hell.

Mandy thrust her tail for him to grab. He didn't hesitate. She'd taken him this far through the dark, why not into the light? He stared at the floor or else he'd go blind. They no longer walked, they ran. *Toward* the fireworks. He never doubted Mandy's instinct for a second, only his chances. Boiling. Adrenaline tightened his overworked muscles into a survival mechanism, all of a piece. He was aware of the sharp pain from his ribs at every step, but that, too, spurred him on.

The next spark threw off light with the intensity of a nuclear furnace. Not heat, just blinding, scorching light. He mashed his lips together and shut his eyes tight. Mandy kicked their run into a sprint. Another spark blazed purple *through* his eyelids onto his retina. The source had to be yards away. A deafening roar popped his ears. Lactic acid gripped his left shoulder and squeezed. Bright purple invaded his deepest, most secret retreats. Unbearable. Nowhere to hide. Nothing left, only Mandy's tail jerking him forward, wrenching him on—

Splash!

Water gushed up his nose, down his windpipe. He'd fallen into another channel? Shockingly cool, then sickly, the water felt alien until he surfaced and coughed it out. The light was still as bright. He panted. Mandy grabbed his leg and, allowing him a split second to take a deep breath, yanked him under. Something warm rushed over his head and neck before he submitted once more to the salamander's pull.

The light ahead was dimmer when they resurfaced. A purple canal now lit the way as far as the eye could see. Behind, blistering intensity stepped slowly but surely away until it dimmed to the same benign glow. Jason sat on the side, exhausted, his legs dipped in a pool of purple residue. The firework display they'd admired from the beach had just encored…big time.

"There goes your discovery, Kate. Let's just say I got a ringside seat this time."

Mandy beckoned him to climb on her back.

"Well, no point hanging around," he said. "Nothing to see here, right?" *Only nuclear light shows.*

Viscous residue seeped down the narrow walls. Jason and Mandy were no longer in the sanctum, rather an arterial waterway joining one to the next. As they swam under a chimney, he looked up and saw a nib of daylight at the top. Its fading walls ran with residue. Whatever had ignited the monstrous geysers, he felt sure it took place far below.

Pyrofluvium *was* an energy catalyst, after all. Maybe some part of the craft's engine still functioned, and there was a build-up of this stuff. Then once every couple of weeks, it exploded. And he was walking right over the hot coals.

"What next?" he yelled up.

The water channel stretched a quarter mile. They seemed to traverse it in no time. Mandy scurried onto the metal platform leading to the next sanctum and lay down. Somewhat recharged, Jason took the opportunity to explore. A short, nervous stroll.

He stopped a hundred yards from the water. No change in the décor, but something else. A horrid feeling of being watched. He cocked an ear. A distant scrape followed the squeal of what sounded like an enormous hinge. The hairs on his neck bristled.

A door? Some kind of cage? Definitely on a hinge, whatever it is.

He raced back to Mandy. Heavy, thumping footsteps vibrated through the metal floor. From behind…

He noticed residue streamed from the water channel, across the floor, perpendicular to the direction they'd been heading.

Off to the right. It's running downhill. If we can head downhill...

He immediately thought of the valley he and Kate had wanted so desperately to reach. Was this the way to it? In suggesting the chimneys, had she been right all along?

Thump! Thump!

That squeal of a giant hinge. What had it unleashed? What on Earth would be in a cage that big? On Earth—no, on Kratos. The scale of the place hit him again. He doubled his pace. Mandy already waited for him at the water's edge—her dome halo blinked twice in quick succession. No longer waiting for her lead, he firmed his right arm above his ribs and followed the course of the residue…downhill.

"Come on, Mandy," he shouted. "Follow me."

She scurried to his side as Jason realised the salamander had probably never had a way out.

Thud! Thud!

Her heartbeat had to match Jason's pulse for pulse as they fled.

Chapter Nineteen
The Big Pour

Day 18

A chevron formation of birds streaked across the sky. Kate counted twenty-six, and shuddered at the memory of being clamped in the huge beak during her eleven hour fall, awaiting the crunch, with no way to defend herself or the man in her arms. How quickly horror had turned to hope.

Clouds parted overhead in a stratospheric Rorschach, morphing the heavens into a shape she'd only ever seen rendered by Computer Generated Imagery. She lost her bearings for a moment, forgetting the direction of the *Elemental's* drift.

Yeah, east to west, but which is which?

She couldn't summon the impetus to get up and check. Though bone dry bodily, her resolve remained damp. Two days of lying on her back in a floating limbo had atrophied her every motivation. Eating, exercising, planning ahead, making even the tiniest decision now felt beyond her. At the nadir of existence, it was theoretically the peak test of a survivalist's aptitude. But she couldn't get over how cruelly fate had played its hand against her. Remorseless. Sadistic. From the bottom of the deck.

Just before midday, the *Elemental* turned slowly through forty-five degrees. The sensation wasn't severe, but Kate felt it.

No wind. Some kind of current?

She instantly forgot her maudlin marathon and shot across to the port side. The water *was* on the move; as she dipped her hand, it rushed through her fingers.

"A strong current, too."

No signs of life below the surface, submarine-sized or otherwise, only a full-depth, concerted gush toward the northwest. Toward the precipice...

The entire ocean?

"Okay, think. What could be causing this? Something on the sea bed? Yes, but it's not the sea bed, it's the roof of the craft. Giant craft, roof, precipice…water…emptying?"

Her throat tightened.

"It's like Jason said—this is through the looking glass the other way, quantitatively off the charts. Think scale. Think water in a metal bowl. Why would it gush toward the rim? If the bowl was tilted, or the rim was lower at that point. Yes, that storm must've raised the water level to an overflow. If there's a dip in this side of the craft, *voila!* A big pour. A bloody big pour."

Something walked over her grave. Any trace of the purple Pyrofluvium behind her had long since dissipated. And with it, Jason. Thinking of the best way to secure herself to the *Elemental*, Kate's brain clicked into gear.

"If it's not a sheer drop, if the waterfall isn't vertical, you might get to see the valley yet, Katie girl."

She realised her best chance to avoid capsizing was to cut down the mast. With no wind, it served no purpose anyway. Without it, the vessel would resemble a lifeboat, albeit an improvised one.

The operation took over an hour. She sliced through the stay ropes with her splinter. It proved taxing, and the wing itself almost collapsed on top of her as the last line snapped. She watched the sail float alongside in the water for a moment, before it upended and fell behind.

Two hours later, the rumble was as loud as a Harley Davidson's engine ticking over. The throttle hadn't yet been turned, but her ears felt the grip. White mist boasted a full rainbow and reached high over the precipice. She tested the lines securing her belt one more time. One fastened to each of the four cleats—more than enough.

"It might be for nothing," she whispered, "but nothing *could* mean anything…"

She shook her head.

"A bit late for optimism, Katie girl."

Her muscles clenched as the noise increased. The sea's current now seemed rapid, incontestable. Still no view of the precipice through the mist. Only the non-stop fall of thunder. Billions of tonnes of water pouring into oblivion.

The depth of the ocean did not appear to lessen. She could still see a fair way down. The entire body of water was moving this way. On Earth and other planets, she'd seen waterfalls fed by either a river or a lake; here, a sea at least the size of a continent overflowed. She could barely hold her hand steady enough to scratch an itch on her neck. As the first specks of spray peppered the *Elemental,* the cascade roared with the power of a rocket launch.

She screamed at the top of her voice, but no sound escaped.

Oh, Christ, this is it. Here we go.

The veil of no return. A film of cool moisture covered her hair, face and neck. Visibility was now that of a white, backward balaclava. She felt the boat move quicker and quicker through the water, and the dread welled up as hot oil in her gut. Her eardrums rang. She fought giant, panic breaths with all of her pride.

The *Elemental* now hurtled faster than it had ever surfed as a sand yacht. Kate's hair flapped wildly, and the spray drenched her eyes shut. Still louder, still faster, then suddenly…

Ugh!

Her stomach vaulted. The boat took flight for a second, and a raking wind lifted her from the deck. On landing the vessel spun and skidded at a sixty degree angle. It sent a shock up her spine. She spread-eagled her legs and lay back as the current swept her down the steep gradient. All she could do was grip the ropes and hang on. Saltwater flooded over the raw, peeling skin on her palms and fingers.

Hang on, damn it. Just hang on.

Down, down into the roar. A broad-arm current heaved the boat to one side until she was sure it would capsize. But the buoyant vines were stubborn. The spray eased long enough for Kate to see a breaker the size of the Statue of Liberty explode onto a massive metallic wall. Each drop of watery shrapnel could have filled a swimming pool. The *Elemental* barely escaped a blitzkrieg.

For the next minute, she was able to keep her eyes open. Wide open. An arcing torrent—half a whirlpool—shot her around a dark brown column that scraped the sky. A series of underwater humps the length of the Tower Bridge accelerated her until g-force creased her cheeks and her stomach slapped and floundered against her spine.

She caught glimpses, snapshots of the full-scale pour. To her left, a dome-like metal shield repelled the surge, throwing up a riot of white liquid debris. *Any* such resistance yielded the same result. Even farther across, the slope of the craft dropped almost vertically; the water there fell into a deep, mile-wide chasm. A mind-boggling waterfall—beyond comprehension. Kate tore her eyes away. For some reason, that abyssal drop left her panicked. Was it the suddenness? Perhaps the sheer size of the hole? Or something deeper in *her*—a genetic, ingrained fear of the void?

The *Elemental* listed at a dangerous angle. Sideswiping rapids thrust her into a cauldron between two semi-circular structures. Buffeted about in the foam, Kate cracked her head on the deck. Heavy spray pounded the boat. Through it all, her mind was a blank. An instant eraser of any and all horrors.

A spindrift avalanche tossed her from the cauldron onto a long, steady slide that fed into a deep trough two football fields wide. The momentum increased. Her neck and jaw muscles ached with constant tension. Her biceps shook to preserve the hold.

It's all part of the craft, she had to remind herself. *If the water can get down, you can. Nothing but obstacles on a slalom.*

"Ah, hell."

She braced herself for a huge impact. Gathering velocity on the slide, she hurtled toward the trough at a sixty-degree angle.

"This one's gonna be rough."

She accelerated still further. The silver-green flow appeared smooth and mossy. With three hundred yards to go, the *Elemental's* keel hit something underwater. *Crack!* The huge beak ripped in two, hurling Kate sideways into the cascade. Water flooded up her nose until her brain felt like splintered chipboard. Cool water pooled inside her suit, making her twice as heavy. Meanwhile, half the boat was still fast on whatever had impaled it. She quickly came to and pulled the emergency knot to untie the lines holding her belt.

Splash!

She met the level trough at seventy miles an hour. It knocked her for a loop. The slow-moving current seemed akin to drifting backwards. Her hands bled and stung in the saltwater, but she still managed to swim for the nearest tentacle. Nothing else entered her mind. It was the last trace of their vessel. A lifeline. She wrapped the vine three times around her waist and tried to fight the current. No good. Giving up reminded her of taking too many sleeping pills; she simply sighed and acquiesced to the drift—a long, semi-conscious netherworld of autumn and Oregon timber lakes.

This is it…one more obstacle and you're done for. You gave it a heckuva try, though, Katie girl…one for the record books. Rest for a moment now. You've got all the time in the world.

The thunderous noise might have drowned her shout but it couldn't touch the voice inside her head. Kate smiled at the idea.

That's one thing they can't take from you...from Kate Borrowdale.

Memories of the past few weeks flashed by, merging together in her mind. Two stood alone, though she couldn't understand why. The first was of her lying on the deck of the *Elemental*, doing nothing but tell herself how stupid she'd been to fall ill. Food poisoning, of all things. The second—her fight with two barracudas to procure a much-needed meal—made her shudder.

Surely there are better things to remember than that.

But nothing else sprang to mind. The easy, constant drift soothed her, and she grew fond of the stillness. In the midst of hell's torrent, a breather.

Realising she'd spun to one side, Kate jerked herself around on the surface. She bobbed there for a moment. Suddenly, the lull let go...

She plummeted, full speed ahead. This slide skimmed inches over the metal surface. Still as steep—fifty to sixty degrees—it nonetheless felt more tactile, more real to Kate. Her boots and the butt of her suit periodically scraped the metal. A giddy, powerful sensation. No longer on the shoulders of an ocean pour, she could now touch the spout, as it were, and engage for the first time, however ineffectually, with the flow.

But the exhilaration didn't last long. Another enormous vapour cloud loomed below. For as far as she could see, miles across, the slope began to concave. The inches quickly deepened to metres. The slick film of water converged into a white-water torrent. Kate spun and bounced like a tyre on the rapids, thanks to her buoyant lifebelt. She swallowed the Amazon and spat back the Nile. Mountains of water piled onto her, while a hundred currents met simultaneously to jet her forward. Into a raging fjord. No sky, no air, just an ocean spilling its full fury on top of her.

Then the mist broke. She saw a purple sky. The deluge seemed to spread beneath her as fizzy soda. Colours fought through the torrent's final spits. Kate barely remembered where she was as the current settled into a steady, flat stream.

A river? Is this…is this the other side?

Her vision made out a vague reddish expanse. Tired limbs weren't much help as she paddled to the left bank. The buoyant vine wouldn't let her break free of the current, so she untied it. A series of coughs and retchy inhales followed her final exertion—hauling herself onto dry ground. The first in nearly three weeks. Her tired head sank onto a firm, dusty surface. As her heavy eyes finally closed, red dirt under her fingernails reminded her of nail varnish. The kind women used to wear…a lifetime ago.

Chapter Twenty
Indigenous

"So this is the real Kratos."

Twilight.

She knelt upright and stretched until her arms and shoulders were tight as leather, on the verge of cramping. An otherworldly perfume scented the air. It piqued her senses as she inhaled. On this side of the river, hundreds of skittish tumbleweeds wandered a rouge dustbowl which stretched from the mist behind to an orange forest many miles ahead. Not much of a celebration after her ordeal.

On the other hand, the dead celebrated even less.

The river continued to widen as she walked, forcing her northeast, until it grew so large Kate decided it qualified as a sea, or at least a big lake. No sign of life breached the surface, and she didn't care to inspect closer.

I've seen enough goddamn ocean for a lifetime. And desert for that matter.

She found herself steering farther and farther from the water. Why not? She couldn't drink it, anything in the water would undoubtedly be hostile, and it had almost killed her on numerous occasions.

"No love lost."

Except one.

She blanked the past utterly from her mind and trudged on. The suns rose low in the west. How long had she been asleep on the river bank?

No, don't think about the past. Ahead. Look ahead.

The orange forest was still many miles away. She perspired pints with exertion and the heat. Stopping for a rest, she climbed out of her suit. Cocooned for days, her legs now felt limber and revitalised. She removed her vest. The warm breeze wafted across her back and her breasts as she twirled, eyes closed, like a tired ballerina. There was no joy in the sensation, only relief at it being different. Fresh. Unrestrained. After feeling so ineffectual for so long aboard the *Elemental*, a tingle of freedom suited her like no body-caste survival suit ever had.

"So this is the *real* Kratos."

She folded her suit and vest and slung them over her shoulder. Walking was now a pleasure. No real hope. No expectation.

Just don't dwell in the past. No good'll come of it.

Despite the caveat, Kate did glance back from time to time. The alien craft's mind-bending proportions demanded it. Even though mist covered two thirds of the big pour, she could still make out individual obstacles and the white water breaking on them.

How in the hell did I get through that*? It's like white water rafting…on the slopes of Everest. Better make that Olympus Mons. Luck doesn't even begin to cover it.*

Either side of the cascade, the craft appeared perfectly sturdy. Its walls stood vertical beneath the rim, and Kate surmised that an entire panel of the exterior must have collapsed outward to create such a long, chaotic slope for the pour.

Ripped open during the crash landing?

Whatever the cause, she couldn't quite get her mind around the idea of all that water—a dozen seas' worth—collecting like drainage in a puddle on the roof of a manufactured object. She remembered Babylon Wall and the fast-flowing channel inside. What was the source of that flow? How many tributaries fed how many rivers to this ocean? Might there be even bigger oceans on the craft? If so, how big *was* the craft? And if that volume of water could gather on an artificial surface, what would a *real* Kratosian ocean be like—one occurring naturally? And what might she find in those depths?

Kate's imagination sent her dizzy.

Alright, seriously no more of that. Brain tranquilizer needed pronto. Come on, Katie girl, focus. What was that cheesy jigsaw metaphor Yeltsin used to trundle out…something about the big picture. "Keep your mind off the big picture and on your own little piece…one at a time." Or something. You might as well recite a goddamn nursery rhyme. Did that guy ever get to go out in the field, because he sure came up with some shit.

The suns arced three quarters of the way across the sky in the time it took Kate to exhaust herself. Still on the dusty plateau, she now glimpsed definite shapes in the orange tangle ahead: giant, green, pulsing things hung, like arboreal hearts, on a web of vines and ventricles; bizarre brown drapes dangled from the tree roof, darkening every ingress. It was a forest the likes of which she'd never imagined.

"But why am I not surprised?" She sighed, put her vest back on. "When this place seems normal, maybe I'll start to worry."

Food, water, shelter, companionship. Kate shrugged, realising she had none of those basic survival means.

"Time to improvise, then. Come on, Katie girl, it can't be that dire. It's bound to rain sooner or later, the forest has all kinds of potential for food and shelter, and you're not in bad shape." She fingered a bruise on her lower back. "The place is an open book."

But she couldn't drum up much enthusiasm. The rumble of the waterfall had all but disappeared behind her. An eerie silence filled the plateau. She gazed back over her footprints in the red dust. *Looks familiar,* she thought, recalling her endless trek across the high altitude desert and the number of times she'd shaken her head at those higgledy trails she'd left. *Too bloody familiar.*

Something made her look toward the river. Perhaps to distract from dry memories. It was a half mile or so to her left, creeping as a glacier. She guessed its width had nullified the current almost to entropy. Almost.

But her eye caught something on the bank. First a line at a tangent from the flat course, then an incongruous shape jutting up. She rubbed her eyes and pulled focus.

Couldn't be a part of the Elemental, could it? No, it's too big—the deck split in two. The wing-sail? Nah, it's way too big for that. What then?

"Whatever, it's worth a detour," she said aloud, now quite curious.

Butterflies roused in her stomach as she approached. It was a charred metal shell, partially silver, partially scorched to a crisp.

A fragment of the alien spacecraft?

No, the metal bore little resemblance to what she'd seen either under the desert or under the big pour. Warped, riveted, a different colour entirely, this needed another explanation.

She knew at the back of her mind what it *could* be, but she'd long since buried that part of the expedition. It would complicate things too much. There was an easier-to-swallow, mundane answer. There had to be.

But it's the right size and…and it's charred like the Monique. But how…?

She traced the nearest blunt edge with her fingertips. Solid, smooth, silver. Only tactile physical contact seemed to forge any real connection in her mind.

A landing craft?

She stepped back with a start. Where currents veered around the object, one or two constant gushes betrayed the silence of the slow-moving river. If this craft escaped the *Fair Monique,* who escaped with it? Did they survive the crash? If so, where were they now? If not, might they still be inside?

Kate dropped her suit and dove into the water. Her eyes smarted as she opened them, but the craft had clearly ripped open on impact. An entire side was missing, and water now filled the interior. But she found no sign of any dead bodies.

Back ashore, she sat cross-legged, rocking forward and back as she looked out over the river. Everything suddenly seemed so uncertain. Like a twist at the denouement of a play, finding the landing craft forced her to reconsider everything she'd felt over the past three weeks.

How did they escape? Why hadn't she seen them escaping? There was so much debris, but even so…maybe if she'd kept a sharper eye. But all this time? Yet…who was to say they hadn't just died on impact? The craft had ripped open, they'd floated out, *hasta la vista*. Yes, but they might've survived. They might have.

Whenever Kate tried to simplify it, to decide once and for all what had happened, she ended up shaking her head.

"Dilemmas. Nothing but goddamn dilemmas."

Jason might know what to do. If only he…

"Yeah, a lot of help that is right now." She punched her own arm for thinking of him so flippantly.

Dusk nodded. She pressed on toward the forest, her head a pinball machine of regrets and sunken hopes. And every now and then, the feeling that she was not alone nagged her.

It occurred to her survivors would leave footprints, but also that weeks of wind and storms would have erased them. Being unable to determine anything made her furious. Especially after feeling so carefree during the day.

Okay, playtime's over. First thing first, you need to find yourself a weapon. Nothing doing without a weapon.

She chewed her lip as she approached the tall, densely-tangled forest. The orange trees were more like buttressed beanstalks—without bark or boughs or branches of any sort. In the fading light, they resembled drooping wax figures, cursed to hold the entire forest roof on their shoulders.

"Atlas trees," she dubbed them.

She chose to steer clear of any blue webbing—the pulsing centres looked ominous—and made her way to a large opening which appeared to stretch quite a distance inside. The white, mossy floor was damp as she stroked her palm across it. It also wiped away without effort.

Kind of hard to stay inconspicuous. Not exactly the—

A trail caught her attention a few metres to the right. The moss was badly damaged, as if something big and clumsy had trampled it. The hairs on her neck tickled. Metre-wide prints lay adjacent to the trail on either side. As far as she could tell, it was a heavy two-legged creature with a sizeable tail.

As big as a dinosaur.

She'd tracked game animals before as part of her interactive survival program, but nothing bigger than an ibex. The gait of this creature suggested it took massive strides while always keeping its tail on the ground. Something about the tail's motion didn't quite sit right, though. Kate bent down for a closer inspection.

What were these indentations over...almost over the trail? If they were made by something attached to the tail, then why did they occur outside its groove, and why were they indents and not drag-lines. Almost like they were separate prints...made by another creature entirely. She tiptoed alongside the tracks. A tricky but constant rhythm...six prints repeated. A smaller, scurrying creature...had its own tail that hit the ground periodically.

What about the bigger creature? Definitely two legs. Its tail seemed erratic, though—no kind of rhythm. And there were zigzagging grooves inside the trail. *What the hell?*

She followed the tracks deeper into the dark forest. A humid atmosphere developed under the translucent roof. The perfumed air grew more intense, forcing Kate to muffle a few sneezes. The light remained surprisingly adequate, however, due to the white moss reflecting it at every turn. Almost like snow. She saw no movement through the Atlas trees and none on the path ahead.

Deeper.

No hint of the red dust remained, not even in her own footprints. A few delicate thumps, pulses of the blue hearts-in-webs, distracted her whenever she stopped.

Out of sight, out of mind.

She pressed on, undaunted, on the trail of the creatures. The path narrowed. Black creepers squeezed some of the thickest Atlas trees, some even reaching between two trunks, visibly pulling them together with iron will. It gave Kate an idea.

They could make a decent weapon. The material certainly seems tough enough.

She managed to snap a length free, but it took an almighty effort, and the black vine quickly coiled and petrified in her hand as she let go.

Not willing to accept defeat, she snapped off two more lengths and, using all the strength in her wrists, twisted them around one another, tying the ends with shreds of orange skin cut from the trees. When the vines tried to recoil, they tensed into each other. They thus twined, hardened into an extremely solid weapon. She banged it into her open palm and winced. Then coiled another, slimmer vine around one of the ends, making it into a deadly club. She had to use both hands to wield it, but its striking power would be more than worth the extra weight.

The path curved to the left. Kate kept one eye on the tracks, the other on the shadows ahead. She imagined herself in a Brothers Grimm fairytale for a moment, before the trail grew chaotic at a sharp bend. The larger creature's tail had scraped an arc in the moss totally inconsistent with its footprints.

What the hell? Almost like something was being dragged. And another creature scurrying in pursuit.

She didn't see the clue until it was two feet in front of her. Then froze. Dead silent. Not even a breath. Her temples throbbed with the weight of a thousand denials.

Was her mind playing a trick? She shifted position and read the word over and over.

"Kate."

Kate. Her name. Written in the moss. *Her* name written in the moss. It *was* her name. As clear as her own footprints behind her.

"That's me," she insisted. "Kate Borrowdale."

The forest now opened up into veins and arteries of possibilities. Jason's athletic figure sprinted through her mind. She imagined him after the sand yacht, before his full beard, when the potential of crossing the ocean had lit a fire in his eyes. A fire for her.

"He's here," she said. "Jason…he's here."

She dashed on. The moss proved quite slippery and she fell. But it only made her more determined.

He must've made it inside the chimneys. Survived the fireworks. Made his way under the ocean. Maybe the big pour is the only hole in this side of the alien craft…maybe it was inevitable that we'd both emerge in the same river. So why didn't I see his footprints before the forest? Okay, they might've easily been covered by the wind. I was out a long time.

She thought about Mandy, his trusty companion who never went anywhere without him.

Yes, that accounts for the second creature. The second tracks in pursuit. Jason was dragged by something, and Mandy followed. That's all there is to it.

Kate had never been as excited in her life. Nor as terrified. That Jason was likely in the clutches of huge predator filled her with dread, but the creature had also dragged, rather than killed him. A thread of hope, then, but enough to hang her rekindled excitement on.

Kratos had flipped again. A graveyard one minute, perhaps inhabited by human survivors the next, desolate once more, and now this.

Forget the big picture, she told herself. *He's your reason to keep going. He's the love of your life.*

Over a hundred yards on, she found his survival suit festooned on the creepers between two Atlas trees. Her heart sank. She feared the worst, but only for a moment. The damaged moss had recorded a chaotic struggle, scrape by scrape, after which the tracks continued exactly as before. Two giant, clawed prints, Jason dragged behind, struggling, and loyal Mandy scurrying in pursuit. She knew it was Jason by his second message scribbled in the snowy moss:

"Find me Kate. J."

She pursed her lips and raced on. Lactic acid tightened her shoulder but the adrenaline didn't abate. Her fingernails dug into the club in her grip.

All she could see were the tracks in the moss and her black weapon jerking forward as she ran.

Jason, she repeated. *Jason, I'm coming.*

Then, at the next bend, another white passage spilled onto her path from the left. She kept her course, but not without pausing to swallow. As the light dimmed further, she could hardly believe her eyes. Instead of three tracks, there were six. Three new sets of footprints had joined the chase, adjacent to the others.

Human footprints.

* * * *

BOOK THREE
KATE OF KRATOS

"Now this is the law of the jungle,
as old and as true as the sky;
and the wolf that shall keep it may prosper,
but the wolf that shall break it must die.
As the creeper that girdles the tree trunk,
the law runneth forward and back,
for the strength of the pack is the wolf,
and the strength of the wolf is the pack."

– Rudyard Kipling, The Law of the Jungle

Chapter Twenty-One
Kate in Flight

The denser the forest became, the more desolate it seemed. No colour escaped through the charred tangle of this woodland underworld. The orange Atlas trees lay many miles behind. These new black, gnarled trunks and limbs soon closed in about her, tapering the white path to a dead end fifty yards ahead. Kate's bonfire of a cough raged and cracked and really started to hurt. The oxygen had thinned considerably over the past hour or so, and her efforts to maintain a steady pace had flagged. But nothing could make her stop. Not while there was a chance Jason might still be alive.

A single beam of sunlight penetrated the forest roof about seventy feet above the dead end. Pale, purple sky suggested dawn had just broken. The branches thereabouts, torn, damaged in a haphazard ladder all the way up to the opening, indicated something huge had climbed and broken through not long ago.

Hang on, Jason. Just…hang on.

Kate readied her two-handed club—hewn from the dark trees—and mapped her route up through the branches. Eyeing the many tracks in the ground moss spurred her on.

Hell, the salamander made it up, and it looked like three other people had managed the climb. If they could do it, she definitely could. No one got the better of Kate Borrowdale.

The first few steps up proved easy, like the rungs of a ladder. She puffed after the fourth, however, and had to swing for the fifth. With the club in one hand, she only had one to spare; reaching for handholds, supporting herself while clambering soon taxed her left forearm and shoulder. This she remedied by switching hands periodically. A canny conservation of strength.

Not that I'll have any strength left after this. Christ, what's a girl gotta do?

Basking for a moment in the warm sunlight, she placed her free hand over her chest to still the heavy, painful throb inside. The pursuit had now lasted half a day—a marathon in itself under normal circumstances, but to Kate, on Kratos, merely the latest leg in what had become a punishing pentathlon. Hiking for minerals in the snowy mountain peaks; skydiving for dear life, in tandem with Jason, for eleven gruelling hours; traversing a desert; sailing across an un-crossable ocean; and now this, a grim chase through woodland straight out of a gothic nightmare: her survival had been nothing if not varied.

But as her heartbeat softened and her cough burned out, the thought of being alone spring-loaded and shot her aloft.

Out onto…a wonderland.

The forest roof rippled and groaned as a stiff breeze swept across it. Translucent, skin-like membrane, a giant sheath, heaved and settled in segments, as though it was the fallen canopy of a circus Big Top. Gashes in the skin here and there gave entry to the wind, which flexed acres in creasing, channelled waves. Kate pulled herself up and looked again. The entire ceiling seemed alive, respiring—an ocean with pulsing veins and gasping airways.

Time was running out. So how the hell could she track them over this?

Her first step felt incredibly soft, as though it hadn't touched a surface at all.

Great. Is this thing even going to hold my weight?

To test the canopy's tautness, she bounced it with an extended foot, ready to balance herself or wedge her club between branches should it cave in. *Okay, springy, some give, seems strong enough.* A heavier bounce. *Still good.* She then ran a few steps and bounced with both feet, to the same result. *We're in business. Now where the hell are they?*

The forest stretched for miles in all directions. Beyond it, directly ahead, a staggering mountain range pierced the clouds. Those foothills would take a week to reach, at least. To her left, sunlight reflected off the surface of a huge lake—the end result of the big pour. Where this skirted the mountains, tiny streams trickled through fallen rocks, and for a moment she thought she saw a fast-moving herd zigzag among the debris, as though evading a predator.

The edge of the forest to her right was a day or two away. A series of crescent fissures in the ground thinned the trees episodically, until only a remote archipelago of foliage remained amid a sea of red sand. Unlikely a large creature would take its prey there, given the unsheltered locale and distance from water. The mountains? Hopefully not—she was tired enough already. That left the lake, or rather the dense woodland at its edge, where any Kratosian creature could make a living if it were deadly enough.

"West then."

The decision did not fill her lungs with hope. It seemed too…irresponsible…like an all-in gamble on an already weak hand.

"What's happened to the science, Katie girl? You used to be pretty good at making choices, weighing the evidence. What the hell is this? Drawing straws? Think. Think hard. A creature that size is bound to make an impression on a surface this giving. You've seen its footprints, you know its stride. So where the hell…"

She noticed a tear in the translucent skin a few feet from the opening, and a sizeable depression…where the monster must have stepped. Kate traced the direction of the imprint. A few feet farther on, she found another. Bravo. She had a track. But the colourless membrane, darkening and lightening with the density of trees beneath, proved tough to read. Like following fingerprints across a window pane, she had to inspect the surface from close to. And if her constant crouching weren't enough to make her curse, the distance between the creature's footprints, in less than a dozen steps, increased tenfold.

"How?"

She scanned the canopy ahead. The skin tautened, ached as it filled with wind, almost exploded, and then settled with a sigh. Her own segment of the roof lifted all of a sudden, vaulting her ten feet into the air. Her stomach elasticised for a second, after which the most sublime feeling enwrapped her. Like floating, only with no force to hold her airborne. Or at least none that she could tell. She landed gracefully seconds later, and set about investigating the phenomenon.

A hop, a skip, and an upward leap.

Where each would have lasted but a split second on the ground—as the sequence of a triple jump, say—the same actions had extraordinary consequences on the forest roof. She covered a height and distance over ten times the capability of human limbs. The lightness, the ease of effort, the shock of taking flight, all reminded her of the first time she'd tried a trampoline as a seven-year-old on her granddad's lawn. But when she wheeled sideways through the apex of her leap, afforded time to breathe in and out twice, the realisation hit. It was not the bounce that held her aloft, it was low gravity.

"Okay, what could be causing it?" She parted the hair from her eyes after landing headlong.

Deep purple veins coursed through the entire canopy. The gravity seemed weakest above them. Pyrofluvium again? That was reddish, bordering on purple, and it had been abundant on Kratos ever since Pyromere. Something told her there was more to that element than they'd been made privy to. Maybe it had something to do with the crashed alien ship. Those ocean chimneys, the bonfire night firework display—some kind of exhaust perhaps? Pyro was an energy catalyst, but the briefings had been pretty obtuse. Who knew what the hell it could *really* do?"

Her next leap covered half the length of a football field. Despite flying slowly, Kate couldn't stop herself somersaulting through the arc. "It's all in the take off," she decided.

Six jumps, a mile later, she had the knack. Whenever a gust caught her leap, it changed her course. When the canopy swelled, she tiptoed. All the while Kate trained her eye on a fixed spot in the distance—four clusters of tall, orange trees rising over the lakeside. That had been the direction of her quarry back at the tear, and that was where she had to reach.

Three people, a scurrying salamander and a biped the size of a tyrannosaur: how hard could they be to spot? Was it too much to ask? "Give me a glimpse…just one glimpse." Mid-flight, Kate gripped her club and swung it with both arms. "Just one little glimpse, and I'll…we'll do the rest."

She stopped here and there, or ran back to inspect any rip she'd spotted from aloft, and threw a fist every time it tallied with the creature's tracks. At this rate, it was only a matter of time.

Three or four leaps from her goal, she landed a short distance from a large tear. The roof instantly collapsed under her weight.

Thud!

The downward slide threw her into blunt, jutting branches. She winced through every blow, but the pain was not her biggest concern. Below—a scene of utter carnage. Dead animals as big as rhinoceroses strewn across a two acre hollow on the forest floor. Their blood had collected in black pools, resembling a kind of crude oil swamp. Dozens of uprooted trees had collapsed, barring what appeared to be a path to the lake. Kate couldn't take it all in. Around twenty feet above the nearest monster, the slide fell away and she plummeted onto its torso—a smooth, leathery hulk.

Scurrying onto its leg folded back at the knee, she'd never moved as fast.

"Who are *you*?"

Kate spun round. The shock of hearing a human voice left her poised on the balls of her feet, ready to flee.

"Who spoke?" she shouted. "Who's there?"

"Over here."

The voice was male, deep and sonorous, not exactly young. She crept toward the southwest corner of the hollow, away from the dead creatures, where a single fallen tree had created a rudimentary den in the bracken.

"Hello. Where's Jason? Is Jason there?" She scanned the entire battleground for signs of human casualties. There were none.

"Are you Kate?"

"Yes."

A figure popped out of the bracken—a shortish man around forty, with a full beard. He wore a headscarf which looked suspiciously like a red handkerchief, smart trousers, survival boots, and a t-shirt saying, Omnipod, More Dreams Than You Can Imagine, that had started out white and become…murky. Kate pegged him right away as someone profoundly out of his milieu—a city boy forced to play Rambo in the jungle. The omnipod was fancy VR tech, a rich person's toy. But good on him, surviving out here all this time.

"Kate Borrowdale," she said with a smile.

"Lucas Revere. Man, are we glad to see *you*."

"You are? Likewise. Where's Jason?"

"In there. He's done nothing but say your name over and over."

Thank God.

"Fever?"

"Either that or deep shock—he's been through hell."

Hurry up already, for chrissakes. She felt like barging OmniRambo out of the way; he walked too damn slow. After an entire day of running, fretting, climbing, low-g vaulting, all she wanted was to hold Jason. The guided tour could wait till later.

The den was dark and moist. Two others—a man and a woman—shuffled out of the way to let Kate pass. As it was too low to stand, she sank to her knees and crawled the ten feet to his body.

"Jason, Jason, we made it." She kissed his forehead, then his warm, chapped lips, reached for his hand and kissed that, too. "Jason, I'm here. It's me. It's me, Kate." Leaning in, she whispered, "Never again. We're never leaving each other again. Okay?"

He didn't reply. His eyes were open and he blinked as she blew a cool breath across his face, but something held him captive inside. There was distance between them. Kate stroked his bearded cheeks. Flicking her hair back the way he loved, she imagined herself as an object of pure femininity—a woman just for Jason.

From outside, the three rescuers observed Kate and her two-handed club lying at her side. To the men, she might appear sleek, cold, athletic, a small yet formidable Amazon huntress. The woman no doubt eyed her with disapproval, as though Kate were a tomboy gatecrasher at the Selene pageant. Yes, this one had the look of Selene about her—middle-aged but stacked the way most men seemed to go gaga for.

When Kate emerged from the den, none of them offered to shake her hand.

"Looks like you've got a story to tell," said Lucas.

"As have you."

"Indeed. Introductions first, though," he said. "This is Javier Inarritu, mechanic. And this is Cecelia Benedict."

"How do you do? I'm Kate Borrowdale, terrain scout, and a tired one at that."

Though she wore a survival suit two sizes too big—she'd peeled it down to her waist—Cecelia, a middle-aged redhead, stepped forward with the poise and grace of a Selene contestant. That or a very high-priced escort at *Pont de Reves*, the hoity-toity premier lunar resort. "Pleased to meet you, Kate," And she gave a polite embrace, hardly making contact.

Definitely an escort, thought Kate. *She touches only when she needs to.*

"Hey, Kate." Javier looked at her askance. Shy. Still no handshake, no gesture of welcome. Trim, in his early twenties, he had striking brown eyes but otherwise very ordinary, boyish, Latino features on a round face. His blue overall had fared well in the weeks since the crash. Unusually for a mechanic, he seemed pretty clean, too.

She nodded in reply.

"So what on Earth happened here? I expected a helluva fight, but it looks like I missed the ten-count. Who…or what did all this? It's unbelievable."

"I think we'd better go inside." Lucas checked the perimeter of the hollow. "This might take a while, and we don't have long."

Chapter Twenty-Two
Three From Seventeen

"We lasted the best part of a month, in a hollow only slightly bigger than this hole." Cecelia thumped the nearest tree trunk with her side-fist, "on the southwest edge of this forest...death trap."

Kate admired the woman's pluck—to have lasted so long, so far from mirrors and push-up bras and satin nightgowns, was a commendable feat for an escort. And she'd clearly not just pouted her lips to let the men-folk bear the burden; no, Cecelia had pursued the monster as doggedly as Lucas or Javier, perhaps even more so, as her lot on board the *Fair Monique* could hardly have prepared her for such extreme physical exertion. Unless you counted the sex.

"How many of you survived the crash, initially?" asked Kate.

The five of them sat together inside the bracken den, close enough to smell each others' body odours. Javier, seeing his companions locked in deep contemplation, answered, "Seventeen, I think. I'm pretty sure we counted seventeen that first night. No one slept, I can tell you that much. It wasn't just the shock, either. Man, every ripple in the water, every time a goddamn twig broke, whenever one of those assholes broke down crying, every little distraction...I'm telling you, it reset my clock. Must have been three days before I literally *fell* asleep, in the middle of a hike, just fell down. These guys had to carry me back."

"Exhaustion under stress. I've seen it more than you'd think," Kate said. "You three have done extremely well. Without training, to last as long as you have…in such a dangerous place…it's amazing." No one acknowledged the compliment. She cast a wary eye over each of them in turn. What weren't they saying? "So tell me how the others died. Was it soon after the crash, or was it recent?"

"Both. Throughout. Hardly a night passed without a close scrape of some kind. The giants came every night." Cecelia's fingers trembled as she scratched an itch on her wrist. "That's why we had to follow the one that took your man. We knew the only way to save ourselves was to find their lair, to wipe them out. They…they came every night."

"Came? So you're not expecting them back?"

Lucas waved himself into the conversation. "I wouldn't say that, no. I'm sure they'll be back. All she meant was we're getting out…we're hauling ass from this forest as soon as we can…as soon as your man's fit to be moved."

Kate sensed they were hiding something. Sure it was hard to talk about dead companions, but what had prompted Lucas to butt in like that, and why had he and the escort both become nervous at Kate's mention of the past tense?

"Sounds like a plan," she said.

No one followed up. The silence thickened between them, forcing Kate, now a little unnerved, to think on. They'd been a little stand-offish ever since they'd met her. Was it guilt? Trauma? Maybe they just didn't like her—they wouldn't be the first. The escort probably thought she and Jason were some kind of Tarzan and Jane. *She* was all wrong for starters—three survived from seventeen, and one of them was Pretty Woman without a single mark on her. No chance. And who the hell was this Lucas? Christ, he'd just met two survival experts and *still* hadn't thought to ask their advice. He was clearly the one calling the shots. But not for long.

She picked up her club and lay it across her lap, spun it slowly at both ends. "Okay, I really have to know how you killed all those giants, as you call them. Just the three of you, together, when one of them is bigger than all three of you together. Another amazing feat. You're quickly becoming my new heroes."

She realised how thickly she'd laid on the sarcasm. But with them being unaccustomed to her dry sense of humour, they might mistake it for a genuine compliment.

Again, no answer.

"How did you do it? Spears, bullets, the common cold? Come on, guys, I'm dying to know. Or do I get three more guesses?"

Cecelia took a deep breath. "You have a lot to learn about tact, Kate."

"It's a simple question, Princess."

"Don't talk to her like that," snapped Lucas, a vein on his forehead almost popping. "We killed them. Is that not enough?"

Kate couldn't believe her ears. "Javier, what about you? Can *you* tell me how you disposed of…sorry, brought the bastards down? And don't say 'with tact.'"

The Spaniard shrugged, retreated into his boyish reserve. Kate blinked, incredulous. If she hadn't been so tired, hungry and thirsty, the dark bracken den would have become two humans lighter in the time it took to lift an injured man. Jason's saviours were secretive. Keeping things from one another was the surest way to end a survival plight. As soon as he was up and about, they'd all leave the forest—the Three Musketeers and their secret pact in one direction, Kate and Jason in the other. No sense quibbling. Kratos was too big for the five of them to ever have to cross paths again, and that sounded like heaven right now.

"I'll leave it at that, then. I still owe you one for saving my man."

My man.

Lucas and Cecelia whispered together, each keeping an eye on Kate. A few shared nods later, he said, "You're right, Kate, there's no sense keeping secrets. Not now. It's just that…you wouldn't believe how hard it's been for us to make it this far. One of the survivors was a corporal, a head of security back on the *Monique*. Anyway, he had a way about him…a serious chip…and when it came time to leave the crash site, he wouldn't budge. Not for anything. He absolutely refused."

"He lost his nerve?"

"Not exactly, no. He…he was armed. The most powerful hand-weapon I've ever seen. And when someone so bull-headed is armed, you don't have a big say in the matter. He would *not* let us leave. But when the monsters kept coming, and he could only bring down one or two at most, we knew it was time to mutiny. Like Cecelia said, the creatures came every night. We lost at least one person every night. Corporal Rappeneau would *not* budge. He insisted we hold the fort, as he called it. At any cost. So one morning, while he slept, five of us took his weapon and I…I killed him. I'll not deny it. I shot the bastard to kingdom come…and two others besides. They tried to make us stay, so I did the only thing I could…for chrissakes, just to keep us alive."

He shook as he finished his story. His darting eyes were wide, full of fear. Neither Cecelia nor Javier made a move to comfort him.

He'd done an awful thing. But sometimes that was the only way. Should she give him the benefit of the doubt? Survival of the fittest held true until there was a gun in the equation…then it was the Wild West. He may have been right, he may not, but there was no use arguing with a trigger-happy mutineer.

"Sounds like you did what you had to do, brother." She gave a reassuring nod. "And you brought *these* monsters down admirably as well. Good for you…all three of you."

"Thanks, Kate. I'm glad you're here," he replied.

Silence.

Jason fidgeted, groaned, then changed position so that he lay beside Cecelia Benedict, his head inches from her hip. Kate waited for a raised eyebrow, a doe-eyed glance, the slightest of smiles from the shapely redhead. Any excuse to distrust her even more. But none came. The escort was either too tactful or simply not interested in Jason.

Hmm, that's like saying a vampire isn't interested in a jugular.

Each curled in his own corner of the den. Javier kept the first watch. Kate held Jason's hand while she imagined them lying side by side on the deck of the *Elemental*, drifting under a wizard's cloak of stars and purple dusk. They were the only two people left alive on Kratos, and it was bliss.

* * * *

"Water…water…I can't…" Jason retched as he tried to swallow. An awful smell of gutted fish stung his nostrils. His chest-boring coughs woke everyone in the den, but Kate was the first to comfort him.

"That's where we're going right now." She tilted his face delicately in her hands. "We're going to find you some water."

It had been an age since she herself had eaten or drank. The U-fish and a few cupped handfuls of rainwater, days ago. Thinking about it accentuated the physical effects—dry throat, gnawing stomach, leaden limbs—and she wondered what the others had lived on all this time.

"Where's the nearest drinking water?" she asked Lucas, quietly so that Jason couldn't hear.

"The lake, I'm afraid."

"What do you mean? That's saltwater."

"Yes, but we have a still. It's only foldaway but it produced enough for all seventeen of us that first day." He retrieved a bright orange, cylindrical shape from the back of the hollow. An emergency survival bag. The cylinder itself was made of protective foam rubber inside a nylon sleeve. She wondered which other items they'd brought along.

"One of the guys rescued this from our shuttle before it sank," he said. "It's the reason we're still here. As well as this…" He unclipped a silver rod from a holster attached to his belt. Its exterior was grooved like the inside of a rifle barrel, and a series of red and green L.E.D. lights pulsed in a coil around its circumference. No longer than his forearm, the thing resembled a musical instrument as much as a weapon. "*This* is our advantage over this world. *This* is going to keep us alive."

In that case, enjoy it while you can, because the first time you make a boneheaded decision, I'm taking it.

"Are you able to walk?" Cecelia crouched at Jason's side and offered him her hand. To Kate's chagrin, he took it.

"Thank you," he said. "Yeah, I think so. Just parched, that's all…and…dizzy." Clutching his ribs, he stumbled into the daylight and bent forward, bracing his knees with his arms, to survey the site of slaughter.

Several eviscerated hulks were sprawled across the hollow before him. He remembered the creature's upright shape and the rhythm of its stride in vivid detail, as if from a recurring nightmare. His shoulders tightened. The *thump, thump* of enormous clawed feet pounding first the metal floor of the alien ship, then the red dust of the desert, filled him with hate. He'd been so helpless. Dragged for miles and miles, from unknown to unknown, by a monster he could barely even see to an end he couldn't imagine. How he'd cried for help. How he'd shifted position at every opportunity during the drag to prevent friction from burning holes through his survival suit. The hot metal still scorched his thighs and arms, the dust blocked his nostrils and coated the inside of his mouth, and his ribs still crunched as the monster's momentum flung him around corners into countless tree roots.

He remembered writing Kate's name in the white moss as the creature paused to look up. He'd almost managed to wriggle out of his survival suit, out of the creature's clutches, when the fight began. Not much of a fight really—more the monstrous tantrum of a child seen through the eyes of a ragdoll. But the thing had left Jason's suit behind, festooned on the branches. A trace that he existed. A glimmer of hope that Mandy…or Kate…might be able to follow.

How stubbornly that hope had stayed with him as the creature had climbed up, bounded across the forest roof with him in its claw, until he'd blacked out. The sensation of floating through the air after being dragged across Kratos for so long…hit him now with wheeling, nauseous insistence.

Kate knelt beside him. "What happened, Jason? What happened on the *Elemental*?"

He collapsed sideways into her, shivering. She caught him.

"It was awful," he groaned. "There were monsters…all around you, monsters from the deep. Mandy and I fought…hey, where *is* Mandy?"

Ashamed for not having asked before now, Kate shrugged. Despite following the salamander's tracks for a full day through the forest, she hadn't thought of her since the forest roof.

"Lucas, what happened to the small creature chasing Jason? It looks a bit like a large chameleon with a funny-shaped head. Did you see it?"

"I think I scared it away," he replied.

"What the hell for? It was trying to protect him."

"How was I supposed to know that? As soon as the monster dropped Jason, the little critter ran straight for him. Looked like it was about to attack, so I fired. Didn't know it was a pet."

"You'd better not have hit her?"

"No, it clean got away."

"Which direction did it run?" asked Jason.

"Toward the lake—that way." He pointed to the pathway blocked by fallen trees.

"Then that's where I'm going." Jason rose, staggered to his feet. "I owe that little critter my life ten times over."

Javier and Cecelia glanced at each other. A cruel frown appeared on Lucas' brow, while his right hand twitched over the powerful weapon tucked in his belt.

Uh-oh. It was starting. Too many chiefs and not enough discussion—this was going to end badly if they weren't careful.

"Okay, everyone take it easy," she said. "Darling, first we'll find a proper shelter, then you and I will find Mandy together. We need to get these people to safety. It's what we've been trained for. And Lucas," she turned to the others, "promise me you'll be careful with that thing."

"Course."

She stood facing them, hands on hips. "Now listen up, I want no arguments on this—we're going to drink from the lake, then we're heading for the mountains. This forest is just too unpredictable for us to live in, and you've already indicated how dangerous it is to camp permanently near the lake. Our best bet is to find somewhere controllable, somewhere defensible from an elevated position. A mountain cave, perhaps. Trust me, it will increase our chances of survival beyond measure. I also saw streams among the rocks, which might prove crucial as a water supply. Jason?"

"Count me in." He placed his hand on her shoulder.

"Guys?"

They each nodded, but with less conviction.

She spied Lucas' weapon. *You're going to have to figure a way to take it, Katie girl. He's far too trigger-happy. And he's already got the taste for killing.*

"Give me a day's rest, then I'll see if I can manage the hike." Jason masked a yawn with his hand.

"Deal." She supported his weight as he hobbled back into the den.

The three accomplices were already whispering together inside. Hmm, she couldn't have laid the situation out any clearer. The rest was up to them. For the time being, at least.

"How long did you chase after me, Kate?" Jason propped himself against her, rested his tired head on her shoulder.

"For over a day. I never gave up hope."

"And probably set a few records on the way, too."

"You bet your sweet ass, Bub."

He chuckled, winced when it hurt his sore ribs, then sank until he was prone. He rested his head on her lap, sighed with contagious contentment. His dumb, lopsided grin left her beaming like a twelve year old.

"Wish I'd have seen it," he whispered.

Stroking his dusty hair, Kate thought back to her endless nights on board the *Fair Monique*—empty, future-less hours spent utterly alone. All she'd had was her work, and no one to share it with.

"I love you," she said softly.

He was already asleep.

Chapter Twenty-Three
Leading Man

"Nobody make a sound." Kate knelt at the den's entrance, alert to a peculiar *whump-whump* that didn't sound anything like the motion of the canopy roof. It was rhythmic, controlled.

Holding hands, the others—including Jason, in consoling form—watched her reconnoitre the hollow. The *whumps* seemed to descend from the roof. A series of scrapes and scrabbling across the glade kept her on tenterhooks. Almost pitch dark outside. She strained to see what was causing the furore when, from out of nowhere, an enormous shape flapped down a few yards in front of her. It kicked up a blizzard of ground moss in a sudden hurricane of wind, knocking Kate off balance. The others covered their faces as particles filled the den. The huge shape then lifted and flapped twice more.

I'll be a son of a...the eagles!

The creatures' low purrs seemed to support her theory, as she'd discerned their dialect on the beach at Dolphin Cove. And the size of the wing also tallied.

But what an awesome sight, that she couldn't see, that she daren't risk venturing out to see. Giant eagles feeding on *those* carcasses.

The forest hollow remained a whirlwind feeding frenzy for hours. A sweet smell none of them had ever encountered before stung their nostrils and pervaded every breath.

"Rancid meat never tasted like that," whispered Javier, closing his eyes to savour the flavour.

"Feel free to tuck in," replied Cecelia.

"Yes, if I'm not tucked into first."

Kate and Jason sat side by side away from the others, touched foreheads.

He whispered to her, "The lad's got a point. We'll have to take whatever's left before we leave—dead flesh or not."

"This time, we'll try and cook it." She recalled her horrid bout of food poisoning on board the *Elemental*.

"Well, we *are* the survival experts."

"And them?"

"I don't know yet," he said. "Without the gun, I just don't know."

"When shall we take the gun?"

"When we're out of harm's way. No sense disarming a gunslinger while we're under siege. Let's see how he does."

"Yep."

Lucas didn't say a word during the night, though he had plenty he wanted to say to these two arrogant, condescending...okay, maybe Remington wasn't so bad. But that Borrowdale—an absolute cow, insufferable even in small doses, the kind of person who'd stop at nothing to make sure she called the shots, till all lives were subordinate to hers and she wielded absolute power. Not again. He'd already seen Corporal Rappeneau blow that kind of autonomy in a big way, with nightmare results. And he'd had to step in, kill a man—more than one—to ensure no one had that power over him, over the others again. Ever. Borrowdale might be a professional drop scout, she might have all the knowhow in the world to keep them alive, but she also wanted his weapon in the worst way. Why? Two guesses, but he only needed one. God, he could smell it on her, practically hear her teeth gnash in frustration.

Yes, she was going to try and take it soon. No, he'd never let that happen. One Rappeneau was enough for any planet, and he owed it to Cecelia and Javier to—

But—what was he becoming? Seriously? He'd kill to remove another's authority but also to retain his own? What was he if not the one calling the shots now—at gunpoint—over these four people who all had the right to decide for themselves how best to survive?

He twined a loose bit of stitching from the waist of his T-shirt around two fingers, tightened until it bit and cut off the circulation to his fingertips. They tingled, throbbed when he untwined it.

The son of a Beta grade ISPA officer—his father had been a chef in the veterans' hospital at Med Lake before he died—Lucas had always wanted to join the Service, make a name for himself, maybe one-up the old man and become a Delta or higher, a leader of men into combat. But the sad fact that he'd flunked almost every academic qualification he'd tried for, again and again, had kept him a civilian for life. Not his fault. Just inherited his mum's slow learning, that was all. His first eight business endeavours had flopped within a year on Jaguar, Mars, Ferrer Five, and even Kappa Max, the scummiest shack-sheik colony on the 100z border. So winning a co-op contract to run a fast-food diner on the *Fair Monique*—one of ISPA's Pioneer class starships—had in fact been the biggest break of his life, one he'd loved every minute of…until, yeah…

But he'd *proved* his ability to be in charge of others, albeit flipping burgers, and he'd been good at it. The captain himself had commended Lucas's conduct during a fire evacuation drill, when he'd gone out of his way to extricate a deaf customer who'd wandered into a storage room during auto lockdown. A proud moment. Not that these drop scout assholes cared a snot who he really was, what he could do. All they saw was his weapon, and his non-rank.

Boy, had Borrowdale underestimated him. She'd best watch who she tried to lord it over—he knew how to take care of himself, how to take care of those who got in his way.

He kept his hand close to the trigger of his weapon tucked safely away…but easily retrievable. For tonight the darkness smelled not of rotting flesh but of mutiny.

It could come at any time.

* * * *

They gathered their supplies at first light. The eagles had long since left, and all that remained in the hollow were the monstrous bipeds' skeletal remains, their black blood spattered across the white moss. The bones had not been picked clean, though. Kate,

Jason and Javier managed to pull a few loose chunks apiece from the giant ribs—more than enough to feed the five of them for a few days.

"Come on, this is taking too long," snapped Lucas, throwing the survival bag over his shoulder. "We need to get moving a.s.a.p. Trust me, you don't want to be around when more of those bastards arrive. Come on."

Jason rolled his eyes at Kate, who twitched a knowing smile. Lucas saw it, and Cecelia saw that he saw it. But true to form, Kate observed all.

Though the twin suns were visible between clouds, Kate sensed that they were farther apart in their orbits than usual. She perceived her four companions—not speaking, barely cooperating, thrown together by cruel necessity. Back on the *Fair Monique*, they would not be friends. Their footprints from the den in the glade had diverged almost straight away; those seeds of mistrust replaced the uprooted white moss in her mind.

In truth, she wanted the split.

Beyond the two toppled trees, the lake path consisted of bare, dark red soil damaged by innumerable heavy footprints. Lucas led the way. His hi-tech weapon flashed red and green as he held it out to probe the unknown ahead, to give him the edge over fear. Cecelia and Javier, arm in arm, followed close by. Kate observed the Spaniard's sly glances at his glamorous companion, and the fact that Cecelia revealed no hint of reciprocity.

She wanted the lad's protection.

It led Kate to consider...Through all their dangers shared on Kratos, she had never resorted to seeing Jason in that light. An equal partner and lover, yes, but never a masculine crutch. For some reason the notion left her feeling bitterly cold.

Hmm, she might be the lady, but I've got the man. Oh, give over, Katie girl; give the poor lass a chance. Not every woman can take care of herself. So she's beautiful—so what? That's no reason to dislike someone. And after all, Jason would never stoop so low as to fall for an escort. He probably doesn't even like redheads. He…he's hardly looked at her. And she's arm in arm with the Spaniard. Yep, that's it—nothing more to it.

A low foghorn groan tugged their attentions northward. It may have been distant, but it was unlike anything they'd heard before. The black trees thinned after a few hundred yards. Stumps or fallen trunks, formerly orange Atlas trees, sketched a modicum of colour amid the gothic woods, and farther on Kate glimpsed a cluster of giant, living Atlases. A blue heart suspended by sinuous webbing throbbed in the centre. She'd seen these in abundance during her first day in the forest.

Whatever they were, they seemed to be relegated to the outskirts of the forest.

Jason winced whenever he stumbled, favouring his left side. Each time she touched the bruised area over his ribs, he clenched his teeth, held his breath.

"That doesn't look good," she said. "You need some serious rest soon."

"Aye." He kissed her hand. "Soon as we find somewhere safe."

"What happened on the *Elemental*, Jason? How did you make it?"

A part of her didn't want to know, didn't want to hear how the man she loved had suffered, but his being here alive was so miraculous that dispelling the dream, grasping the reality seemed the only way to bridge the rift she perceived between them. How *had* he survived the deadly crossing without a boat?

Jason fastened his stare on Cecelia's careful steps ahead. "By a thread, I have to admit. I tell you now, I'd never have made it on my own. No chance in hell. When you became ill, and I…I thought you might not make it…something died in me that day." He gripped her hand. "Daniella was always so safe, never risked herself a day in her life after the big sacrifice on Fourmyle. She used to be my life-line. She was what I looked forward to after every expedition—sweet perfume. Dependable, away from survival. But *you* were in the thick of it with me. You're my huntress. And I've nowhere to go if anything happens to you. That would have been it. Jesus, Kate, this *is* it. This is the land that time forgot."

Though he was trying to emphasise the hopelessness of their being marooned, Kate loved that thought. Edgar Rice Burroughs' story brought a German U-boat to the fabled island of Caprona, where Germans and Allied captives were forced to co-operate in a prehistoric land where evolution had gone berserk. In the end, only the hero and heroine survived, stranded, forced to head ever northward on the long-lost continent. *That* was Kate and Jason. She remembered the final romantic passage in the book, when Bowen and Lys looked up to the heavens and exchanged vows—companions, survivalists for all time. She took his arm and breathed in the new world.

Kratos was their Caprona.

"Mandy was extraordinary," he went on. "She recruited our dolphin friends to fight the behemoths, then she carried me under a typhoon to the great chimneys. You remember those things? They must have been pyro exhaust vents of some kind—they exploded while I was *inside*. We hid in a water channel, barely escaped. After that, Mandy led me on until…that bastard found us. It was hiding in an enormous cage inside the craft. We had no chance. It dragged me for a lifetime…to this place."

"My God." She couldn't picture it, or perhaps didn't want to. "Mine seems almost laughable in comparison."

"Tell me."

Kate relayed her ordeal, starting with waking up alone in the middle of the storm. He kissed her for every triumph—her improvised fishing strategy, removing the *Elemental's* sail, clinging doggedly to the deck for as long as she was able during the big pour, tracking him through the forest. But a much louder, guttural foghorn curtailed his final kiss. Its frequency resonated with a tickle in their ears. They tried to rub, scratch the itches inside, but they were too deeply embedded.

"What the hell is that?" Jason asked the others. "You three have lived here for weeks now; have you heard it before?"

Cecelia answered, "We haven't, no, but one of our first hunting parties reported something similar. They followed the forest border toward the mountains…I think it was on the third day…and one of them never made it back. The others all said they'd heard a deep moan coming from the forest—a booming choir, I think was the phrase they used.

That was it. We never imagined going that far again."

"But here we are." Lucas shook a fist. "Thanks to you and your so-called survival expertise, Kate. If you ask me we should have climbed back up to the canopy roof and gone in some other direction. We're heading toward the most dangerous part of the forest."

Kate stormed toward him, her black club slung over her right shoulder. "That's genius. You tell us that *now*, when we're almost at the lake. Why don't you just admit you didn't have a clue what to do, instead of pointing out how dangerous my path is *after* we've taken it?"

"Easy, Kate." Jason held her shoulders.

Fingers twitching at his belt, adrenaline shaking his arm, Lucas clearly wanted nothing more than to silence Kate…for good. "We were better off before you came along." His voice trembled.

"Oh yes, you were in grand shape—three from seventeen. I have to hand it to you, that's some tiptop marksmanship."

Cecelia ran between them. "What's that supposed to mean? Lucas has done his best. He's no murderer. How dare a roughshod suggest—"

"I don't suggest, Princess. I say what I mean. Not that a cheap clip-a-lay would understand."

Both women glared, nodding the acknowledgement of their mutual dislike. Their cards were on the table—no longer tarot, they were now open Cydonia Face cards with hate in the margins. One was a prostitute, the other a 'roughshod'—damaged goods, a shack-sheik's cast-off with a history of childhood abuse. But neither assumption was correct. The conclusions had merely been convenient, an easy fit for their instant hatred of one another.

"This has to stop…now," yelled Jason. "Lucas, lead us on. Cecelia and Javier, keep walking. Kate, *stow it*."

Lucas pursed his lips but walked on. Incensed, Kate left Jason's side and fell back to bring up the rear. He was right, of course, but she had to sulk all the same.

It was that hotheadedness again. Now she'd even turned Jason against her. *Nice going*.

The trail finally opened up to a shimmering lake. A mossy white gap between the bank and the border of Atlas trees was no more than thirty feet wide. The giant footprints headed left along the bank, toward Lucas' camp somewhere to the south. Vast and still, the lake itself shone green under the twin suns. Jason inspected the ground, then the water, for signs of Mandy.

"Here. Is this what you wanted?" Javier pointed him to a few tiny prints amid the stampede.

"Yes. *Mandy*." He followed the trail to the water's edge. "She went in here." He paused. "At least we know she's still alive."

Kate kept her distance from the group but her heart swelled as she heard Jason's voice lift.

"Okay, Lucas. The still—you can hand it over," said Jason.

"What for? I know what I'm doing."

"Oh? What was your job on the *Monique*?"

"I owned a café bar."

"I see. Hand it over."

Lucas shook his head as he unpacked the lifesaving still. A small metallic object, resembling a cigarette lighter, fell out of a torn pocket inside the bag. No one else saw it, nor, apart from Kate, would they have known what it was, but Jason picked up the emergency transmitter and placed it in the pocket of his shorts. Without the launch tube on a shuttle craft, it was next to useless; any message he recorded would never reach space. But it was a private memento, a link to the past, that he felt like keeping for himself.

In minutes, he had the saltwater still set up and functional, droplets already forming above the collection basin.

Probably realising how ridiculous her stubbornness was under the circumstances, Kate rejoined the others. She sat next to Javier, the only one who hadn't displayed hostility toward her so far. No doubt his body odour would made up for it. Jason smirked to himself, then went on explaining the ins and outs of life as a terrain scout to Cecelia, who seemed interested in everything all of a sudden.

"Hey, Javier."

"Hi Kate. Everything alright?"

"So-so. I was wondering what you made of the forest roof—that low gravity phenomenon. What do you think could cause something like that?"

Javier shifted position to face her. Moss had stuck to his palms, so he rubbed his hands together, allowing the breeze to whisk away the white specks like pollen over the green water. He had pleasant wide brown eyes and the beginnings of a goatee. Though he wasn't exactly Kate's type, a little immature, he would probably be nice, down to earth company in the real world.

"That low-g was awesome." His glance skimmed over Kate's breasts. "I heard the others say it has something to do with that red-purple element I can't pronounce—the deep colour running through the arteries. I guess the whole roof is like some kind of skin. Pity there's so many monsters running about. You could invent some extreme sports with that thing." His eyes lit up at the thought.

"I know. I broke the triple jump world record by about a quarter of a mile."

"I beat the high jump ten times over." He leaned in close to whisper, "And on the way down, I squashed Cecelia."

Kate laughed. "Yeah, and I'll be *that* was an accident."

The Spaniard placed his finger over his mouth.

After a few hours, the apparatus had provided enough pure moisture for them each to drink a cupful. With a weary sigh, Lucas packed it away for the next leg of the trip. There had been no further signs of Mandy, nor of the monstrous bipeds.

"I'm sure we'll see her again," Kate said to Jason.

"Hope so," he replied. "I wouldn't be here if it wasn't for her."

They trekked along the lakeshore until nightfall, ever alert to the rustling canopy above, mindful of the constant boom-song emanating from the forest. Lucas' mysterious weapon reminded Kate of a battery-powered Star Trek toy, its red and green lights flashing in a tacky helter-skelter sequence. But it staved her fear…up to a point. Out front in the dark, it lit their way reassuringly—a behemoth killer—but, by that same token, it stood out like a beacon in the night. It was a repellent *and* an invitation to the forest dwellers of Kratos.

With nowhere safe to camp, they pressed on. The foghorn noise dissipated as they reached the first boulders at the base of a scree slope, and here Kate scrambled ahead, guiding Lucas' light while she quested for an easy upward route.

A cave, a hollow, a sheltered gap under a rock…come on, give me somewhere safe, somewhere out of reach.

Lucas and the others aped her every move. Her sheer tenacity, her boundless energy as she scrambled over the rocks, was clearly good for them, survival of the vicarious proactive kind. She daren't give in. Panting, her chest churning heavy, wet sand, Kate darted about in the blackness for over an hour. Her gaze lighthoused at every turn. Finally, she bade them stop to concentrate on a sound that was barely audible—a light trickle through the rocks.

"It's ahead, to your right," said Cecelia.

Kate cocked an ear. "Right you are. Good hearing."

They followed the tiny rivulet a few hundred yards up the slope, where they discovered a vertical rock face with a small ingress. Though the gap was only three feet high, dark, and part of the water course, Kate wasted no time in tossing her club inside and crawling after it on her hands and knees. The tunnel lasted eight or nine feet, after which it opened up enough for her to almost stand tall.

Chilly inside, the cave sounded quite deep; the timpani echoes of dripping water seemed spread out, acoustically channelled. There was no light and no smell. Though damp, it suited Kate's frugal checklist superbly.

It was high up, solid, enclosed, easily defensible, and it was a water source.

"Come on in, guys. I think we've found our home."

The others crawled nervously through the stream. Lucas knelt, roved his weapon about the cave for a few moments, before lighting the way for Cecelia. Kate helped her through. With all five now inside, close together, it seemed a little warmer.

"Make yourselves comfortable if you can." Kate huddled next to Jason. "Get a good night's rest. Tomorrow we've got work to do."

Javier inched closer to Cecelia. "What sort of work?"

"Ever heard of Robinson Crusoe?" asked Kate. "Well his job was a walk in the park compared to this."

"But there's five of us."

"Five times the work."

"So what's the good news?" the Spaniard groaned.

"The good news," answered Jason, "is that we've got one crucial advantage. In case you hadn't noticed, her name's Kate—Kate of Kratos."

Chapter Twenty-Four
Brinkmanship

The sound of creaking fabric woke Kate. "What…?" It was the sleeve of Cecelia's oversized survival suit snagging on the rock wall above.

"Ssh! It's hiding."

"What is?" No sooner had Kate opened her eyes than a streak of light shot across the cave in front of her. She sat up with a start.

"Cecelia?"

The men were sound asleep. None of them even twitched. In the pitch ahead, a dim glow, nothing more than the faint corona of a light source hidden behind a promontory on the rock wall, flittered about. What was it? The streak had moved so fast it couldn't possibly have belonged to a land animal. And the corona pulsed, swelled, almost as though the light itself were respiring.

"Cecelia? What is it?" Kate's lowest whisper. The squeak of sodden boots replied. Then a scuff on the rocks.

"Kate, come—follow me. We're not alone. Whatever it is, it's been checking us out."

The word *it* goosed Kate from knees to neck. This was an alien presence, a new life form no human had ever seen, in the cave with them. Something bioluminescent? The way it had streaked across the darkness a few feet above ground suggested it was airborne. Some kind of giant firefly? On the verge of rousing Jason and the others, she turned toward Cecelia, whose silhouette now blotted out the corona. Her dainty footsteps weren't in the opposite direction, as Kate would have bet beforehand, they inched toward the thing, intrepid, in the name of discovery. It reminded Kate of herself, and the notion intrigued her.

Let's see what this princess is made of.

They crept in single file. After a few higgledy ridges in the floor, the rock became flat, slippery. "Easy, Cecelia. Don't get too close." The most air tasted fresh as a mountain tarn. Water droplets echo-popped farther in, suggesting a large hollow. Kate manoeuvred herself into the trickling stream and felt her way along the right hand wall, opposite the strange glow. The thing definitely pulsed. Its corona was now a luminous yellow. Its shape grew with each step she took. Suddenly the light darted across the passage like a midnight sparkler, an indelible snake that seared Kate's retina.

"Did you see it?" she asked.

"No. What was it?"

A tart aniseed smell tainted the tarn freshness. The creature's residue? Something like a slug's silver trail…only through the air instead? With Cecelia along, the expedition felt more juvenile than scientific—the way midnight hikes in the forest used to be when Kate had been a Girl Scout. Strangely, she didn't feel threatened by the thing at all. Perhaps because it was eluding them—a sign of fear—or because Cecelia herself seemed unafraid.

It upped and zigzagged away, bright as a R.A.M. generator light, until it snaked out of sight. This momentary illumination showed Kate plenty of the geography. "There's a crossroads up ahead," she said, "where the roof lifts into some sort of chamber. This passage continues on a fair way beyond that, cylindrically. The stream veers right when we get to the chamber, and I think there's a slight waterfall."

"How could you tell all that? It was only lit for a second."

"It's my job."

Cecelia touched Kate's shoulder in the darkness. "There you are. Jason was right, you are handy."

"And there's more to you than meets the eye, Cecelia. I'd have bet krugerrands to credits you'd be the first one out the door back there. Good for you. I think we'll do fine."

"Me too."

Kate switched hands on the slippery wall as she turned to retrace her steps. "What do you say we bring the men along tomorrow…so we can explore properly? Lucas and his ray gun."

"Sounds good."

"Tell me, Cecelia, what did you do on the *Fair Monique*? I've been meaning to ask."

Cecelia paused. "I was a part-time schoolteacher. My husband was a security officer."

"Schoolteacher. What subject?"

After a quick, rehearsed chuckle, Cecelia sighed. "Art, I'm afraid. I teach art."

"Really? Well, that's something *I* could never do."

And probably the only thing she can do that I can't.

"You really think we can last here, Kate?"

"Yes, I really do." She still didn't care for the word *we*. Any way it sliced, it was a euphemism for Kate, Jason and so much dead weight.

A sluggish, ultra-violet dawn loomed over the cave entrance while Kate crawled through. The entire forest canopy, indeed the whole of Kratos appeared in hibernation as the suns began their indomitable climb. The burbling stream coursed between her feet down the slope of slate and scree. To the north, a low-lying mist skirted the bases of four towering mountains. Long, sweeping valleys and islands of orange vegetation, perhaps Atlas trees, hinted at an ecosystem dribbling its way through the mountains. No signs of animal life, though. And the mist shielded the lake to the south.

"Where to start," she muttered.

Hours later, Jason draped his arms over her shoulder from behind. "The way I see it—three choices." He kissed her neck. "One, we venture deeper into the cave after those glow worms. Two, we scout these valleys." Head resting on her shoulder, he pointed to the veins of vegetation among the rocks. "Or three, you and me head back into the forest."

Kate tensed. "For food?"

"Uh-huh." He slid his fingertips over the undulations of her clavicle and shoulders, down her triceps, in onto her waist. It tickled her for a moment, she laughed, before his coarse hands began to peel her vest up. She arced her neck back, breathing heavily. Jason spat her hair out of his face. It didn't break the momentum. Gently letting the folds of fabric fall, his hands were now inside her vest, sliding upward. With one arm Kate held his face near, and, closing her eyes, kissed him. Her ecstasy didn't remain static at the meeting of lips, it continued on as sunlight through a magnifying lens, scorching, combustible. Her entire body clenched as he took handfuls of her breasts, caressed her stomach and waist, and finally, manfully, spun her round by her hips.

She whispered, "Jason." Seeing his mouth ravenous and agape, she hiked his shirt up to his chest, ready to strip him naked for all the planet to see.

"Uh-hmm." Lucas cleared his throat behind them.

Jason snorted, shook his head, while Kate scowled with a hateful gritting of her teeth. "Can't we just...dump them somewhere?" she said.

"Tempting." He straightened their attire before throwing Lucas a wave. "Very tempting."

By the time Jason and Lucas returned from their sojourn to the northern foothills in search of food, it was late afternoon. Fell weather followed them.

"There *are* herds around, but they're so alert and they dart away so quick, we'd need the Bow of Odysseus to hit one," explained Jason.

Lucas wheezed, gathered his breath. "Yeah, my gun isn't much use at long range, I'm afraid. There's no sight and no way to target in. It's kind of like the pulse equivalent of a shotgun—deadly only at close quarters."

Heavy hail thrashed the rocks as they huddled together inside the cave. The temperature fell below freezing, and with all three men now without survival suits, the time came to light a fire.

"W-we've got p-plenty of incendiaries." Lucas opened their emergency bag and held up a fistful of silver metal sticks.

"Yeah, to burn what? Stone and water?" replied Kate.

Shivering, Jason scraped her club toward him across the rock, handed it to her. "How about this?"

"*That's*…worth a try." She loathed having to give up her weapon, but if it would keep Jason warm, so be it. And she could always make another. She snatched an incendiary from Lucas. "Rip the strap off that survival bag," she said.

"How will I carry it?"

"I don't give a shit. Do you want a fire or don't you?"

Kate also tore a strip from the midriff of her vest. This she set alight to hold under the club. But the wood was stubborn. She tried the strap next, which burned hotter and longer. Seconds before that frazzled out, horrid smoke columned from the black club. Kate bent low to fan the heat, and the first flames crept up to envelop the Kratosian wood.

"N-nicely done, Kate," said Javier.

Jason kissed her on the cheek.

"Hmm, we'd better work out what to do when this thing dies out." She noted how quickly their smiles vanished when she spoke.

"Oh, give us a moment, for chrissakes," snapped Lucas.

"Whatever."

The wood spat, crackled. Cecelia coughed, moved out of the path of the rising smoke. "Right, Cecelia and I have the only suits," said Kate. "We're going to rotate them until the weather passes. An hour each. The others will have to huddle together, share their body heat. Also, I want this entrance plugged up, so when it's your turn to wear a suit you'll have to sit here and shield the cold air. Maybe spread the survival bag and hold it as a canopy over the hole. Other ideas?"

Cecelia thought for a moment before responding, "We could always explore further inside the tunnel."

"Hey, not a bad idea," said Lucas.

Jason nodded, rubbing his hands in the heat. "Now's as good a time as any. And at least we'll be away from the storm."

"But we don't know anything about what's further in." Kate's knees ached from her kneeling position, so she sat cross-legged instead. A curious smell, rather like newly-laid tarmac, rose with the smoke. "I wasn't going to explore the tunnel before we procured a food supply. Provided it doesn't get any colder, we could probably survive right here until the weather breaks."

"*If* the weather breaks," said Cecelia.

As much as she hated acceding to the princess's logic, Kate had to admit it was worth the risk. The storm might very well last for days, perhaps fatally.

"Very well—good call, Cecelia." She feigned diplomacy with a twisted, stitched-on smile. Jason sniggered when he saw it. *He* knew how much it pained her to be undermined, to be second best.

Kate went a little light-headed, disoriented when she rose. The red and green lights on Lucas's gun barely illuminated the sides of the tunnel as he crept forward. He staggered twice during his first dozen steps. After the third stumble, he stopped and turned to them. "Is it just me, or is anyone else feeling a little…dizzy?"

"Yes," replied Javier.

They all agreed.

"It must be the fumes," said Jason. "Whatever's inside that black wood, it's…what's the word…part…port…*potent*. Some kind of drug. Kate? Love. Where? Stay close. Celia, give your hand. Everyone…stay together."

The number of loose rocks quadrupled underfoot as the tunnel wheeled, swayed, flexed like a giant artery. Clinging to one another for guidance, the five explorers zigzagged insanely through the dark. Kate couldn't stop giggling. The staggered blur effect whenever she glanced from side to side tickled her, made her think of Mandy the salamander's precognitive spectral twin. So this was what it felt like? Then Cecelia's hand squeezing her arm struck her as the funniest gesture since her sister's Angelina Jolie impersonation in front of the entire class at school.

"Jesus, that's some strong SUCSUB," slurred Javier. "Even Kate's having a good time."

"Yeah, she issss," Kate replied. "But what d' y'all mean by SUCSUB? Sounds like…like a hiccup underwater."

"Ha! Close. It means Smogged Up, Can't See You, Bitch," answered Cecelia, a hipper, chipper chick all of a sudden.

They reached the hollow, where a short but fierce waterfall shot out from a crack in the right hand wall and pounded the bare rock floor, feeding the watercourse. The ceiling was twenty feet high at most. To the left, another tunnel burrowed into the darkness, while straight ahead, the route declined steadily. Jason, the most resistant to the hallucinogen's effects, thought he saw a faint yellow glow pulse from time to time in the pitch black.

"That's what whorl saw…we saw," said Kate.

Cecelia added, "Then it's…probably penis sass by now."

"Huh?" Javier looked at her.

"Seen us pass, I mean."

Kate erupted hysterically. It was such an infectious, from-the-gut laugh, it tickled Jason too, and he couldn't help but join in. Soon, all five were in hysterics at the crossroads in the dark.

Fizzzzzzz

Jason spun to face the passage ahead. A faint yellow glow seeped down the right hand wall, sneaky, like syrupy sunlight, pulsed for a moment and then zapped across to the opposite wall. The luminous whip blazed onto Kate's retina, leaving another streak she couldn't blink away.

Fizzzzzzz

Another light shot across the passage. This one hovered, danced over the first as a honey bee of blinding intensity. It quickly uncoiled into an airborne snake. All eyes now observed the bizarre phenomenon. More lights entered the fray, each bolder, sprightlier than those before. A swarm of erratic slithers began to inch forward toward them.

Arms outstretched, Jason backed his friends away and whispered, "No sudden movements. We don't know how they'll react if we surprise them."

"Cecelia and I saw one last night," said Kate, now almost sober. "It avoided us like the plague when we went after it."

"But it came to us first. It was definitely checking us out," replied Cecelia.

The rugged walls and ceiling of the passage jived, swung shadows—a hyperactive discotheque all around them. The explorers crept back, and the swarm followed. The smell of aniseed filled the air again. A little warmth now touched their faces, and where the creatures belted in concert over the water course, the first hints of steam emerged.

"They're creating tremendous energy. Must be scorching hot," said Kate, ready to turn and run for it. But Jason's grip on the back of her neck stayed her impulse. Yep, what if the things took her sudden flight for a threatening gesture? What were they capable of? Obviously timid when alone, the bioluminescent oddities had a hive confidence, a strength-in-numbers instinct. There were dozens of them, but only five humans.

Back, back toward the cinders of her slow-burning wooden club, they waited for Jason to give the word to flee outside. The grim veil of a thunderous downpour loomed not far behind. Cecelia held onto Jason's arm. Caught between the chill and the char-grill, they bunched together as closely as the flying lights. Then…the creatures stopped advancing. Their chaotic swirl slowed. Strong heat no longer emanated. Jason made ready to speak when…

Thud!

The swarm dispersed when a ripple of energy fanned out from Lucas's weapon. The blast hit the ceiling not twenty feet from the cave entrance, shaking the sanctum with the force of an earth tremor. Three or four stone pieces crashed to the floor as a cloud of pulverized rock blanketed the passage.

"Nice shot." Cecelia placed a hand on Lucas's shoulder.

Javier agreed. "Yeah, that gave 'em what for."

"It…it was the only thing I could do. I didn't mean to…you think they'll be gone for good?" Lucas bit his lip and looked at his feet as he awaited harsh words from the two professional survivalists. Sure, he'd got rid of the creatures, but was it really necessary?

"Yeah, you already know what I'm going to say, so I'll let Jason do the talking." Kate, hands on hips, kicked the remnants of her club angrily against the wall.

"This is crunch time, I'm afraid." Jason stood tall over the cowering gunslinger. "Lucas, we know you mean well, and you've done a commendable job of keeping Cecelia and Javier alive up until now, but I'm afraid you're not fit to be in charge of that weapon. This little stunt might have ruined our chances of living here."

"What? He just saved us," insisted Cecelia. "Those things could have killed us all."

Kate replied, "Yeah, but they stopped. There's intelligence behind that rationale. We wandered into their domain, and they warned us away. Why do you think they haven't killed us before now? We're allowed to stay *here*, at the entrance, just not any further in. That's why Jason warned us not to alarm them. This is brinkmanship, Cecelia. We need this place to survive, and those creatures need us to not venture into their habitat—live and let live. But what do you think they'll make of our cohabitation now? Bang, bang, boot hill."

"You're guessing at all that," said Cecelia.

"All right, but we've just turned a potential enemy into a definite one," said Jason. "And we can't afford to take those kinds of chances. Not in the shape we're in. If the things hadn't stopped at the end, if they *had* tried to evict us, Lucas would have been right to fire. But they were probably communicating. And we just answered back in the *worst possible way.*"

"So hand that thing over." Kate held her hand out to Lucas.

"Not to *you*. No way, Jose," he replied. "I screwed up, I admit it, but there's no way I'm trusting our lives to you."

Jason sighed. "Then what do you suggest?"

"I think we should vote on it. Kate or Jason. All those in favour of Kate, raise your hand."

Only Jason voted. Furious, Kate glared at each of the others in turn.

"All right, all those in favour of Jason?" Three hands went up, and there, between the miniature cave-in and the gargantuan downpour, they had a new leader. Lucas handed Jason the firearm and the gun belt with a curling grin, his sly glance at Kate Borrowdale a final, spiteful gesture of defiance.

She wanted to rip his head from its stubby neck. "Glad that's settled," she said, swallowing her homicidal urge. "No more assholes with itchy trigger fingers. And Lucas, now we're even. That is I can kick your ass all over this mountain without worrying about being shot. Think it over, creep."

Jason had to turn away to smile. He knew Kate's threat was genuine, and she might very well win the fight at that. Knowing he knew that lifted her spirits a little. She was the worst loser he'd ever met, hell, that she'd ever met. Amused by the staring contest between her and Lucas, Jason draped his arm over her and kissed her cheek. "You're cute when you're angry," he said.

She shrugged him off. But as soon as the others turned away, she clasped her hands around his. A tingly touch of magic. Outside, the rain eased, the temperature rose a little. Inside, the smell of aniseed lingered.

Chapter Twenty-Five
Wisdom of the Owl-Men

A dour drizzle slicked the rocks as Kate and Jason made their way down to the foot of the mountain. Jason glanced back, threw a wave. The others were standing just outside the entrance to the cave, or the 'Mile High' Clubhouse, as Javier had dubbed it, referring to both its altitude and the 'high' they had all experienced after inhaling the fumes from Kate's burning club. And though none of them said so, each had to have cottoned onto the irony of that nickname, since sex was the last thing on their minds. Or was it?

"They're all going to have to pitch in." Kate eyed the three civilian dots as they disappeared inside the Clubhouse.

"Yeah, they will," replied Jason. "We need to get them off to a good start, ease them into a routine. But they'll be okay. This next step is the trickiest. Did you see any of those heart shapes they mentioned, hung between the orange trees?"

"Uh-huh. Atlas trees. I steered clear. The ones I saw pulsed, so I didn't stop to find out *what* pulsed."

"Like Javier said, there has to be something alive inside. They only found empty ones, but something had broken out. Like some kind of hatching."

"Great. More new creatures to contend with. I'm telling you, we'd make a fortune as xenozoologists. I should've kept a diary on board the *Elemental*. I literally lost count of the sea life, the new species."

"Mine would have been a single entry—bastards."

Kate snorted. "I still think we made the right choice, though, attempting the crossing. Otherwise we might still be traipsing about in the sand."

After sliding down the last scree incline, Jason paused in contemplation. A peculiar rain pattern emerged over the forest roof, the low gravity veins slowing the downpour so that, high up, the falling droplets accumulated into airborne rivulets. He pointed the phenomenon out to Kate.

"I've been wondering about that—the yacht, I mean," he said. "It would've been a hell of a gamble, but we could, at a pinch, have fashioned it into some kind of glider. You know, to fly down to the valley floor."

"Thousands of feet…straight down? Hmm, I've had my fill of falling, thank you very much. I'm keeping my feet firmly on the ground from now on. Besides, gliders are tricky to balance; I think we'd have plummeted."

"Not much faith in my engineering skills, eh?"

"Is 'splat' a word in your dictionary?"

Cecelia had kindly lent Jason her survival suit for the hunting expedition. It was in good nick, whereas Kate's was battered and discoloured, the green pigment of the sea and the bark of black trees having dyed it an Earthly camouflage. But in the forest outskirts on Kratos, she didn't blend in. The muscular Atlas trees were orange and densely clustered. Between the buttressed roots, white moss carpeted the ground. Heavy drizzle tickled the canopy roof. The sound reminded her of surf receding over a sandy beach above. Streams of water pounded the moss here and there as Kate and Jason looked for signs of blue webbing, the cradle of their proposed food source.

For over an hour they found nothing, and Jason was about to suggest they try further south, when Kate grabbed his arm and nodded toward a teardrop-shaped gap between two wax trunks.

"Gotcha," she said.

Suspended in the midst of a disgusting tangle of blue vines, the heart was triangular, about the size of a human torso, with rounded corners and wrinkled skin.

"But this one hasn't hatched." Jason pointed out its slow pulse. "Do you think we should?"

"Are you kidding me? We might not find another. And besides, Kratos has made it pretty clear where we rank in the food chain."

"Agreed. There's no prize for second place."

"Everything battles lest everything dies."

"What?"

"Nothing." She readied the empty survival bag. "Just something I read once—a law of the jungle."

"Okay, I'm going to cut this thing open. Whatever's inside will just have to spill out. Ready?"

"Go."

He slashed the skin with his knife, a deep cut right across the centre, then stepped to one side, his gun trained on the wound. The thing's pulse stopped. Kate's own heartbeat galloped. What form would the emerging embryo take? She leaned forward onto the balls of her feet, ready to dodge.

Small chunks of light blue flesh fell to ground. The object quivered. Something was definitely alive inside. But how much alive? Would it survive this premature hatching?

"Give it a nudge," she whispered.

"You give it a nudge."

She did. The heart twitched. A few more fleshy chunks spilled out as if squeezed from inside. Jason whipped round, his gaze darting about the trees behind. A craggy frown appeared on his brow.

"What's wrong?" she asked.

"Listen."

The drizzle eased aloft, and through the drumming streams of rain cascading from the roof—the low foghorn boom. Not as loud as the last time they'd heard it, but the acoustics seemed to pinpoint it…not far ahead.

"We're too far north," said Jason. "This is precisely where they told us *not* to explore."

Though she was warm inside her suit, Kate shivered. "North, south—coming back here at all was a risk. No use crying about it now. Cut this thing down."

He shook his head and gibbered to himself as he sawed through the webbed vines holding the heart up, one by one. "They're bloody tough," he said. "Here, take the gun." Kate pressed the warm metal handle into her palm and held the flashing barrel in a cautious, spidery grip.

The boom-song rose an octave, seemed closer still. Another twitch from the blue heart made Jason jump back. "Christ." He sawed vigorously through another four vines then started on the fifth, and final, support.

An ear-splitting shriek forced them both to cover their ears. Vanishing into the upper harmonics, the sound left behind a terrible, gruelling pain deep in her inner ears. The boom disappeared. In its place, a muffled ring at a frequency she perceived as dangerous drowned out everything else. They clasped their temples with rigid palms. The old titbit about a ring in the ears denoting the death of that particular frequency struck like a gong in Kate's mind. She shouted to Jason at the top of her voice. No sound emerged. She saw his lips move.

Shit, she thought. *Are we both deaf? For how long?*

Picking up the gun she'd dropped, Kate suddenly felt a hard blow to her stomach. She crashed backward to the floor. Jason landed on top of her. He'd dived to knock her away, but from what? She couldn't see. His face creased with fury, Jason snatched the gun out of her hand and blasted the ground beneath the heart. Red earth, white particles, hunks of blue flesh exploded into the air.

"What the hell is it?" she screamed. But no sound came out. Jason didn't acknowledge her either. *Okay, so we're both deaf. I need to know what he's firing at, though.*

Before the dust settled he sank to his hands and knees and began to gather the steaks strewn all about. Kate joined him, one eye ever on the cloud in case whatever *it* was returned. Had Jason hit his target? Getting his attention, she mimed the action of firing a gun, formed an 'O' shape with her thumb and forefinger, and then shrugged, as if to ask, *Did you hit it?*

He nodded. Her sigh tickled a windpipe full of dusty phlegm, and she coughed. Soon, the emergency bag was chock full of odourless blue meat. As they jogged back through the orange maze, Kate checked behind them every few seconds. There was no wind to preface any monstrous threat by its smell, so without hearing, she had only sight with which to detect the dangers of the forest. These multiplied exponentially in her mind. What of the foghorn boom growing nearer? Had the hatchling responded to that call, the call of its kin, deafening Kate and Jason with its high-pitched cry for help? If so, what might its brethren do? Self-defence or not, had Jason shot their offspring and stolen the egg? She quickly overtook him, keeping a frenetic pace through the waxwork stalks.

They soon ground to a halt. A number of Atlas trees had collapsed, barring their way ahead or to the north. Jason shook his head and motioned for her to lead them south, further away from the Clubhouse. She spat, bared her teeth, angry at herself for getting them lost.

She could have sworn this was the same way they came. They'd only retraced their own footprints. But the tracks ended at the fallen trunks, and Kate didn't remember this obstacle. Plus there was no way they could climb back over; four or five Atlases had fallen together and snapped, creating a gargantuan thicket. *That's bloody odd. It's happened since we passed, or else these aren't our footprints.* She measured her boot against the smaller prints, and bade Jason do the same against the larger ones. Perfect matches. She cleared her throat and shook the puzzle from her head. There simply wasn't time for problem-solving.

The giant orange trunks seemed to sweat, to droop as the streams from above eased to drips and beads of rainfall. When Kate finally came across an easy right hand turn, she cursed their luck, as another blockade of Atlases barred their way north. Beyond these, more had fallen, to form a conspicuous barrier in the forest.

Jason grabbed her shoulder from behind. Wild, wide eyes accentuated the worry-lines on his forehead. She yelled at the top of her voice, "What's wrong?" But again no sound emerged. After swinging the bag of meat from over his shoulder to tuck under his right arm, he pointed high up into the trees, then roved his finger through three-hundred-and-sixty degrees of the forest. He pointed to both his eyes as if to tell her, *There's something watching us from up there; keep a sharp lookout.*

She hadn't noticed anything, but then again her attentions had been localised on the few feet ahead, on the maze. Kate's left shoulder throbbed as though in a steel clamp. Days without food and a proper rest were taking their toll. Exhausted, she leaned forward to brace her arms on her knees, and panted. Jason handed her the gun.

Where the trees stood upright, their buttress roots conspired to barricade any possible way through. More fallen trees. The first black trunks suggested they were entering the forest interior. Kate ground her teeth as she jogged. These were no accidents. They were being guided. She turned to Jason. He gaped in horror. They both knew it—craft and intellect were behind this maze.

Oh God.

Above the next blockade, the canopy roof sagged half way down to the floor. Tonnes of rainwater had collected in its depression, stretching the skin to its limits. As the surrounding membrane flexed, this giant saddle-bag groaned, even bounced for a moment, its contents swilling, threatening to collapse in a torrential flood. It was here that Kate first glimpsed the pursuing creatures. *Almost* out of sight behind the upper tree trunks, two man-sized forms clutched at the smooth bark. Each had sharp talons that dug into the orange trunk, and fingers on the tips of its wings which gave it poise. Dark grey, its body appeared bulky, clumsily so, as if it frowned on exercise and was a glutton, but the fact that it had climbed so high suggested otherwise.

Kate ducked behind the fallen Atlases and, through a slight gap, observed the creatures as though they were the quarries. Jason joined her.

One of the things leapt from tree to tree, not bothering to use its wings. There was a practised stealth, a sly, sneaky methodology in this highborn hunting, as the creatures kept exclusively to the rear side of trees, poking their heads out only for a split second at a time. This jittery head motion seemed very bird-like, and from her brief glimpses she thought they resembled giant owls. Four over-sized eyes, flat faces with hooked beaks, tufts of spiked down, and a sly awareness that she didn't like and didn't trust. But were they hostile? So far, all they'd done was sing in deep, monotonous foghorn voices and follow Kate and Jason from on high. What if the vicious hatchling didn't belong to them? What if the Atlas maze was not their design? Could she take the risk of not firing if they came close? Or would firing be an even greater risk, assuming there were more? She thought back to Lucas's disgrace in the Clubhouse. He'd acted rashly, fired when there was no need, but she now felt that same constricting dilemma.

It was a gamble either way. Without knowing for sure if a thing was hostile or not, it was best to be safe. There came a point at which she would have to fire, before her opponent gained the upper hand. If she let it get too close, she might lose that ability to defend herself. But where should she draw the line? *How about a warning shot first, to disperse them? If that doesn't work, it's more likely their intentions are hostile. Best to be safe.*

The owl-men chose not make their way directly toward Kate and Jason. After circumnavigating the bulbous sag, they split up, leaping southwest and southeast through the trees. Kate was about to yank Jason up when a tremor shook the ground. They both spun round.

A standoff.

Three owl-men had landed nearby, barring the mossy path. Seven-feet tall, heads hung forward without necks, they held their rigid wings out horizontally behind their backs, to keep them from touching the ground. Their black eyes didn't blink. Slowly, arms at her side, Kate raised her gun at the owl-man in the middle. One false move and she'd blast it to kingdom come.

Jason flinched as the one on the left opened its beak. She thought his hearing might have returned. Hers definitely hadn't. That same irritating, muffled ring, as if everything was distant behind a single xylophonic note.

What the hell do they want?

The eyes had no pupils, so Kate couldn't tell what they were looking at, but her intuition told her they were cognizant of the weapon, not least because it flashed in her hand, and it was the only thing she'd moved. Had they observed its power back at the blue webbing?

With a languid wave the owl-man on the right brought his free wing forward. Kate stepped back, and right away the creature paused. A few tense moments later it resumed, as though it knew it was a suspect held at gunpoint by a nervous policewoman, and any sudden movement might waive its Miranda Rights, permanently. The creature's bare wing was ten feet long, the three fingers at its end spindly, with four or five knuckles each—these digits unfurled as they approached the ground. To Kate's surprise, they began to draw a shape in the moss. She studied it, one eye ever on the owl-man himself.

A single vertical line, a connecting, sideways 'V', a separate upside-down 'V', another vertical line capped by a horizontal one…

Her tight face lifted, cool realisation flushed through her. A tingle in her ears. She nudged Jason. His scowl appeared equal parts acknowledgement and intense puzzlement, for the owl-man, improbably, had written a word:

K-A-T-E

Too much for her tired brain. They'd been watching the whole time? Or maybe they'd back-tracked the human footprints out of curiosity and had come to that spot where Jason had written her name. Either way, they were smart…too damn smart. But why would such sneaky creatures make themselves known, put themselves in harm's way? What were they trying to say? There was no such thing as communication for its own sake in a situation like this. They wanted something—but what?

The Clubhouse dilemma again reflected her predicament, a two-way mirror for doubt and certainty. Now that she was face to face with them, the creatures didn't appear hostile. They'd initiated the meeting with courtesy. But there was rumour to contend with—other survivors had ventured into this part of the forest before, heard the foghorn boom and vanished. Kate kept her gun trained on the enigmatic scribe.

With the tip of a single sharp claw, it added to its inscription:

FIND ME KATE. J.

Those uplifting words she'd read a few days ago now dragged her down to the unfathomable. The owl-man's eyes were black, impenetrable like potholes at night. No trace of emotion. Its companions looked on with a frightening apoplexy. She didn't know how to respond. So what point was there in staying?

Another tremor spun her round. *What?* She swallowed hard. *Trapped?* Two more owl-men stood twenty yards ahead on the path. One of them drew a shape in the moss. Grabbing Jason's arm, she pulled him on while watching both alien parties. The new creatures stepped back as Kate and Jason approached. Her shoulders remained stiff, poised, her legs were dying to bolt. The inscription read 'KATE'. Nodding at them as she passed, she also held her sweaty forefinger over the black button on her gun. *Just one false move...*

But the owl-men let them pass. She'd seen no malice in their behaviour...yet. Round the next bend, Jason spotted another identical inscription on the ground. And fifty yards on, another. The owl-men were showing them the way out, a path through the maze?

He slung the emergency bag full of food over his shoulder and, with his free hand, accepted Kate's invitation for them to hold hands. Their palms were hot, moist. Occasional amethysts decorated the canopy roof, welcome glares of sunlight breaching the forest, while the upper orange trunks glistened. It was no longer cold. Though they kept tight vigil on the trees, they saw no more owl-men. This convinced Kate that the creatures were benign, that their communications were indeed to show the way out. An eastward turn confirmed it. For an ordinary traveller it would be difficult to keep a steady bearing, but Kate's compass was magnetised by memory, intuition, a subconscious grip on the turn of each path. Without hearing, her world was a map of fluid visuals with a beginning, middle and end. A northeast turn told her they were headed back for the Clubhouse.

All this for one meal? It'd better be the gourmet equivalent of a Jason Remington kiss. I'm not kidding. All right, Katie girl, you're going to have to find another food source. But where? The lake? Not recommended.

A few dozen yards ahead, the barricades ended at what appeared to be another hollow in the trees, and she looked forward to seeing a passage leading to daylight. Once more her name appeared in the moss. She really was a celebrity. As Jason had said, Kate of Kratos. She forced an artificial grin—a half-hearted attempt to lighten her inky demeanour. *Nope, just dour old Kate Borrowdale.*

Taking Jason's arm, she leant her head against his shoulder. There were many pores in the swaying roof. Fluvial sunlight illumed the hollow. Kate skipped just before they entered. Exactly why, she didn't know. A glad impulse? A subconscious desire to get home? Jason laughed at her girlishness. She watched his well-kept teeth part sublimely in the midst of his dark beard, and his skin wrinkle underneath his brown eyes. Lovely. While swinging her hand, he turned to face forward.

His bag dropped quicker than his grin.

The next thing Kate knew, she was blasting away at a horde of monstrous bipeds rushing towards them. Though he was armed only with a knife, Jason readied it in his hand. Stepped forward. Adopted a sideways fighting stance...

...to face the three dozen shapes of his kidnapper.

Chapter Twenty-Six
Tigress, Tigress Burning Bright

The owl-men had led them into a deadly trap. Each pulse of energy from Kate's weapon fanned out with devastating force. The first few attackers lost limbs and half-torsos to the blast. Thirty feet tall, their slouched, muscular frames bombed forward as sprinters out of the blocks. In every direction Kate glanced, dozens tore towards her with piston-powered legs and outreaching arms. The four arms—two attached to wide shoulders, two at the hips—were not long in proportion to the creature's size, hence the need for four. Upper and lower body limbs, for climbing and gathering.

She pulled Jason to her side, shielding him from the nearest foes.

She fired. Twice. Couldn't hear the pulses, but felt every joule. Whip cracks of adrenaline lashed her to the spot. The shots didn't perturb the juggernauts *at all*. Blast after blast eviscerated them, explosions of dark blood flooding the hollow. Jason tugged her arm, pointing behind to where three more rushed in single file. She kept a steady arm, zeroed in on the leader's exposed, vertical ribcage arranged like organ pipes over its chest, and pushed the black button. In mid-lunge not ten feet away, two halves of the brute flew back into its cohorts, knocking them off their feet. Another two shots finished them.

How many more?

Dozens skidded through the blood, scrabbling over the bodies. Some even advanced on their bellies, using all four arms to scurry. The tops of their heads were ridged, sloped like a tyrannosaur's; their mouths were giant suckers which, when riled, flared open to reveal a single sharp tooth, maybe poisonous, attached to the back of the throat. This would impale any prey for the flexible jaws to do the (unimaginable) rest. Disgusted, Kate kept her trigger finger busy. The half second between blasts while the cylinder recharged was too long. It gave the onrushing teams a greater chance of dodging, confusing her aim, of utilising tactics to overwhelm her by sheer numbers. Luckily, the beasts were single-minded. Predictable. They never veered, nor did they stop to think.

In a far corner of the hollow, a pile of tiny carcasses resembled the gentle salamanders—Mandy's kin.

The attack was relentless, her aim unwavering. Then a tremor between shots kicked her off balance, and she spun to see five monsters almost on top of her. Light blazed through a tear in the canopy roof—the creatures had jumped down. More piled through the hole. Way too close. Even the fan of the energy blast was insufficient to engage enough of them in one go. The nearest two exploded completely.

Holy shit.

The weapon's effect at point blank range was unlike anything she'd ever seen—chunks flew in all directions, while even the blood flash-boiled, its putrid fumes making her gag.

Her back crumpled under a heavy blow. Winded, she could barely kick at the clawed hand grasping for her legs. The hideous thing bent low over her. Drool from its quivering sucker-mouth landed on the belly of her suit. A crushing grip from behind clamped her shoulder, pinned her to the ground. "Bastards. Get off!"

Kate lifted her arm to fire, but another claw grabbed it and pulled. She screamed. No sound emerged. The first brute now clutched both her legs. Blank panic, then sickening revolutions overwhelmed her. The final drawstrings of her hips and shoulder sockets felt like they were snapping. She was helpless. One violent pull apiece from the things and she'd be in the alien garbage. In pieces. But life returned to her legs. Her heels hit the ground, and she opened her eyes to see Jason's knife slash open the creature's throat. As dark blood spurted all over her, he dived at the claw of the brute holding her firing arm. Stabbed down with all his might. The blade passed clean through the monstrous, fleshy palm. It let go and careered backwards in agony, knocking two of its brethren onto their backs.

One more creature still had hold of her by the shoulder. It hadn't been able to pull before because of the throng piling behind. But with a little space it darted backwards, yanked Kate across the detritus—blood flooded over her face and up her nostrils. She flung her arm blindly behind her and fired. No effect. She fired again. The creature hurled her into the air, and she threw up; before it could impale her on the horrific poison spike in its mouth, she seized her chance for a final, desperate shot.

The creature's head disappeared in a blast of energy. The impact gouged a crater in the ground five feet wide, throwing red dust into the faces of the other beasts. As the headless biped toppled, she prepared to bend her knees for a heavy landing. Luckily, another dead body broke her fall, and she leapt to the ground once more.

"Jason?" Seeing him alive—fierce relief; seeing him sprint for the Atlas trees, chased by six bipeds—a fiercer call to arms. She'd take down a planet full of the sons of bitches first. Four from the north had to suffice, blasted to bits as she sped after Jason and fired at anything that moved through the snowfall of moss, the rainfall of blood.

"*Jason!*"

He was at the trees. One of the beasts bulldozed straight through the first orange stalk, smashing it into spark-like splinters. Kate fired, but it was too far away. The energy pulse dissipated by the time it reached. Faster than she'd ever ran in her life, she swallowed the distance to the tree-line in a single breath. Hit another two monsters as they struggled to barge through the wall of the maze.

Yes. She got it. He was heading for the path they'd traversed, where the Atlases were clustered thickest, nigh on impenetrable. Places to hide. Obstacles for the lumbering things to negotiate. Away from open ground, where human smarts might come into play. One biped on its own found it tough to barge through the trees, so the forest did help to slow the predators. She shot one in the back, punching a hole right through it. Its innards festooned on an artificial blockade of Atlases.

Go Jason, go. She winced to see him holding his ribs, but he was making better progress through the tangle than his pursuers. It was being small, niftier, that gave him the edge. She checked behind her, nodded at the sight of half a dozen bipeds struggling to negotiate the woods at any real speed.

There.

Jason was now *on* the path marked by the written series of 'KATES'. His idea sparked one of her own. *Right, the quickest way out of here is…the roof. Let's beat them at their own game.* Taking down the last three predators between her and Jason, she joined him over their old footsteps…to what should have been doom. They hugged each other, but still couldn't hear.

No time to waste.

She waved him out of the way before blasting repeatedly at the canopy above a pile of felled Atlases. Eight or nine shots did the trick, as the height permitted the energy pulse to fan out, enough to cover a wide area while still inflicting enough damage to breach the membrane. Her crescent curve of carnage managed to collapse the skin enough for them to clamber up using the Pyrofluvium veins. Rainwater cascaded over them. The rubbery veins were slick yet soft hoses for them to grip. Kate's heart leapt when she saw the twin suns high over Clubhouse Mountain. Every time Jason slipped, she willed him on. Bursting to tell him, "We're nearly there—just one last effort."

Without warning the canopy wrenched to the vertical. An enormous weight of some kind had collapsed it further. *God help us.* Grasping the purple vein with one hand, Kate dared to look below. Fired three times…straight down. The blast annihilated the skin, sending five or six monsters with it, but that was only a small portion of the flap. Seeing Jason clamber up onto the roof itself, she ground her teeth and resumed the climb. A few more metres. The membrane strained, swayed under tremendous pressure. Almost there. A strong arm extended down for her to take, and lifted her onto the rain-minted wonderland.

Very little wind disturbed the shimmering expanse. A thousand pockets of water reflected the purple suns, while a low-lying mist, here and there feeding into pores in the skin, ceiled various sections of this upper world. Spindly, wispy joints over the veins connected the mist as sketched highways between cities.

Kate shot away the rest of the draping skin so that the predators had no way up. But Jason wasn't convinced. His determined frown and finger, pointing at the Clubhouse, lit a new fire under her. She located the nearest Pyrofluvium vein and took a quick run-up. *Jumped* for her life. The sensation of being airborne again rushed frosty mountain dew inside her from scalp to toes. Jason was also in mid-air. A delightful ache-cum-pins-and-needles blossomed from her shins to her lower spine. On landing, her legs gave way and she rolled, slid over the canopy until she splashed into a pool of rainwater. It shot up her nostrils again, and Kate coughed through a clear-headed vibe.

Yep, for drinking, Katie girl, not snorting.

Jason flew past, waving her on vehemently. But any newfound optimism sank into the cold puddle when she glanced behind. A horde of bipeds bounded across the roof, parting the mist with an urgency to match hers. *Bastards. What's wrong with you?* Rising to flee, she slipped face-first into the water. Punched the surface. *Of all the goddamn times*...Luckily the cylinder's green and red lights told her exactly where it had sunk. She plucked it up and sped off. Leapt above the mist, the breeze blowing her hair in an exhilarating stream behind her. But the monsters' leaps far exceeded hers. The way they bobbed up and down through the mist would be comical if it weren't for their desired goal.

What now, Katie girl? Think.

She could try to turn and face them, pick them off in mid-air. That would give Jason more time to get away. But he didn't have the gun. She did. If she fell, he would have no way of fending them off.

No, hold steady. Jump for your life. You might make it.

It stoked her every time Jason glanced back mid-leap. He was a half mile in front by now. A dozen more jumps and he'd be home free. But her odds weren't so hot. One more valiant vault kicked her hundreds of feet into the air, the highest she'd ever jumped. Her fingertips tingled, a gust of wind pushed the suit's fabric tight against her breasts. This effort *had* to edge her away from her pursuers. But no! The first ones were within spitting distance, arms cupped at their sides.

How powerful were these bastards' legs?

She shot one at the apex of its leap, knocking it way off course. The next she hit from above as it reached up for her ankle. Square in the tyrannosaur brainpan. The slow-motion shower of skull fragments and blood resembled a comet's coma as the creature arced out of orbit. But with every airborne second the horde gained. Their propulsion was that much more powerful, likewise their acceleration through the air.

She bullseyed another beast before the situation became desperate. Around thirty flying enemies now closed in from various angles behind her. Had other tribes joined in the hunt? If a few of them reached her at the same time, she was done for. Holding her weapon to her bosom as tightly as she'd held Jason gave her poise. She faced forward. Christ, still another half dozen jumps.

Then it occurred to her—what if she took away their trampoline? Landing with a bumpy roll, she scrambled to face the monsters. Shot after shot tore through the particular Pyrofluvium artery that was giving them lift. Soon, a twenty-foot circular hole gaped behind her. Stepping back, she continued her handiwork. The first biped dropped straight through. Another tried to grasp the edge but plummeted. A third almost landed on top of her, but she fired up, rending it apart in mid-air. "Eat that." More fell in, jerked out of their low-g floats into unseemly flops. The snare had taken eleven or twelve when she careered backwards, the skin having bulged significantly behind her. Four enemies had landed ahead of her, possibly before she'd even finished the snare, and had come back to find their quarry.

Two snapshots. One monster fell, but the others stalked her with erratic shallow bounds. A shadow reared up behind her. One had climbed out of the snare. *Shit*. She took another run-up. Hurled herself into the air...

The nearest giant almost grabbed her leg as she took off, so she blasted it farewell. Above the mist again, her stomach shrank to an icy cube—the sky was now full not only of leaping beasts, but scores of the treacherous owl-men as well.

This was it. Despite her crazy efforts, she'd failed. The owl-men glided and swooped far above the effects of low-g, so it was only a matter of time before they swamped her. No doubts. But, through the blackest thoughts of what the predators of Kratos might do to her, she grinned, for if nothing else, she'd saved the man of her dreams. He'd gotten away. Her last stand had allowed him to reach the Clubhouse, the mountains where he would find sustenance and a beautiful lagoon and build a home for the others. Mandy would come to greet him, and they would spend the rest of their days contented, together, and would have great adventures.

She sobbed approaching the pinnacle of her leap. Tears misted her vision, so Kate shut her eyes. Tight. The air resistance on top of her scowl pulled at her scalp. Her ears popped in the high altitude. The wind's howl deafened her—the first sound she'd heard since the hatching. She swallowed hard. Several times. This helped equalize the pressure, and her next exclamation was a thrilling one, at full volume, "Come and get me, you cowardly sons of bitches!"

A rock hard vice grabbed her from behind, and she shot upwards, her stomach left far behind. The force was too strong for her arm to aim, so she glanced sideways instead.

You?

Her mind wheeled, unspooling déjà vu. "Your Majesty?"

The magnificent eagle was far from fully-grown, but Kate recognised the scar down its breast and the pride in its eyes. It had her by the thighs, just as its big cousin had during her eleven hour fall. She twisted herself to look behind. The owl-men were retreating from a flock of giant eagles, and the hideous bipeds had already vanished.

No way to comprehend what was happening. Constant shock and horror had no outlet—they had to eat themselves away before she could think straight. Meanwhile the eagle prince carried her safely to the stream just outside the Clubhouse, and set her down.

"If ever you need me," she vowed, looking him in the eyes, "I'll be here." With that the eagle took flight and soared high above the mountain. Its kin followed, victorious.

"Kate, are you Okay? Kate?" Cecelia's posh, silken voice was oddly welcome. Trying to stand upright, Kate's tired legs give way and she fell. Cool water streamed inside the neck of her suit, ran over her breasts and pooled at her midriff. Her eyes closed of their own accord. The purple sky and the white mist over the forest blurred into a hazy, candy floss dream in the corner of one eye. And faintly, far below, she heard another voice grow nearer—a man's voice full of relief, of disbelief, a voice that would ensure her dream was a sweet one. However long it lasted.

Chapter Twenty-Seven
The Propagators

"How did you come by these?" Kate blinked up at Lucas when he dropped a few dozen white stalks beside her. After her own disastrous hunting expedition in the forest, how on earth had Lucas Revere, unarmed and incompetent, managed to succeed where she hadn't?

"A stroke of luck." He untwisted the shoulder strap on Javier's navy blue overall, gave the youngster a pat on the back. "Remember the miniature waterfall we saw in the Clubhouse tunnel? Well, it suddenly occurred to me—if the stream's travelling downhill, there might be a pool or a tarn further up, and there could be vegetation in it. We saw plenty at the bottom of our lake after the crash. Getting to them was the problem; the water there was so deep. But we lucked out this time." He glanced down at his puffed-out chest—Kate thought he was going to pound on it—and tightened his bandana around his forehead.

Yeah, lap it up, Rambo. Your work hasn't even started yet.

"Whereabouts is this tarn?" asked Jason.

Javier stopped gnawing on his half-eaten plant. "Quite a long way up—about an hour's climb. We did good, huh?"

"You did spectacularly." Jason shook both their hands in turn. "And there's plenty more?"

"And then some," replied Lucas. "It's a grocery store that sells one product, but we *know* these stalks are edible. We practically lived off them for a week at the lake, before we found the blue hearts."

"And none of you got sick?" Kate lurched from the memory of her toxic food poisoning on the *Elemental*.

"Not a one," said Cecelia. "They weren't tasty, but they stayed down."

Kate sat up, excited. "Say no more." Her first bite produced a watery crunch—rather like celery or a leek. The plant wasn't chewy; rather it softened in her saliva, thinned into wet paper that she felt compelled to either swallow or spit out, its texture being unpleasantly soggy on her tongue and not like any food she'd ever tasted. "Whoever tried this first was a brave one." She pulled her face. "I've eaten tastier bugs." Then she remembered how lucky she was to have any food at all, and added, "But good on you, gents—you've just made things a lot easier."

Lucas threw her a superior wink, and she was too tired to deflate his gloating pomp. For now, they had food, and the ex-gunslinger had earned his spurs…and his right to brag.

An early evening chill precipitated a night of inconstant winds and icy howls. This time they had nothing to burn, so Kate insisted her roster of suit-swapping be adhered to religiously. When her turn came to plug the entrance, to shield the others from jabs of wind, she realised that would have to be foremost in the Clubhouse renovations. They wouldn't get far with a frozen workforce. Her thoughts turned to the Atlas archipelago winding through the valleys to the north. Plenty of fuel—if the orange stuff burned, that was—and plenty of timber, even rocks for building. So food, water, shelter, enough work to keep them busy…was she forgetting something? She traced her knuckles down the arm of Jason's suit. The other survivors were invisible in the shadows, curled together for warmth. Then there was the problem of men…and women. Not exactly a part of her expertise. No, defending the Clubhouse was concern enough for all of them.

For the time being.

"Prioritising is everything," Jason had the centre spot as the five survivors sat on a ledge overhanging the Clubhouse entrance the following morning, dangling their legs. The twin suns winked through roving clouds, sparking a violet magnesium lightshow in that ionised cumulus, a brainstorming of the heavens. The mist over the forest had cleared. They could now see miles to the south, to the shoulder of the giant craft, while spray thrown up by the big pour curled into an apostrophe thousands of feet high. Otherwise Kratos appeared settled, deserted, waiting.

He continued, "Now that we have food and water, I think we should rig some sort of shield for the entrance and then set about making defences."

Kate smiled, pleased that he was thinking along similar lines. "So it's pretty much all haul 'n' crawl for the first few days," she said. "Who's up first?"

"Crawl? How about the one with the tightest ass?" said Javier.

Everyone laughed.

"Someone might as well say it," he added, looking at Kate and Jason. "Was it a part of your job description? 'Cause you two have the best asses I've ever seen. Seriously, it's not fair."

Kate blushed, while Jason stared at his feet and grinned. "There were no buts in our contract, no. We managed to shape pretty good back-end deals, though."

Javier playfully shook Jason's hand.

"Okay, who else gets to go?" asked Kate, eager to deflect her embarrassment.

Cecelia half-chuckled. "How about the biggest asshole?"

Everyone looked at Lucas, who shrugged—whereupon all five of them erupted in a blaze of laughter.

"Gotta love our democracy," said Jason. The laughter subsided when he rose. "All right, Kate and Cecelia stay here, see if you can fix up the place; this is our home from now on. Lucas, Javier, come with me." Kate was about to protest when he added, "Just for today. We'll rotate in future." He winked at Kate. "And I think you could do with the rest for once."

She flipped him a salute and, watching him leave, blew a kiss to his back...and his backside.

"Now that's what I call a man," said Cecelia.

"Hmm, he's a man all right. Now all we need is a woman's touch." Kate dropped down to the Clubhouse entrance and proceeded to roll a two-foot high boulder out of the path of the stream. Meanwhile, Cecelia tiptoed down the rocky slope at the side of the drop. Daintily shifting the odd stone or pebble, she soon cleared a flat workspace around the entrance. By late afternoon, the interior and exterior of the Clubhouse were unrecognizable. No obstacles of any kind were evident, apart from the odd jutting bedrock they couldn't remove without heavy duty machinery. Kate even built a rudimentary cubicle out of piled stones, thirty feet to the west of the entrance. This doubled as both a toilet, which could easily be washed clean, and a private changing area for the women.

Inside, Cecelia cleverly marked out areas for sleeping, dining, food storage and building materials. Talking about warm beds, furniture, cups and bowls, even pots for cooking over the fire, seemed to keep her in high spirits. When the men finally returned carrying an entire orange Atlas tree between them, she rubbed her hands with glee and set about apportioning the wood for its various uses. Kate joined in.

"I reckon about this much for the door." Kate measured a good-sized length of trunk with the edge of her open hand. "Maybe a bit more."

"And I'd say twice that for chairs and a table. You could cut decent bowls from this diameter as well," said Cecelia.

All three men collapsed, flat on their backs after their World's Strongest Man event—log-lifting. Jason stared up at the clouds, trying to catch his breath. "Lads, I think we know where we stand in this little community."

"Say what? Stand?" said Kate. "Not even half a day's work and you're all three mummified. There, there. You have your little rests while we women see to the *real* work."

Cecelia brought out jagged-edged stones she and Kate had splintered by throwing against a boulder and then partially sharpened by scraping them against other rocks. They would eventually make useful cutting tools. She then retrieved two leeks apiece for the men, and the Perspex cup from the emergency still, which she filled in the stream for each of them in turn.

"We're off to a good start," said Lucas. "We'll have this place liveable in no time."

Kate rolled her eyes. She saw Cecelia do the same.

* * * *

"Ninety-seven."

At the start of each morning Kate added a stepping stone to her private staircase up the mountain—a little hobby she'd devised to heighten her sense of progress. *Three months.* Almost a hundred days in the Clubhouse. No predators had ventured so high in that time, and the only sign of the tyrannosaur bipeds was the occasional long-distance glimpse of one lumbering across the red desert beyond the far edge of the forest, dragging its poor victim through the dust. Jason couldn't bear to watch. He'd suffered that same fate, and the memory was clearly still a puncture wound on the tip of his tongue—he couldn't talk about it without dampening his spirits. But the bipeds no longer dared to vault across the forest roof. Had the great eagles perturbed them?

Three months, she thought. *I should be due for parole about now.*

Despite carrying her brand new black club wherever she went, her hands were bruised, calloused and cut. Her elbows and knees were red raw. Weeks of continuous, strenuous exertion had damaged her ribs and lower back. Despite it all, Kate hadn't slowed for an instant. The Clubhouse defences were almost complete. Descending her staircase, she surveyed their rock-fall snare perched precariously over the steepest part of the southern slope. A single gunshot to the keystone would bring that entire avalanche down upon any attacker. She crossed her fingers and whistled the tune to *Surfin' USA* by The Beach Boys, relieved, as the snare had taken them two weeks to rig and had inflicted multiple injuries on her.

Next, on the northern slope, a number of branches from the stubborn black trees lay bent, taut between boulders, ready to be sprung into deadly action. Kate had remembered how powerful the recoil was during the making of her club, and that same methodology—drawing the branch back as far as it would bend, then releasing it—provided a killing force. Over a dozen "bowties", as she called them, waited for any attackers from that route. She kept well clear. The things had never looked fully secure.

And now for the masterpiece.

Funnily enough, the quietest member of the group had conceived the greatest contribution to their defences. Javier Inarritu, a repair shop mechanic, still only in his early twenties, knew nothing of survival. He was a hard worker, diligent, a team player who learned skills quickly and never opted out of a tough assignment. But in his three months' stay in the Clubhouse, Javier had made only one real improvisation of note.

And it was a corker.

"Morning, Kate." Cecelia, in her tattered yellow blouse and panties, stood hands-on-hips, overlooking the work in progress.

"Morning."

"Come here for a second. I'm being a bit slow…there's no…how will this thing work again?"

Kate cocked her head to one side, bit down on her sarcasm. Though Cecelia was the heart and soul of the Clubhouse—food preparation, nursing injuries, keeping everything tidy and accounted for—her acumen didn't extend beyond its confines.

"Don't worry about it. We're not finished yet." Kate watched the acre of membrane fidget under a sudden gust, but its edges were fastened down well enough. "I tell you what, though—you remember how high we could jump over the forest roof?"

"Yes."

"Well, imagine reaching the highest point of one of those jumps, and then suddenly you're not floating, you're dropping like a rock."

"Splat."

Kate clicked her fingers. "Exactly. We're hoping this skin might catapult those monsters high enough so that they splat…big time."

"How will it do that again? I get that the purple veins create a low gravity effect, but how can you throw them so high if they don't jump? I don't quite get the spring part."

"Yep, that's the trick." Kate rubbed her aching abdominal muscles as she explained, "We explode them. You remember those experiments Javier did with Pyrofluvium, the red element found in the veins? Well, when it ignites, the kinetic energy unleashed is far more powerful than any leg muscles. That upward thrust, together with the low gravity fumes from the explosion, should propel *any* creature high enough for it to splat. Javier calls it 'the sucker punch.'"

Cecelia raised her chin in a cute, haughty fashion, almost looking down on the idea. "But won't those fumes still be there to cushion the monster's fall?"

"Not if we drag the canopy away right after the explosion. Jason's going to rig some kind of counterweight. If we cut the weight on one side, the other side should drag the skin away. We might even have it be part of the explosion. We're not sure yet."

"You lot are far too clever. I get it now, though. Thanks, Kate."

"No problemo. We still on for our soiree?"

"Absolutely." Cecelia tossed her long red hair over her shoulder as Javier and Jason approached. Her pale skin was smooth, impeccable for her age—mid forties. How had she stayed so meticulously clean and unblemished? By keeping to the sidelines. But Kate didn't begrudge her that. She'd had it as rough as any of them…in her own way. Their roles were different, that was all, and there was no longer any animosity between them.

That evening, Javier started the bonfire early. He created a spark in the usual way, by clashing two flint rocks together. This ignited the few drops of Pyrofluvium he'd collected in his palm-sized stone mortar. Next, he lowered a strip of Atlas bark into the flame, and when that lit he placed it under three black branches. The hallucinogenic fumes soon emerged. The smoke columned high over the Clubhouse entrance, out toward the suns setting in the northwest.

"Where were we last time?" Jason inhaled with enthusiasm. "Monte Carlo was it? Or Pont de Reves?"

Lucas rubbed his hands in the heat. "Pont de Reves. I'd just won at roulette—two hundred thousand dollars. That puts me at…eighty-three million two hundred thousand."

"That's just your weight, bro," said Javier. "I say we let the ladies choose a venue tonight. Somewhere sultry, sexy."

Kate's throat was sore, so she let Cecelia go first.

"Hmm, bear with me a second." The redhead closed her eyes and hummed with contentment. "Okay, we're all dancing together to the soothing lilt of gentleman jazz, in an elegant speakeasy where tuxedos and ball gowns go together like long-sleeved gloves and glasses of champagne. Kate and Jason waltz gracefully, athletically, while Javier and Lucas tango together for a bet." Everyone laughed. "And me…I have Jimmy Stewart whispering sweet nothings as he twirls me close enough to taste his aftershave, and I melt away into the warm, smoke-filled background. There's liquor being served at the bar, even though it's the Prohibition. But a cop bursts in, we all stop at the pop of a champagne cork. Lucas thinks about offering him a bribe—eighty three million two hundred thousand dollars." More laughter. "But the cop smiles and pours himself a double whisky, and we all live happily ever after. The end."

"Bravo."

Reckless applause filled the night.

"You're always the best at this, Cecelia," said Lucas, "but I was wondering, who do Javier and I end up with? And don't say each other."

"Tana Lurner for me," replied Javier.

"I think you mean Luna Tarner," corrected Jason.

Kate snorted. "Or even Lana Turner."

Lit from beneath, Lucas' glaring eyes and pout appeared quite hideous, as though they ought to be on a poison label.

"So that means I get Cecelia." He gleefully rubbed his hands in the heat once more.

Cecelia glanced at Javier, whereupon they both exploded with laughter.

"What's so funny?" asked Lucas, happy as a lark. "You don't think a millionaire can afford a redhead?"

The black wood snapped, spat out a few sparks.

"It's not you, bro," said Javier. "You just touched on something we were talking about the other day is all."

"What which?" Jason untied his tongue. "Which was?"

Javier thought for a moment. "Preparation…propitious…no, prep, prop…propagation, that's it. The propagation of the species."

"In what sense?" asked Kate.

Cecelia answered with her schoolteacher matter-of-factness, "In this sense. Right here, right now. We're the propagators, the hast lumans…the last humans on Kratos. When we die, there'll key low one neft to Larry on the species."

Jason interrupted, "Translation—there'll be no one left to carry on the species. And she's right."

"I am? How cool."

"Actually, it's pretty hot," added Lucas. "It's for our own good to propipulate. Pronto. That means we need to whose chew we saw hexes with…choose who we have sex with." He cleared his throat. "Who wants to go first?"

Javier shuddered. "What are *you* looking at me for, bro? I'd rather go extinct first. Why don't you dick a pame…pick a dame? Sorry, folks."

Jason laughed until his eyes watered. Kate, not amused, inched away from the fumes. It might only be idle banter, but this was when inhibitions got nixed, and relationships got de-refined…redefined.

"Okay, I'll nay right sow…Cecelia is the girl for me. There, I've said it. I'll happily propitiagate with Cecelia." Lucas closed his eyes, sighed with utter contentment. "Away, cuckoo's next?" He thought for a moment. The question was too important to leave in drug-addled jabberwocky. "Okay, who goes next?"

"No hard feelings?" asked Javier.

Everyone assured him it would be all right; everyone but Kate, that was.

"You asked for it, fellows," he said with a giddy, posh enunciation. "I'll take Cecelia *and* Kate. And not necessesorily in that order."

Jason cleared his throat before giving Kate a pathetic, sheepish look. She wanted to shear his every lascivious impulse from across the fire before he joined in and said something he might regret. If Kate hadn't felt so drowsy herself, she would have kicked the conversation into touch without thinking twice. But strangely, even dangerously, a part of her needed to know…

"My turn now." Cecelia was sounding more like Marilyn Monroe on helium than a sultry femme in a speakeasy. "Can I have a double 'J' and tonic on the rocks? Double 'J'—Jason and Javier. These rocks right here dull woo…will do." She closed her mouth to stifle a laugh that shook her entire scantily-clad body.

The two 'J's chuckled to themselves, sporting grins as wide as the Kratosian horizon, while Lucas, spurned, swallowed bitter phlegm and turned away, horrified. *Okay.* Kate was about to end the exchange right there when Jason, eyes closed, let slip three little words that froze the blood in her veins:

"Kate and Cecelia."

Without saying a word, she grabbed the end of a charred branch and tossed it behind her, down the eastern slope.

Jason's high jinx dropped anchor. He had to know exactly what he'd done.

Bastard.

Kate lobbed the second branch even further before kicking the third at Jason—with venom. He winced as it scolded his leg.

"Hey, Kate, no hard feelings, babe." Javier's conciliatory plea was curtailed by a boot load of cinders flung into his crotch.

The others backed away, fearing an equal dishing of hot ash.

"You had to go and do it, didn't you," she yelled at them all. "Just when everything was settled, you had to screw it all up."

"Sweetheart, we mid…didn't wean it. I didn't wean it…mean it! Come on, Kate, we're still alive aren't we? All five of us. We've loud fuck here together. I mean *found luck here together.* Shit."

Cecelia tried to keep a straight face but it was no use. With a splutter of saliva she doubled up in blind hysterics, taking first Javier, then Jason with her. Only Lucas failed to contract the hilarity.

On the verge of tears, Kate stormed inside the Clubhouse, grabbed the gun and the nearest survival suit, and, slinging her black club over her shoulder, marched away up her mountain staircase into the sombre, lonely night. After the ninety-seventh step, she doubled her pace. It was as if the mountain lifted her invitingly onto its shoulders. She didn't stumble once. Her footsteps crunched on dirt and loose rocks, while a refreshing alienation smoothed every gritty sound. And the gun's helter-skelter lights showed her the way.

Chapter Twenty-Eight
Despatched

It wasn't that he'd betrayed her trust or even disgraced himself. No, Jason Remington had simply reminded Kate of what her mind had bricked over all those months, of what her bitter experience had tried to effervesce, and that she had lately forgotten. He was a man from Earth, just like any other. And he did not have eyes only for her.

Asshole. After all I went through to keep him alive.

She felt unwanted like the bare rock overhang up here, too high and too secluded for life to touch, unsupported and forgotten. The wind grew fierce as she reached the tarn. She climbed into her survival suit. Well, hers or Cecelia's, it sure as hell wasn't Jason's; his was still festooned across black boughs somewhere in the unforgiving forest. The chill subsided. Skirting the edge of the wind-whipped water, she swung her black club into the shallows and shut her eyes as icy droplets peppered her face.

She cackled insanely. None of it made any sense, so why not press on a little further?

White vegetation, dislodged by the choppy brew, gathered like jellyfish at the shore. They inched forward and back on the shoulders of muscular swells.

Why did you have to do it, guys? Why couldn't you just let me have my Jason?

She realised how dark it had become. Holding the gun behind her back, she gazed ahead. Nothing. Irrevocable night. She could be stood on the lip of an abyss, at the foot of Babylon Wall's big cousin, on any part of any planet in any galaxy in all of creation. So why Kratos? Why had destiny plonked her down a hundred light years from Earth, gifted her the man of her dreams, and then left her to stare at the dark side of a mountain, all alone?

No, not fate. Katie girl, you did all this. You left home to travel the galaxy, you saved your own neck and *Jason's, and guess what, you're the one acting like a Dairy Queen grounded on Prom Night. It's all you. Fate just coloured in between the lines. Jason still loves you. He might fancy her as well, but it's you he loves. Jason Remington. It's just the end of the fairytale, that's all.*

She screamed into the wind, "Ha! Some fairytale."

The higher she climbed, the colder it became. The odd loose speck of dust or dirt lodged in her eye as the wind raked the mountainside. Even when she sheltered in an alcove between two domino rocks, the constant gusts slashed outside, the cold aching inside her ears. Missing the giddy tingle when she'd warm her hands over the fire after they'd almost frozen only made her more miserable, so Kate bunched her legs up to her chest and rocked back and forth, resting her sore cheek on her knees.

"Out there somewhere, there's a Kate Borrowdale who wasn't born with a self-destruct device in her chest. Show me the way to go home…I'm tired and I want to go to bed…I kicked a little ash about an hour ago…and his balls are burning red."

She didn't even smile. Poor Javier had not deserved that. They'd all worked tirelessly on a diet of leeks and little hope for over three months, and for what? In the long term, what would happen to them? If Cecelia wasn't too old to bear children already, she soon would be. Javier could do the honours. Heck, they both wanted it. But what if he didn't get her pregnant? Should Jason try? A smell of stale liquorice blocked her nostrils, made her cough. She'd rather kill him first. She shook her head. Despite the deep space, cryogenic logic—the fact that humans would be extinct on Kratos if neither she nor Cecelia gave birth—her selfish exclusivity with the man she loved superseded it all. She frowned and switched cheeks.

"Is it really too much to ask? One woman, one man. Some couples never have children anyway. It's not like we'd damage the universe if we all died off without leaving any heirs. We're not indigenous. We shouldn't even be here. No, sleeping around is never right, not under any circumstances. Not when there's love in the equation.

"Kate of Kratos…Kate of Kratos…" She repeated Jason's nickname for her until its every nuance was wrung dry. "It's this place," she said. "It strips away your morals until you're nothing but a pack of wolves." She pursed her lips, sucked steady breaths through her nostrils. "So it's ultimatum time, Katie girl, as soon as I get back. They either accept that it's Jason and I *only*…or Jason and I leave the Clubhouse for good. And if *Jason* doesn't agree to that," she looked out into the pitch void, "then he'll never see me again."

A jittery promise. Not one she could live up to, but the sentiment held true. A bittersweet warmth in her chest began to squeeze, and she felt Jason's gentle caress on every part of her. She tried to exhale slowly, but the breath juddered. She sobbed. *Why did you have to say it, Jason? Why?* The salty frame around her eyes reminded her of all the nights she'd cried herself to sleep on the *Fair Monique*. The view was the same.

And so was the company.

* * * *

Infinitesimal foils clashed somewhere in her subconscious early the following morning. Last night's drunken tomfoolery seemed so trivial, and as she yawned and rubbed her eyes, the clearest vista she'd ever experienced on Kratos told her that her point had been made. Without the hallucinogen, Jason and the others would be embarrassed by their behaviour. They had to be.

That was the last they'd hear of propagation.

Kate had encountered this phenomenon before—the optimistic sluice of a wakeup, when all burdens of the previous day were washed away by a cleansing stream of *carpe diem*. A transfusion. And that each morning offered a fresh start was perhaps the secret of her mastery over survival. No matter how bad things got by nightfall, a good sleep always tilted her resolve toward the horizon. It was a rejuvenation of hope by natural means.

He, on the other hand, wouldn't have slept at all. He'd have been too worried about her.

Serves him right.

She got up and stretched. The bruise on her lower back was more painful than ever, probably due to her unorthodox sleeping position. And given how warm it was now compared to the last night, her lips were swollen, chapped as she tongued them. Sharp changes in temperature often had that effect. She swallowed, thirsty.

Quite a distance past the tarn, she realised this was the highest she'd ever climbed up the mountain. *Spectacular.* The entire forest roof appeared as nothing more than the skin shed by a passing reptile. The southern lake, fed by the big pour, was even more vast than she'd imagined. It formed a moat around the base of her mountain range, then disappeared. She reckoned it formed a gargantuan alien river network to the west, which would course, arterially, through the various dells and foothills.

The big pour itself was still hidden by the comma of mist. Either side, the panels of the huge craft didn't appear quite so adamantine as they had when viewed from below. Kate frowned at a bulge in the metal three quarters of the way up, partially hidden by the mist. How long had that been there?

Downhill footing had always irritated her. A propensity to slip on loose scree or infirm rocks was far greater than when she slogged uphill. Perhaps it was the same for everyone. She dusted her backside off after slip-slide number three. But she hadn't missed her footing *once* last night—

"What was that?"

Dirt and tiny rocks danced for a moment all about. She spun round fearing an avalanche. No? "Then what...?" The weather was fine with no clouds to create a thunderstorm. No follow-up aftershock to suggest an earth tremor, and nothing below seemed out of place…other than a tiny column of purple-grey smoke rising from near the Clubhouse.

"Idiots. They've exploded some Pyro."

Good god, if she'd been there, she'd never have let them be such numpties. The 'sucker punch' snare hadn't been activated, as the explosion from that would have simulated a thunderclap. What she'd felt was more like a murmur.

She ignored her need to rest, tore down the slope, half-dancing, half-skiing until she reached the cool tarn. Didn't look at the food or the water; her stare was locked—radar—on three or four dark shapes flying low over the forest roof, toward the Clubhouse.

Kate wanted to punch herself for not being there. The impromptu explosion had aroused interest from these forest dwellers which, airborne like that, flying craftily low, could only be one species—the sly owl-men.

Right, everyone needs to be inside. Please don't let them find the hideout. God knows what they're capable of.

It was the first morning she hadn't laid a new stone at the top of her stairway. She flew recklessly down the steps, tripping before she reached the bottom. The survival suit shielded her from the brunt of the fall, but her left knee smashed into a jutting rock. She groaned and ground her teeth through the pain. Her kneecap rang, throbbed. Enormous shadows now roved over the mountainside. As she looked up, the owl-men circled high above, and she hated them for staying out of range of her weapon.

They'd learned.

Instead of swooping to attack, they began to sing—that awful, low, foghorn boom which resonated inside her inner ears and quickened her heartbeat to an audible thump. For she knew what the song meant, and which creatures the owl-men were in league with.

Knock, knock, knock.

Light reflecting off Jason's wide eyes shot out like flashes of cannon fire as he undid the latch and opened the black, wicker door.

"Everyone stay here," she whispered, crawling inside.

"Where've you been?" asked Jason.

Her sharp glance averted his stare. "Never mind that now. We're in trouble."

The other three eyed the flashing metal weapon she held up in front of her.

"I don't know what the hell that explosion was for, and I don't care. But it sounds like those owl-men are calling for reinforcements. I hate to say it but I think this is the day we've been dreading."

"It was a quick test. What do you want us to do?" said Lucas.

Kate had to do a double-take. Was this really the same obnoxious power freak who'd loathed giving up his autonomy, now asking *her* to lead *him*? "All right," she said, "we need to be smart about this. No martyrs and no panic-buyers."

"What does that mean?" asked Cecelia.

"Panic-buyers—the crowd mentality. You need to think rationally and keep control of your own actions. Don't let yourself be swept up in the big picture. Remember, panicking buys you one thing—the farm."

"Succinctly put," replied Javier.

Kate threw aside her mattress of twined orange bark. She grabbed the five spears she'd made and handed them out. "Let's hope it doesn't get so desperate. We should be safe in here." She looked to Jason for reassurance. He nodded. "But if you do get cornered, go for the throat. Those bipeds are massive, but they're pretty dumb; they don't learn in a hurry. Right, I'm going to keep an eye out at the entrance. Someone else take over in an hour or so. If they do show up, I'll yell right away. And then I'll take care of the flank defences. Jason and Javier, be ready to light the 'sucker punch' if all else fails."

The others might've thought she stopped to mouth a prayer, but, strangely, the words to *Wouldn't It Be Nice* by The Beach Boys jaunted into her mind.

"I'm coming with you." On his hands and knees, Jason pressed past her.

A grim determination constipated any emotion she ought to feel. Instead, Kate hummed her tune as she crawled behind him through the tunnel. No sooner had he stood upright when Jason hurled himself to back to the ground, almost clashing heads with her, and shouted into the Clubhouse, "They're coming. Everyone get ready."

Her scalp buzzed—a mixture of fear and pent-up excitement as she rose beside the man she loved. He stood tall, legs apart, strong arms akimbo, his ferocious stare fixed on the rapid stream of creatures approaching by the lakeside route. More and more owl-men glided low over the forest roof. This concerted attack had the smell of despicable design, a rank orchestration by those calculated cads the owl-men, for whom Kate now wished only one thing—annihilation.

"K-A-T-E indeed." She spat. "I'm taking as many of those shits with me as I can."

"Me too. Good luck, Kate." He kissed her cheek. "See you shortly. Be careful."

With that Jason rushed to the bowties, the black catapult snares waiting on the northern slope. Owl-men circling overhead were not sleek like the eagles, they were dumpy, awkward, high school bullies who just happened to be smart as well.

"Not that smart." She eyed the steep southern decline. "Bullies fall hard."

A thunderous cavalcade of displaced rocks and debris made her grip the metal cylinder tightly in her sweaty palm. From her position, adjacent to the rock-fall snare, the lower half of the slope was hidden, and her mind conjured an army of titans scaling Mount Olympus. The noise increased. It sounded like the workings of a colony of ants amplified a thousand-fold. They were having a hard time clambering up the steep rise, but any second now they would appear.

"Steady, Katie girl. Hold steady." She hummed the chorus for *Mrs. Robinson* over and over, ready at any moment to blast the anvil-shaped keystone to smithereens.

And here's to you, Mrs—

There! The first tyrannosaur skull jerked into sight a few hundred yards below. The music stopped and she slid her finger over the black button. *Whump-crack!* She sprinted to one side as the pivotal rock exploded, bringing down the entire stack—over three dozen medium-sized boulders—in an instant. Anything loose in its path was press-ganged into a relentless roll which, though not all that fast, couldn't be stopped. At the first steep hill, it gathered serious momentum and roared on a direct course for the dust cloud kicked up by the assailants. She couldn't see the bipeds any more. The three dozen rocks were now hundreds; the mountainside was shedding its own coarse skin.

Kate threw a victorious fist as the dust cloud reached a hundred feet high. The roar gradually dissipated, becoming a gravel undercurrent far below.

Rather than return to the Clubhouse, she ran eastward to Jason, in case he needed help. But it was all over. The bowties had all been released, and a few bipeds lay splattered among the rocks further down the slope. Jason beamed when he saw her.

"So they worked?" she asked.

"They were awesome. The things didn't have a chance."

She squeezed his shoulder. "Come on, let's get back."

"Right. Sounded like the avalanche kicked up a storm."

"You've no idea. I doubt there'll be *any* of those things left by now."

But the owl-men still glided and swooped overhead, ever out of range of Kate's weapon. What else had they got up their sleeves, seeing as they were too cowardly to join in person?

By the time Kate and Jason reached the Clubhouse, the frantic scrabbling had resumed…directly below. And this time the huge bipeds were not hidden. Her head chimed as though she'd dunked it in a trough of icy water. This was it. However many the avalanche had wiped out she couldn't be sure, but at least fifty now tore up the slope toward them.

"Javier, you ready?" yelled Jason.

"*Ci*," came the reply.

"Right, come on out, quick. It's time."

The gap between the edge of the Pyrofluvium canopy and the Clubhouse entrance was around ten feet. They'd folded the membrane together so that very little space existed between the purple arteries. Thus, the explosion would precipitate even greater propulsion. It covered almost a full acre, and there was no way around it to reach them. The monsters had no choice but to cross the trap.

"It's all right guys, I'm…I won't miss, I promise," though the young Spaniard shook with a mortar full of flaming orange bark in his hand.

Jason was about to take it from him when he saw the lad's unsteady hands, but the look of determination in Javier's eyes stayed the protest.

"Good luck, amigo."

Kate said, "Don't dally. The moment you've thrown it, get into the tunnel."

"Yes, ma'am."

Kate and Jason crawled back inside through the cool stream that felt sublime on her bare skin. Cecelia helped them both inside, while Lucas held his spear tighter than a long-lost sweetheart on Valentine's. Their homely decorations—orange paint on the walls here and there, chalked picture portraits that resembled no human who'd ever lived, rudimentary wicker chairs, and a table fashioned from the black wood—suddenly seemed absurd. But, and Kate felt it stronger than she'd ever expected she would, it was a home worth saving. It was *their* home. She glanced at Lucas Revere who, despite his natural bull-headedness, had learned to play as part of a team; at prissy Cecelia Benedict who had made a home for them in the ribs of a rock cave; she thought of shy Javier Inarritu lighting the spark to save them all. *These* were people worth saving, worth fighting for.

And then there was Jason Remington. By God, the more unkempt he became, the more handsome, enticing he seemed to grow. As he knelt down beside her, crouching to see events unfold through the tunnel, she couldn't imagine life without him.

"Come on, amigo, come on," he whispered. "Not too soon."

"Where are they?" asked Cecelia.

No reply. Everyone waited for the rumble to erupt. And waited. Only Javier, poised to watch the bipeds approach, knew when all hell would break loose. Kate kept her eye on the flame in his hand. That would signify the Fourth of July. She daren't blink. The rumbling grew louder.

There. The flame disappeared into the air and Javier dove back into the tunnel. The monstrous horde was almost on top of him. Kate's every muscle clenched in anticipation. Any second now, the roots of the mountain would be wrenched.

"Quick, Kate, get me another," screamed Javier. "One of those bastard owl-men snatched the flame."

Chapter Twenty-Nine
A Day To Remember

There wasn't time. Fire-lighting without the incendiaries required preparation, a few moments' procedure. The first bipeds crashed into the Clubhouse wall, scraping at the rock to widen the hole. Grey, fleshy arms reached inside the tunnel, though not very far. They splashed, gouged, poked blindly. There was no way they could get in.

"Now's the time," said Lucas. "While they're all gathered in one place—we could blow them sky high."

Jason scoffed. "Be my guest."

Monstrous, shuffling feet and low grunts were constant; they seemed to rotate as though the bipeds took turns at trying the impossible.

"There isn't a brain between them. What can we do to trick them?" asked Kate.

"Some kind of decoy?" proposed Javier.

"Yeah, but what, and where? We're stuck in here."

Lucas crouched beside them. "Then it's attrition. We have to wait it out. We've enough food for a few days, and all the water we need."

Water? It gave Kate an idea. "Guys, correct me if I'm wrong, but doesn't our stream flow directly under the canopy…I mean close enough to almost touch the Pyro."

"Yeah, it does," replied Javier. "So what?"

"Well, this is a long shot, and we might have to try it a few times. Amigo, can you make me a few more flames to burn inside the bowls…to float down the stream?" It was the first time she'd called him amigo, and it sounded nerdy.

He nodded, puzzled. "How are you going to get it past them? They're swarming around out there."

"Like I said, it's a long shot. Either it'll frighten them and they'll back away—*boom*—or they'll ignore it and trample it into the water."

"There's also the owl-men," said Lucas. "They snatched the last one, so they know how dangerous fire is."

"Yeah, but we're talking ten feet here, through a crowd. They probably won't even see it in time."

"It's worth a try," agreed Jason. "Let's do it."

Cecelia fetched four bowls carved from the orange wood. As these would incinerate immediately, Jason lined the base with a handful of small, flat stones. Javier then lit a strip of Atlas bark and placed it onto the stones.

"We need to give it a chance." Kate took the bowl in one hand and placed the gun in her other. Crawling through the tunnel, she didn't hesitate, even when a gigantic hand scraped inches from her face. *Whump-crack!* She sent a pulse blast through the entrance, instantly clearing the mouth of the tunnel.

Go.

She let the bowl loose. The candle bumped and bobbed along the stream under stampeding limbs. *Come on, just ten feet.* Ferocious blows pulverized the rock wall above. Mouth agape, Kate held her breath.

She'd scurry back inside at the first hint of a purple spark. Seven feet now…eight. A pair of muscular legs stomped astride the stream. Then another monster barged into view. They clashed. The first biped tripped forward, landing on its side…on top of the candle.

"Shit. Pass me another."

The creature rolled itself upright, so Kate cast the second bowl loose. Another arm reached inside the tunnel, missing the candle by a claw's width. Three or four monsters barred the way beyond, but she prayed the flame would get through.

After five feet, the splash from a single footstep dowsed that hope.

"Another!"

This time, urgency dug her nails into the rim of the orange bowl. The second one had upended, become wedged. It now blocked the course of the stream. *Right, this has to be quick, Katie girl. On three: one…two…*three! She shot the nearest monster full in the groin. It exploded, and the nearby attackers staggered back from the same impact. Kate wasted no time. The brief window in the assault allowed her to dart outside, fire four shots to provide enough space and, after tossing the bowl like a Frisbee so as not to tip its contents, dive back inside. It was all over in a matter of seconds.

"Get back. Everybody back."

Two strong clawed digits gripped her ankle but she kicked them upward against the roof of the tunnel. The creature winced and lost its grip. Kate scurried through the stream and huddled low at the back of the cave with the others, beneath a pronounced jut in the rock wall. That would shield them from a cave-in, or so she hoped.

But nothing exploded.

"Oh, Christ. What now?" Lucas tore at his hair.

Jason pressed all their heads down. "Give it chance."

Still nothing.

"I might have to try again," said Kate. "Let go. Javier, make me anoth—"

Boom!

The floor itself cracked apart, while rock dust showered from all across the ceiling. The devastating crash of thunder forced each of them to press their palms tight against their ears. Cecelia fell backward, hit her head on the wall as a tongue of purple fire roared into the cave. Everyone else leapt to their feet ready to bolt. The heat was tremendous—like facing the open door of a furnace. Kate thought the entire mountain had lifted off its foundation.

Jesus, what's happened out there?

As the roar subsided, the gentle pit-pat of rain grew to a torrential downpour. Kate rushed across to the tunnel to see. It was raining all right—fire, rocks, blood and body parts fell from the sky. The explosion had annihilated the entire biped horde! For as far as she could see, the hailstorm wreaked continuous carnage on the mountainside.

Her throat tightened. *Oh my God.*

Jason saw the fear in her eyes and ran to join her. "Kate, what is it? What's happened?"

She swallowed twice before replying, "Pyro. The explosion. Look, it's raining down on the forest roof. If just one spark catches an artery…"

"It's *adios amigos*."

Holding hands, the others heard every word. But the news was too much for Lucas' nerves to bear. He flung Javier aside and, grabbing the mortar and a fistful of orange strips, fled deep into the cave.

No one tried to stop him.

As soon as he scrambled over the fallen rocks caused by his own panic-shot months ago—no one had ventured past them since—Kate yelled, "There. It's lit. The forest roof…it's up."

Lucas didn't stop to ask questions. Gibbering to himself, he struck two rocks together, again and again, finally lighting the first orange strips. With his new candle to guide him, he sprinted down the passage and veered left at the crossroads, out of sight.

"That's unbelievable." Kate crouched at the entrance once again. Seeing there was no further danger outside, either from the ground or from the air, she stood upright to watch the awesome firestorm spread across the woodland. The others joined her outside the Clubhouse.

"I've never seen anything like that." Javier placed his arm over Cecelia's shoulders. "It's like the devil reaching up to claim a bit more hell."

The violet arteries erupted with anatomical continuity. Flaming trails branched out over the vast membrane as though the blood flow of the forest had caught fire. Cecelia gasped as the speed of this spread increased southward, and again when it reached the red desert beyond but continued *across* the valley, parallel to the river. Pyrofluvium was everywhere. Like channels of oil just below the surface, only purple, the ground exploded in half a dozen pipelines of fire toward the giant craft itself.

Kate looked at Jason.

"The chimneys," he shouted. "That thing is *full* of Pyro."

"What are you talking about?" asked Javier. "What's full?"

Kate's jaw tightened.

"That entire spaceship." Jason mimicked a mushroom explosion with his arms. "If that thing goes up, *we* all go—"

"Up. That's it." Kate yanked Jason and Javier by their arms and pushed them on up the slope. "If that thing ignites, if those panels burst, we'll be washed away by a trillion tonnes of ocean. We have to climb…*now*."

They didn't have time to say goodbye to the Clubhouse, nor did they stop to gather supplies. Together they reached step ninety-seven, where Kate glanced to the south, in a single sprint. The fire trails were *at* the base of the craft, one east of the mist, the rest inside the mist. Would the moisture be enough to dowse them? Kate thought not. Heck, a dozen fire hoses couldn't extinguish an oil well in full burn; what was a little spray gonna do?

The devastation caused by the avalanche was now clear enough. It had formed a new foothill of piled rocks, under which dozens of monsters were buried. The northern fringe of the forest was charcoal. Awful, towering black smoke veiled much of the rest, while clumsy lines of flame danced, snaked along the northeast extremities like purple dragons at a Chinese New Year.

Jason and Kate could have climbed at twice the speed, but Cecelia was not agile. At one time, Kate would have protested. How dare a hanger-on tarry their crucial bid for safety. But Cecelia had earned her leeway and any helping hand they could give her, through months of patience and marvellous esprit de corps. No, she could never be left behind.

A magnesium flare blazed in the cloudless sky to the west. *Oh my God. It's happened.* Brilliant purple light scorched Kate's vision like a nuclear blast. An agonising metallic groan rattled her shoulders, ribs and teeth, and a piercing, high-pitched screech shot through her brain. The great panels were buckling. Thousands of feet high, they supported an untold quantity of water. One had already collapsed to form the big pour, and the spillage from that fed a lake the size of Superior in North America. So what would happen if another fell, or they all went?

It was as though the planet were tearing apart at the seams. Ferocious hisses struck out above the groans and screeches.

The pressure.

The blunt rocky overhang was now visible above them. If they could just get to the tarn and stay on the northern slope, they might be high enough. Adrenaline lifted her stiff upper body frame on a winged coat-hanger. But poor Cecelia was really suffering now. Her mid-forties stamina was down to its last fumes.

"Come on, guys, carry her. For chrissakes."

Her arms clasped around both their necks, they each lifted one of her thighs, giving her a seat between them as they climbed. It wasn't any quicker, but at least they didn't have to stop for

Cecelia to rest. Kate led them on at a frantic pace. The overhang was twenty feet away when a deep, resonating clang, the striking of a dynastic gong, spun her to the south.

The great panel buckled outward at the centre, and as the rim lowered, the ocean's frightening brow rose and then bowed over the valley. It poured seawater as though from the neck of a continental vat. A cascade of dark green water seemed to plummet forever until it crashed on the metal promontory, exploding white. Then it fell to ground with the weight of an Arctic shelf. The impact caused both an earth tremor and a thunder roll at once. Relentless, muscular, the cascade swept across the valley floor, drowning the forest and surfeiting the great lake many times over. This new pour was a two-step waterfall, though it dwarfed by a fathomless margin Kate's memory of rafting down the big pour. She'd witnessed a dribble in comparison. In between snatched glances of the cataclysm, she kept her eyes fixed on the ground ahead. To the right was salvation. But her left side gaped, felt so exposed. An icy swath threatened to envelope her at any moment.

Come on, Katie girl, keep going. It can't touch you here.

She checked behind. The others lagged. A powerful blast of cold air knocked her off her feet, and didn't abate. She had to stay low and use her hands to grip the rocks. Behind, below, the mind-boggling surge violently birthed a new sea. Nothing remained of the forest except wisps of grey smoke in the atmosphere. Even those swirled in the oceanic draught. The great plateau she'd surveyed every morning from the Clubhouse entrance was now completely awash.

The torrent reached higher up the mountainside, but nowhere near as fast or as high as she'd feared. The mountains lined only the west and northwest of the plateau that she knew, so, in theory, there might be hundreds of thousands of square miles for the water to cover. If that was the case, it wouldn't be a very deep sea.

Still, it was a transference of oceans—enough to send a girl off her trolley.

She waited for the others at the overhang. The wind was still as strong, the waterfall undiminished, but she felt sure they were out of danger.

"I just saw one of those sea behemoths try to surface," yelled Jason. "Remember I told you about those—they almost snatched us from the *Elemental*. Now we've got *those* to contend with. And God knows what else from the depths. Whatever could kill us up there can kill us down here."

Kate threw her hands up. "We're never coming back to this place. There are peaks and valleys galore to the northwest. I don't think the water level will rise all that high."

"I don't know. Who's to say how big that craft really is? I've a feeling this ocean's going to pour for a long, long time."

"All the better to hotfoot it while we still can."

"Agreed."

* * * *

Lucas heard the incredible roar from deep inside the cigar-shaped tunnel that had lately shrank to more of a cigarette. The four-foot diameter forced him to crawl. His knees bled. A sudden blast of cold air almost killed the flame in his mortar. He could think of nothing except the wide open space waiting at the other end for him to flee across. There was no hint of light ahead, but he knew it was coming. Whenever he paused, his head wheeled forward and his arms wanted to collapse with it. He hadn't noticed any downward decline, yet that was the only explanation. The tunnel sloped downhill.

After a sharp curve the passage dropped sharply, diagonally. Lucas peered down and inhaled a smell that made him retch—a lungful of salty seaweed. Water. Impenetrable seawater barred his way. Even if this was the only passage out, there was no way he could *swim* through it—not without light, and certainly not along such a narrow tunnel. He let his face fall to his knees and, child-like, draped his arms backward over his head for further isolation. In the flickering candlelight, he sobbed.

The others might laugh but he had no choice; he had to go back.

"Why's the candle so bright?" he said aloud. A tart aniseed smell made his scalp shiver. When Lucas turned, he dropped the mortar from a rubbery grip. Light snaked slowly toward him. Dozens of the bioluminescent creatures. The closer they got, the faster they circled until the heat was so intense he had no choice but to shield his face.

"Leave me alone. *Get away.*"

Buzzzzzz

The noise and the smell and the burning, acidic heat overwhelmed him. His scream didn't register in the wild swarm of electricity forcing him back. He couldn't breathe. First his hand, then his neck and cheek grew molten. The stench of scorched flesh made him throw up. Inching back, close enough to the edge as to almost topple, he reached behind for a handhold, something, *anything* with which to pull himself away from the heat. The pain stabbed, swelled, throbbed, razor-bladed inside. The last thing he saw before his eyes seared shut was brilliant white light, and the distinct outline of a coiled snake hovering right in front of him.

His T-shirt burst into flames. With charred hands he dragged himself the final few inches and fell into the diagonal drop. The burning heat gave way to sharp slashes as jutting rocks flayed the loose flesh from his back. The second he hit the cool water, Lucas's heart gave out. Above, the swarming lights slowed and diverged in impish formation. The tunnel darkened to an idle glow. Only Lucas' candle remained. And when that flickered out, there was nothing left but the smell of aniseed.

* * * *

At the tarn, they each ate a leek and drank water to slake their hot thirst. Kate guessed they'd only been climbing for half an hour, but in that time fire had predicated a new watery era in the hybrid evolution of Kratos. Mist now veiled much of the two-tiered waterfall. The wind had eased somewhat, yet it still carried enough fine spray to soak the mountainside. Traces of a rainbow appeared over the centre of this new sea, while sunlight and the shadows of violet clouds roved across its surface.

A low, lopsided arch in the rock provided shelter. Jason laid his head on Kate's lap by the water's edge. Javier and Cecelia embraced, pressed their cheeks together. There was a pure, ancient feel about the tarn, as if the first Kratosian life had sprung here eons ago.

"Where to now?" asked Jason. "Before we climb any higher, how about scouting the mountain at this altitude—from the west side, I mean."

"It's a good idea." Kate ran her fingers over his damp beard and through his long hair.

"See what we can see," he added.

After a good hour's rest, they traversed a rocky shelf that skirted a sheer vertical rise. Precarious, yes, but it wound all the way around to the western slope—over two miles. Here the mountainside was very steep indeed, up and down. Kate eyed an exposed pass between the next two crags, many miles away, and they all agreed that was the best course. However, it meant a long, sustained slip-slide down the scree slope before them. Black slate crumbled easily under their weight. The men soon picked up their pace. Kate shook her head and laughed as they seemed to enjoy the rollicking descent.

"Just like Jason and his sand yacht," she told Cecelia.

No reply.

"Cecelia, everything alri—"

Kate glanced back over their route. The redhead wasn't there. Had she surged ahead? Kate's eyes had been on her own footing. No, there was Javier and there was Jason, out in front. Had she fallen through a fissure that they'd disturbed? Been buried?

Kate shouted down to the men and started back up the slope. "Where are you?" Climbing here was an ordeal. For every three firm steps she managed, two slipped from under her.

Her ears tickled. She paused for a moment and heard a scream. "Where are you? I can't see you," she yelled in reply. Another scream. It seemed distant, higher up the mountain. She couldn't be that far back, could she?

Again, her inner ears tickled. She stopped her in her tracks and looked up. Instantly squeezed the gun with aching fingers. She'd forgotten all about the owl-men! Slyly, they'd taken advantage of this noisy descent by swooping to snatch the lagging female. Cecelia. And being unarmed, she had no chance.

Kate wanted wings. All she could do was watch the poor woman disappear high to the west, behind the rocky rise, in the claws of a monstrosity. The screams didn't stop. An awful emptiness swelled inside. She blamed herself for not giving proper protection. After all, who had the only gun? By the time Javier reached her, she knew Cecelia was gone for good.

"It's useless. There's no way to catch them."

"*Cecelia.*" The young Spaniard didn't even look at Kate. Spitting, panting, he tore up the slates far quicker than she had. His trick was to splay his feet with each step, thereby spreading the weight laterally. It wasn't elegant, but Javier didn't care.

"Cecelia."

He'd loved her from the first. Kate had seen that right away outside the bracken den the first time she'd met them. And she recalled the many bone-chafing impulses she herself had endured at the thought of losing Jason.

He'd do anything to get her back.

A convoy of Rorschachs, silhouetted against the sun, flickered into view from over the eastern shoulder of the mountain. Bunched together, their unwieldy shapes nonetheless dove in a clinical arc, carving a rapid path with the authority of a judge's gavel. Directly above Javier.

"Look out." She curled her hands to form a megaphone and screamed, "Javier. *Look. Above. You.*"

He did. The owl-men were almost upon him. He grabbed the nearest slate and hurled it aloft. Clever. He threw it over-arm by its edge so that it spun like a ninja throwing star. It sliced the first owl-man's belly but not enough to stop its swoop.

"Bastards, you wanna be extinct? Well, come on then." He hurled another slate which missed the squadron altogether. The first owl-man lunged for him with clawed feet. He leapt to one side and, jumping up to grab its wing, dragged the creature down onto its back and unleashed a barrage of fists to its face. A second monstrosity swooped but he dodged that, too. A sharp lunge from a third gripped his shoulder.

Kate and Jason were less than thirty feet away. She could take a pot-shot with the gun, but the pulse would hit Javier.

Jason yelled, "Do it. It won't kill him from this range."

Whump-crack! The pulse threw shattered black slate up the slope. By the time it reached the melee, Javier was airborne in the owl-man's clutches. He screamed obscenities. The shockwave clipped his legs, knocking him into a pendulum swing. But the monster held him tightly as it flew away.

"No." Kate fired again. The other monsters staggered back, while a few more landed higher up the slope.

Jason pulled her arm. "He's gone. We have to run…now."

She tasted bitter bloodlust as she watched Javier writhe serpent-like in the owl-man's talons. He *was* gone. They *did* have to run.

"Right, just let them try and take us."

Something hard and sharp hit her in the small of her back as she fled. Kate spun round to blast the monster apart, but there was nothing there. The owl-men were stood in the same spot. *What the hell?* One of them whipped its wing in her direction, and out of its claw flew a piece of slate. The accuracy of the throw took her aback, as she had to dodge.

"Oh shit. They've learned. Jason, wait up."

The next stage of their descent bristled with tit-for-tat exchanges. Kate deflected a hail of slates dropped from above with desperate shots from her gun. Riding a mini avalanche with every step, she felt the weight and crazy pace of a juggernaut take her down the mountainside. The crafty owl-men attacked from every angle. One skimmed slates sideways, another waited for the lulls between shots to drop much bigger rocks from above. They even tried hurling them simultaneously. But Kate kept her composure, and the owl-men feared to venture too close. Jason stayed by her, as close as he could. The weapon's pulses formed a near-constant umbrella to repel the raining stones. Kate's sides ached through an unremitting clench. Half way to the bottom, she glanced up, ready to fire again, but…the attackers had vanished.

"Don't stop. Keep going," she cried.

There was bound to be another attack. The things were simply regrouping, formulating a craftier strategy. She glimpsed their Rorschach shapes high above.

Mid slide, Jason shouted, "Look. To the north."

It broke her rhythm, made her fall sideways into a torrent of sharp edges. But Kate's suit protected her. A skyward glance became a double-looped lifeline of relief. One, the owl-men were headed back to the mountaintop. Two, they were being pursued, en masse, by her oldest friends on Kratos, those proud marshals of the air, the giant eagles!

She lay there for a moment, to let it all sink in.

Unbelievable. She recalled the time she'd rescued the little hatchling prince from a hideous slug. All this for one act of kindness.

As soon as they reached the bottom of the slope, she collapsed onto her back, gasping. The day had been a running nightmare right from the start. She couldn't remember everything that had happened. Somewhere, somehow, a family of five had been reduced to two; their labour of three months, the Clubhouse, was under siege by the sea; Kate and Jason were back at square one on the Kratosian survival chart.

"There's still hope for Javier and Cecelia." Jason collapsed beside her. He sucked in several huge lungfuls of air. "Those bastards might flee altogether if the eagles backtrack them to their lair. Our friends might still be alive."

Kate reckoned not, but she wanted Jason's optimistic words to be the last ones spoken on the subject. Javier and Cecelia deserved it.

"Come on, we need to find shelter," he said. "We're totally exposed."

"And that's not all."

"Huh?"

"How two people can travel so far without really going anywhere." She tossed an angry slate eastward. It failed to dislodge more than a few loose cousins, and soon she couldn't tell it apart from a million others. "It's some kind of sick cosmic joke."

"What is?"

"Progress. We're no nearer to our goal than we were crossing the desert."

"And what goal is that?" he asked. "We're still alive, aren't we?"

"I suppose."

"Well then, we're winning. Look at it this way, the longer we survive, the closer to our goal we get." Jason held her hand as she rose to her feet. "And think how much we've learned, the friends we've made." He looked skyward.

"Yeah, Mandy, the dolphins, the eagles."

"There you go. And this isn't the last chapter, by a long shot."

She almost smiled. "That's what I've been saying. This is the first chapter all over again."

"Maybe that's the secret of survival." He cupped her filthy chestnut hair back over her shoulders.

"What is?"

"The first chapter. We get to repeat it every day. Maybe the trick is to see that as a good thing."

"*How?*"

"Well, we get to refine it together. Pretty lame, huh?"

Kate pulled his head toward her by a fistful of his greasy black hair. She kissed him, and the day's multiple shocks eroded. "Hmm, not as lame as all that."

He paused.

"Kate, can I tell you something?"

"Yeah?"

"I love you."

She knew that later on, when the chaos settled around her heart, she'd cry.

"I should hope so," she replied.

It was the proudest moment of her life.

Jason checked to make sure the tiny metal recorder was still in his pocket, and then he led her by the hand to the next pass. It was flanked by steep, towering crags.

Chapter Thirty
Farewell

"To anyone out there...come and find us!

This will be the only surviving record of our existence on Kratos. And as the recording capacity of this transmitter is limited, I must be brief. For purposes of recall and concision, this message is read from my own handwritten testimony.

I am Jason Remington, formerly a terrain scout on board the Deep Space Explorer, Fair Monique. I confess to not knowing the precise year, month or date in Earth time of this recording. We have estimated thirty months, or two and a half years since the Fair Monique crashed on Kratos. What an incredible story we have to tell, my partner and I. There is no time to recount those precarious early months, and I can scarcely believe them even now. Suffice to say that Kate Borrowdale and I are miraculous survivors on a miraculous world. There is no going back for us. We are bound for the horizon, and that is enough. Here, we have finally reached the summit of one of the highest mountains in the western range we call The Stalagmites. At the closing of this message, I shall secure the transmitter here, where it might be pinpointed from orbit, or perhaps for other explorers to one day find.

Three civilians lived past the crash: Lucas Revere, Javier Inarritu and Cecelia Benedict. We have seen no sign of them for over two years. They are likely dead by now, but we live in hope. Their contributions to our plight were unforgettable, and though we look back on them with fond memories, they are with us every step of our adventure.

And dare I forget the magnificent animals that have shared our great journey: the graceful dolphins to whom I owe my life; the great eagle prince, for whom Kate's brave intervention inspired a lifelong pledge of loyalty; and last but not least, Mandy the salamander, one of the greatest friends I've ever had. Hopefully, she's still waiting for us with her kin when we reach the base of the mountain. I cried at our happenstance reunion four months ago, for she saved my life countless times in the early days. Without her, our adventures would not be the same. These are noble creatures, and theirs is a world of reciprocity, of consequence.

Anyone listening to this will likely already be acquainted with the stupendous dimensions of the crashed alien vessel to the south, and its rich trove of Pyrofluvium. From this high vantage point, we now look down on it, properly, for the first time. Forests, lakes, plateaus with innumerable herds and vegetation, all seem to have grown around this gargantuan craft. It appears to be an artificial ecosystem—not indigenous, that is—sired by the crashing of this ship however many millions of years ago. Life was brought here. We cannot be certain of that, but the fact that it peters out the further it exists from the vessel is compelling. Beyond these valleys, out of range of this localised ecosystem, what indigenous life forms might Kratos hold in store? As we head ever westward, I am both excited and fearful for what the future might bring.

Speaking of the future, I have omitted the most wonderful part of our survival tale. As the twin suns occasionally align to become a single celestial body, so too did mine and Kate's early last year. Our daughter is named Monique, after the vessel that bore us across all those light years to Kratos. She was born in the shadow of a great storm, and I have never looked at fell weather the same way again. She is our miracle, the reason we were spared. I have never been more sure of anything.

Exceptional enough for a child to be the sole heir to the last man and the last woman on a planet, but Monique, I must confess, is further privileged.

For she has Kate for a mother.

As I am reading this message, you might presume that a man, as is custom, was in large part responsible for keeping a woman and her child alive against impossible odds, and that my name deserves recognition in the interstellar chronicles. I dare say it does. I have certainly done my part. But Kate has written this legend. If her full exploits could ever be recounted, they would without doubt fill every man, and indeed every woman, with pride.

She is no longer a woman of Earth, as we are no longer a species confined to that provincial planet. She is so much more. No woman ever went to greater lengths to save the man she loved than Kate for I. And thus I will forevermore be the husband of Kate of Kratos. Yesterday, as the purple clouds broke over a land in constant flux, we looked to the heavens and plighted our troth beneath the eyes of God, parents of the most valuable treasure of all—our fair Monique. And it is here, where I must now leave this message, that I impart these final words to my fellow travellers, words that have inspired lovely Kate through her darkest hours on Kratos, words that we now share together:

We don't stay alive to survive, we survive in order to live.

This is Jason Remington, signing off."

THE END

About the Author

Robert Appleton is an Award-winning author of science fiction, steampunk, and historical fiction. Based in Lancashire, England, he has written over two dozen novels and novellas for various publishers, most recently Carina Press and Samhain Publishing. In his spare time he hikes, kayaks, and reads as many classic adventure novels as he can get his hands on.

Website: https://robertappleton.co.uk
Twitter: https://twitter.com/robertappleton
Blog: https://robertbappleton.blogspot.com

* * * *

Read *Alien Safari,* the thrilling new science fiction novel from Robert Appleton, now available in print, and everywhere ebooks are sold.

Five murders on an untamed world. Two fugitives on the run. The hunt is on.

When celebrated Omicron detective Ferrix Vaughn is called in to investigate a deadly breach on Hesperidia, a protected planet full of indigenous wildlife, he doesn't know what to expect. The place used to be a tourist attraction, but the safari tours were discontinued long ago due to rampant poaching. Only a handful of researchers live there now, including Jan Corbija, the disfigured young woman who reported the breach.

The deeper Vaughn digs, the more the evidence seems to point to a recent raid on a biotech facility in a nearby system. Whatever was stolen from there, it's attracted the attention of major political players in a time of war across the colonies. Vaughn suspects the secret is on Hesperidia, in the hands of the two fugitives who fled the murder scene.

If he wants to get to them first, he's going to need Jan's help. Her *Alien Safari* tour will have to reopen for this final excursion. But to survive it, they'll both need to face their demons, for a predator far deadlier than man roams the wilds of Hesperidia. And this is its killing season.

This way for the ride of your life.

* * * *

A selection of standalone books set in the same universe as *The Eleven Hour Fall* and *Alien Safari*, available as ebooks and audiobooks:

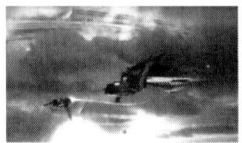

Borderline (only available in ebook format)

Sparks in Cosmic Dust

Pyro Canyon

Alien Velocity

Manufactured by Amazon.ca
Acheson, AB